ON THE EDGE OF UNCERTAINTY

By E.V. Bancroft

2025

Butterworth Books is a different breed of publishing house. It's a home for Indies, for independent authors who take great pride in their work and produce top quality books for readers who deserve the best. Professional editing, professional cover design, professional proof reading, professional book production—you get the idea. As Individual as the Indie authors we're proud to work with, we're Butterworths and we're *different*.

Authors currently publishing with us:

E.V. Bancroft
Valden Bush
Addison M Conley
Jo Fletcher/JL Fletcher
Helena Harte
Lee Haven
Karen Klyne
Sydney Lear
AJ Mason
Ally McGuire
James Merrick
Robyn Nyx/RJ Nyx
JP Preston
Anne Shade
Brey Willows

For more information visit www.butterworthbooks.co.uk

ON THE EDGE OF UNCERTAINTY

This trade paperback is published by Butterworth Books, UK

CATALOGING INFORMATION
ISBN: 978-1-918072-01-3
CREDITS
Editor: Nicci Robinson
Cover Design: Nicci Robinson
Illustration: "Diana" by KC Lylark
Production Design: Global Wordsmiths

Acknowledgements

I am so grateful to everyone who has given their time and expertise to bring *On the Edge of Uncertainty* to life.

Firstly, thank you to Nicci Robinson from Global Wordsmiths/ Butterworth Books for giving me permission to abandon my other project and encouraging me to write my heart's desire. Thanks also to KC Lylark for the fabulous painting of Diana.

Every author needs a person to read and critique the roughest of drafts, and I'm very grateful to Annmarie Llewellyn for ploughing through my ponderous ramblings, challenging and making suggestions. I'm lucky I have some awesome beta readers, in the Swallows critique group: Joey Bass, Valden Bush, Jane Fletcher, Lee Haven, AJ Mason, Maggie McIntyre and Sue Still. I know the book is so much stronger because of all your input.

Thanks to Em, who commented on passages even though romance isn't her thing, and Jerry the cat, who has been a total distraction as I've tried to work.

Finally, I'd like to thank you, the reader, for taking a chance on me and giving me such wonderful feedback. It's such an honour. Thanks.

Dedication

To Em.

And to all the people who believe
they will never love or be loved again.

CHAPTER ONE

Cambridge, England, 1950

A SHADOW FELL OVER Florrie, cutting out the sun and making her shiver. She frowned and squinted at the silhouette. A tall, willowy woman stood over her, blocking out the sun that cast a halo around her head.

"Florence Cooper, is that you?"

Florrie blinked and replaced her teacup with a clatter. She was relieved she hadn't drunk out of the saucer like she preferred when her tea was too hot—she didn't want to be judged in public. That voice, so deep and commanding, with the smoky resonance of 1920s jazz clubs; she hadn't heard it in years, and yet her heart quickened at the sound of it. She caught the familiar scent of ylang ylang and jasmine and immediately craved it, wanting to immerse herself in the olfactory symbol of her youth.

She pushed back her chair and struggled to her feet, determined to see if she was dreaming. The lines on the woman's face seemed to disappear, and her younger eyes stared out, sparkling with pleasure. The whole mask shifted to one that had once been so well known, so familiar, so beloved. "Diana?"

"I couldn't believe it. I thought it was you." Diana reached to touch Florrie's arm but paused before making contact. "How many years is it? It must be over twenty." Her eyes sparkled, and the corners creased in delicate lines. "How lovely to see you."

Florrie's heart fluttered in her chest and she struggled to catch her breath. Was she having palpitations? She leaned heavily on the chair. "I thought I'd never see you again." Her initial excitement deflated like someone had popped a party balloon when she remembered more of their past. "Are you here with your husband?"

A quick frown flashed across Diana's face, before she replaced it with a more sombre expression. "Anthony died at the end of the war. I'm here with my son, Edward, who is up at Cambridge at the moment."

"I'm sorry to hear about Anthony." Florrie's response was polite and what was expected, but Diana must know it was a lie. "Would you care to join us? This is my niece, Cam and her....her Gloria, who graduated today."

Diana's eyes widened, and then she broke into a smile as she offered her silk-gloved hand to Cam. "How do you do, Cam and... her Gloria? Thank you for the invitation, but we're just leaving."

Florrie had forgotten her gentle teasing, showing she understood exactly what Florrie hadn't said. Cam and Gloria shook Diana's hand in turn, and they exchanged pleasantries. Florrie could almost be a young woman again, hanging on Diana's every mellifluous, well-enunciated word, sitting in the cramped offices of Diana's publishing house, discussing books, and philosophy, and writing as if their lives depended on it.

"Do you still have the Euston Press?" Florrie asked after Diana returned her intense gaze towards her.

"No. Anthony sold it to one of the bigger presses. During the war, it was used almost entirely for printing war notices. It closed last year. What a comedown after all our wishes and dreams for it."

Diana spoke as though every sentence had to be forced out of her mouth and snapped into place. But then her lips curled upwards at the edge, and Florrie was dazzled by Diana's beautiful smile.

"I still think fondly of the days we spent putting the world to rights and planning all the things we would achieve," Diana said. "Do you remember how we celebrated when women were finally enfranchised on the same basis as men?"

Florrie covered her heart with her hand. How could she forget? 1928 was such an era-defining year, with the universal votes for women, Amelia Earhart being the first woman to fly across the Atlantic, the publication of *The Well of Loneliness*, and the first talkie being shown in England. They were convinced the world was on the brink of something new, hopeful, and wonderful. And being liberated and professional, modern women, they had surfed the wave of that excitement. After drinking more than one bottle of the champagne Diana had been saving especially for the day of their "liberation," she had pulled Florrie up the stairs of her flat over the printing presses where they worked. Stockings had been shed, petticoats raised, fingers found folds and connections were made of emancipation and ecstasy.

"I could never forget," Florrie managed to say around the emotions constricting her throat. Why had Diana mentioned that time in particular? In three years, they'd had many stolen nights filled with laughter, intimacy, and memorable experiences. But that time was different; reckless and intoxicated, it had been the only time they'd risked their professionalism at the office.

"I need to join my son now, but here's my card." Diana passed over the gold embossed card with her gloved hands. "Are you around for a few days?"

Florrie couldn't help but admire Diana's long fingers, so elegant, unlike Florrie's, now gnarled and twisted by rheumatoid arthritis. How many hours had she dreamed of those fingers and the sapphic symphonies they could play?

Gloria grinned. The sparkle in her eye indicated she was clearly intrigued. She always was a sharp one. Cam would be oblivious as always.

"We live nearby. It's reet easy for us to get into Cambridge," Gloria said.

Diana startled and eyed Gloria as though she'd forgotten they were there. "Wonderful. Shall we meet here for coffee tomorrow morning?"

Gloria placed her hand on Cam's forearm. "Cam and I are busy tomorrow. But that shouldn't stop you two meeting up. We'll get Aunty Florrie here for eleven o'clock."

Diana arched a single eyebrow in the way that had made Florrie's knees go weak so many years ago. She wasn't *un*affected now, and she gripped the back of her chair to control herself.

Cam frowned. "We're not doing anything tomorrow. I thought we'd agreed— Hey, why are you pinching me?"

"I'll explain later," Gloria said in a whisper loud enough for them all to hear.

Yes, Gloria had picked up what was going on. Though nothing really was going on; it was just two old friends meeting up for coffee. Or, more accurately, employer and employee. But Diana did seem pleased to see her. And she wouldn't have invited Florrie to meet up again unless she wanted to; there was no obligation.

When Florrie's heart beat a little faster, she could pretend it was the exertion of rising from the seat without grimacing in pain. Damn this arthritis making her old before her time. "I'll confirm later," Florrie said, trying to right her world.

"Delightful to see you again, Florence. I can't wait to catch up and hear more about what brought you to Cambridge." Her gaze was steady, soft, and searching. "Call me later. Lovely to meet you both."

After a flurry of farewells and handshakes, Diana gently placed her hand on Florrie's arm as she air-kissed her on both cheeks; she'd always been so continental. The second kiss was a feather of lips so close to her mouth that goosebumps shimmied up Florrie's arm. She hadn't had a response like that in years.

Was Diana remembering everything they'd shared too? Probably not. She was just being friendly. It didn't mean anything. Although, now her son was at university, she would be a lonely widow. Not likely. Diana would have filled her life with places to go and people to meet. Yet she wanted to meet Florrie again. Her heart fluttered faster than normal. *Breathe. It would be fine. Possibly.* They would catch up tomorrow and then part ways, ripping apart her carefully curated life and rattling her well-earned equanimity. Again.

Diana snaked her way through the tables of graduates in their gowns with their noisy families. She was still so elegant and turned heads. Florrie swallowed hard. How could she be so raw and agitated after such an innocuous meeting, to be plunged so deeply into the past and the moment her heart had broken?

"Well, there's a story there," said Gloria, picking up Diana's calling card.

Florrie glanced at them both. She needed to smooth her agitated nerves and regain her equilibrium. "Do you mind if we go home now?"

Cam frowned. "Really? We haven't finished, and you said how much you were enjoying relaxing and watching the students punting their parents down the backs."

They stared across the terrace of the tearoom to a family being propelled along the lazy river by a young man who was struggling to stand and maintain the right direction. He almost overbalanced but caught himself in time.

Gloria laughed. "They should've taken a tour. It might have been more enjoyable."

"I hope they've got a change of clothes," Florrie said and smiled.

Cam stared at her, obviously waiting for her response to Gloria's prod. Damn. Florrie thought she'd got away with the distraction. How could she say her past had come screaming in like an air raid siren, warning of disruption to come? She sighed. She was being too dramatic. Coffee with Diana would be fine. Florrie would simply listen to how wonderful Diana's life had been with a fixed smile. But Florrie would bear witness for the woman she had once been, whose world had changed because of the woman she'd fallen in love with, who'd been betrayed and never quite recovered.

"Aunty?"

"Yes, sorry, Cam, darling. I'm feeling rather tired. Do you think they would box up the rest for us to eat later? Go and wait outside, dears, while I settle up."

Cam's shoulders dropped a quarter of an inch. "Of course. Thank you, Aunty."

"Yes, thank you, Aunty. It's been a wonderful, *intriguing* tea."

So she wouldn't be satisfied until Florrie gave her the full story. She was such a cheeky madam sometimes, but Florrie forgave her every time. "You're welcome, and congratulations again on coming top in your exams."

Gloria winked at Cam. "It helped having all those additional tutorials."

Cam rose and helped Gloria with her chair, giving her such a warm and passionate gaze that a man entering the terrace almost snapped his neck giving them a second glance. Was he trying to fathom the nature of their relationship? Cam's dapper, masculine presentation often caused eyebrows to raise and whispers to be shared in gleeful sibilants, but she refused to bend to their judgement. The hackles on Florrie's neck rose, and she stiffened ready to defend them both if he made any comment, but he shrugged and took an empty table.

Gloria took Florrie's arm while Cam asked for their cakes to be boxed up—with continuing rationing after the war, no one wanted to waste food—and they made their way inside to wait.

When a waitress returned with their leftovers, Gloria took the box, and Florrie waved them away. "Off you go. I'll settle this," she said and leaned against the counter.

"Can I help you?" the senior waitress asked as she unlocked the cash drawer.

"Thank you. I'd like to pay for table fourteen, please." Florrie passed the time of day, then rounded up the bill to give a generous tip.

The young woman's eyes widened. "Thanks, ma'am."

"Goodbye." Florrie smiled as she replaced her purse into her handbag then shuffled towards the door. Cam peered in anxiously and opened it as Florrie approached.

"Let me help you, Aunty."

"Thank you, dear." She took Cam's elbow, and they continued down the narrow pavement towards the bus stop, with Gloria clearing the way. When they halted, Gloria grinned and handed Diana's calling card to Florrie. When had she snaffled that?

"So, there's obviously a story there. Who is Lady Diana Packard Smith to you?"

Gloria enunciated the name in faux upper-class English, honed through listening to the well-bred and entitled over the last four years. Gloria intimated she'd been the butt of snobbery at Cambridge, but she'd never let it bother her. Outwardly, at least.

"We were colleagues," Florrie said. "Or rather I worked for her printing press in the twenties in London." Such a bald statement that defined the best time in her life, and the worst. A maelstrom of emotions churned in Florrie's chest. Her hands trembled slightly. Her past had stared her in the face and invited her for coffee. Life was too ordered and safe now. She was happy. And she hadn't yet decided whether she wanted to revisit that time or bury it into the deepest recesses of her mind never to be looked at again. But the question wasn't whether she wanted to sip from that cup again, but whether she was strong enough to resist it.

Chapter Two

London, 1926

THE DAY HAD NCT started well, and they needed to leave now if they were not going to be late for the cultural event at the embassy. Eleven-year-old Cam was hiding under the table in the kitchen—her safe space—and refused to come out no matter how many times her mother called her.

"For God's sake, Camilla, stop acting like a child. Come out of there. We have to go, and we don't want you grovelling on the ground like some animal when the nanny arrives."

"Leave her be, Nora. She's upset about your announcement." Florrie pulled her elder sister out of the room to give Cam the opportunity to calm down and come out when she felt safe. She closed the kitchen door behind them. "I'm happy to stay behind and spend the evening—"

"No." Nora scowled at her. "You're coming. We're being posted, so you need to find another job. You don't want to go back to Belfast, so we'll have to find you something here. This event is the ideal opportunity for making contacts, with all the mix of diplomatic and creative types."

"I'm happy to stay here with Cam."

"You can't. It's a diplomatic house. Camilla is going to boarding school, and that's final."

Why couldn't Nora see it would kill Cam to be at school? "She'll hate it. The other kids will bully her, and it'll all be too loud and the food—"

"Why can't she be normal?"

Florrie frantically waved her hands trying desperately to get Nora to quieten down, not wanting Cam to hear. "She's a lovely child. She's also incredibly bright. Get her a tutor, and she can live with me. I'll get a job in London, and you can see her when you come home. Or maybe we can come out to Egypt and visit at holidays."

"You don't understand how difficult it is."

Nora gave her the same sullen pout she had as a child when she didn't have a logical rebuttal against Florrie's argument. She was trying to carefully navigate the conflicting demands of her husband's career and the requirements of a highly strung child prodigy, so Florrie supposed she should be more understanding. She unclenched her fists. "I only want the best for my niece. It's what she deserves."

"It's not up to me. Charles thinks she'll be better off at boarding school."

Now they were getting to the truth. Where Charles commanded, Nora would follow like an obedient foot soldier. It was infuriating. "Just for once, will you stand up to him? What was good for him isn't good for Cam. She's sensitive and finds other children noisy and frightening. It would be cruel to send her away. She'll be much happier at home with me. We'll get her a tutor who can specialise in challenging her, maybe preparing her to follow Charles to his alma mater."

Nora's mouth formed a hard line of certainty. "Trinity College is a men-only college."

"But there are women's colleges. If you send her to a boarding school, she'll spend all her time playing up because she's so much brighter than her contemporaries, or she'll hide from everyone and run away. How will you deal with that when you're in Egypt?"

"I can't exactly run back to deal with her." Nora huffed loudly. "This is Charles' first senior post, and I'm expected to do my part too. The role of a diplomat's wife is as full as the—"

Florrie raised her hand. "I know. You've told me. But you

also have a lovely young girl who needs love and support. I can give her that. We could live in Charles' second home in Worcestershire somewhere."

"No, that wouldn't work. He'll close it up while he's away. It's too expensive to keep open."

"If you got off your arses and thought about what's best for your daughter instead of thinking about the cost of everything, you'd do a lot better." Florrie always thought of herself as placid, but her sister could get on her nerves quicker than anyone she knew. Nora probably felt the same. Florrie pressed a fist against her thigh and counted to five. This wasn't helping. She needed a different approach.

There was a knock on the door and the nanny, Molly Manders, let herself in. *Good.* Cam liked her. Florrie smiled and gestured for her to hang her coat up in the hall.

Nora looked at her delicate gold watch and sighed. "Let's talk about this another time. We have to be going. Charles will be very cross if we arrive late."

"Please just put your daughter's needs first and give her the time and understanding she deserves."

"I said later." Nora snatched up her sequined clutch bag with a rustle of silk and indignation. "Let's go."

"I'll check on Cam and let her know we're off." Florrie turned to see Cam already standing there, clutching the door jamb, her eyes wide and wild. "Oh, sweetheart, did you hear all that?"

Cam nodded, the absolute picture of misery, her shoulders hunched in on herself and her eyes shiny with unshed tears.

"I'm so sorry," Florrie said. Cam met her gaze and gave her a small, thin-lipped nod.

Nora rushed to Cam and enveloped her in a hug. Cam squirmed and struggled. When would Nora realise Cam hated being touched unless she'd initiated it? Did Nora not know or simply not care?

"Don't worry, we'll sort something out," Nora said. "Now,

pick your feet up, Florrie. We can't keep Charles waiting."

Florrie uncurled her fists. She wouldn't give up on Cam. "I'm ready."

"Where's that nanny?"

Molly bobbed in a curtsey. "Here, ma'am."

Nora kissed Cam soundly on the forehead, despite the girl struggling to release herself from her mother's grip. "Night night, darling. Be a good girl for Nanny Molly."

Still in her mother's vice-like hug, Cam rolled her eyes, and Florrie gave her a conspiratorial wink. They both knew Florrie wouldn't reprimand her for being insolent.

With a flurry of donning coats and hats, they eventually got to the diplomatic car, where the driver held the door open for them. As the most important sister, Nora entered first, and Florrie scrambled in behind. Their journey to the formal rooms at Somerset House passed in a bitter silence, and Florrie wiped away the condensation, wishing she was anywhere but here. When their car arrived, the driver opened Nora's door first, and Charles offered his hand for Nora to lean on. Florrie scurried out of the car and followed a step behind, as was their custom, trying to delay entering the function hall. She hated the trivial conversations and facile comments from dull people boasting about their connections and possessions, and showing no interest in fascinating topics that challenged the status quo and stretched their minds.

She smiled at the valet as he took her hat and coat, then rearranged her gown to make it marginally less uncomfortable, hoping it wasn't obvious to everyone that it was a hand-me-down from Nora, who was taller and thinner. Nora resembled a Hollywood starlet wearing it, whereas Florrie looked slightly frumpy. She pulled at the extra material where she shouldn't have it and tried to stretch it over her unfashionable bosom. She would never be as glamorous as her sister. Not that she wanted to be glamorous; she'd always been grateful she'd been blessed with an inquiring brain rather than Nora's looks.

The room glowed with warmth and life, the low murmur of the crowd muted against the notes of the string quartet and underscored by the clatter of glasses and plates.

A bark of laughter caught Florrie's attention, and her gaze strayed to a group of raffishly dressed young men buzzing around a willowy woman. She was slender and fashionable, complete with the latest flapper costume and short dark hair. Everything about her was completely arresting and seemed familiar, but Florrie had never met her before. Florrie clamped her mouth shut, so she didn't gape.

The group was fascinating and daunting in equal measure. To have that level of confidence, to be heedless of the tuts of disapproval from the diplomatic crowd was something Florrie could never attain. She stared in envy and delight as they laughed again, like they were gorgeous hyenas mocking a funeral, uncaring about the decorum of everyone else.

Charles' lip curled in disdain. "Ah, I see we're plagued by the bright young things this evening. Stay away from them. They're nothing but scandal and trouble."

"Who are they?" Florrie asked, trying to keep the excitement from her voice.

"The sons and daughters of the nobility with more money than sense. They flaunt around London drinking, drugging, listening to jazz, and behaving in a way in which no self-respecting person should act. They're a disgrace. Don't mix with them."

Aside from the drugs, that sounded like an awful lot of fun.

Charles indicated a few sedate groups of people off to one side for Florrie to mix with, then dragged Nora off to meet their important people in the opposite direction.

Florrie headed towards the table where the bright young things were gathered. It was because they were close to the canapes, that was all. They all seemed to be in their thirties and around her age, but they were self-assured and vibrant in a way she'd never been, and they probably experienced more in a week than she ever had in her entire life. She was close enough now that she could almost hear their conversation.

A dark-haired man in his early thirties with piercing blue eyes snatched a glass of champagne from a passing waiter and handed it over to Florrie. "It seems you've been left with the rabble over here. Allow me to introduce myself. I'm Rex, and these are my friends, Diana, Anthony, and Oscar."

Florrie accepted the drink and the welcome with more than a modicum of relief. Hanging around on her own like a wallflower wasn't her idea of fun, and she wanted to revel in their vivacity. "Florence Cooper, but I prefer Florrie."

Rex shook her hand. "What brings you to this kind of occasion, or are you like us starving writers, only here for the free drink and nosh?"

"Speak for yourself," Diana said. "I'm here to cultivate contacts amongst writers and artists for our publishing company."

Diana looked at Rex with an imperious air. It would have made Florrie shrivel had it been directed at her, but Rex laughed and winked. *Publishing company?* Florrie tried not to stare, but Diana was a dead ringer for the woman on the dust jacket of some of her most well-thumbed books. Was Diana the novelist and publicist, Diana Stratford? Yes, it was definitely her. She was one of Florrie's favourite writers. The others were well known too. She wished she'd worn her best dress now. Charles had misclassified them, not that he'd care. These weren't the bright young things. Rather, they were the London intellectuals, the writers, and artists whom she'd read so much about and admired from afar.

She swallowed, feeling out of her depth with her less than complete education. She loved Diana's books; their intensity and longing brought Florrie to tears. These people were publishing royalty, and she was honoured to be included in the conversation, even though Anthony glowered at her for some reason. She didn't dare ask Diana about her writing. Florrie had to be diplomatic and treat everyone with the unenthusiastic decorum that Nora and Charles expected.

All the men swooned around Diana like drones around the queen bee. Some people just oozed charisma. Florrie found herself drawn into Diana's aura like a moth to the flame, except her heart fluttered rather than her wings. "What range of books do you publish in your press?" she asked, hoping she didn't sound too breathless or obsequious.

"The Euston Press publishes modern works by obscure and upcoming authors such as myself," Rex said. "Diana is the most famous author of us all, of course, and Oscar writes dirges and pretends they're poetry."

"You're a fine one to talk. Just because you pander to the masses with your crime fiction, jumping onto the popularity of Sir Arthur Conan Doyle and Mrs Agatha Christie," Diana said to Rex with a twinkle in her eye. She turned more to face Florrie. "We have an eclectic mix of writers, and the more popular books enable us to publish more esoteric works."

Florrie turned to break from Diana's unblinking eye contact. It was too revealing, too intriguing to return it fully. "I've read some of Oscar Harris's poems. I find them very moving."

"I like you already." Oscar fluttered his eyelashes at her and mock-wiped his brow with a flourish of a handkerchief.

He was someone Charles would write off as being a dandy and would want nothing to do with him, although his job as a diplomat was to be nice to everyone—as he stabbed them in the back.

"I feel spurned," said Rex and tossed his head in mock despair.

Florrie chuckled. "I like your works too."

Rex preened his hair. "Thank you. I feel *partially* mollified, which is no more than I deserve since I rescued you from having to talk to the dull as ditch-water diplomats." He leaned forward to whisper behind his hand. "Forgive me, but you don't seem part of the schmoozing set."

"I'm not." Florrie indicated where Nora was hovering with a group of women, all draped with matching polite smiles and expensive pearls. "I came with my sister and brother-in-law who *are* dull as ditch-water diplomats about to be posted to Egypt."

"How tedious," Anthony said. "I'm going to speak to John Wrightson over there."

He wandered off without a backward glance, and Florrie was unsure whether he was referring to the posting in Egypt or their conversation. Either way, the energy lifted in the group and shoulders lowered an inch or two. Florrie grinned and turned to the others.

Diana fixed her with an imperious stare. "So, Florence, are you an author or an artist?"

Normally, Florrie would correct anyone who called her that, but the way Diana said it had an almost French lilt to it, which was very appealing. "Neither. I love to read anything I can get my hands on. I read hundreds of books a year, mainly from libraries."

"And what do you do that allows you so much time to read?" Diana asked.

Florrie swallowed hard. Was this a test? She didn't have a sophisticated career and hadn't been born to the upper classes. How was she supposed to compete when she didn't really know the game? "I look after my niece, as my sister and brother-in-law always have so many diplomatic functions. We had a little altercation before we came out though. They want to send her to a boarding school even though she'll hate it. I said we should get her a tutor, and I'd look after her full time. Not that she needs much looking after." She nibbled her bottom lip; she was rabbiting on again. "Sorry, you probably don't need all that detail." Why did she feel the need to explain anyway? Perhaps she was hoping these intellectual people would agree with her reasoning.

Rex clapped Oscar on the back. "Maybe this is exactly what

you need to keep the wolf from the door." He turned to Florrie. "Our resident poet here is brilliant, ex-Cambridge, but he's struggling to make ends meet. Poetry really is the Cinderella of the arts."

"Can you teach mathematics?" Florrie asked. "My niece, Cam, is a prodigy in maths, and I can't keep up with her anymore."

"I took it at Cambridge as part of my joint honours but much to my parents' disgust, I discontinued the maths and pursued the literary side instead. I am forever a disappointment to them and thus the black sheep of the family." He bowed and grinned.

"Please give me your details, and I'll pass your name along to my sister."

"With pleasure." He withdrew a pristine card from the top inner pocket of his jacket, the gesture so smooth, it seemed rehearsed. "I'm an excellent boy scout and always come prepared," he said, as if he'd caught her surprise.

The evening was turning out wonderfully, and her heart sped up. To have Oscar teach Cam would be thrilling. Maybe they could have conversations about poetry, and he could introduce her to the works of other writers and open new worlds.

"Have you read any of my works?" Diana asked.

Her eyes locked on Florrie's with such intensity that it made her weak at the knees and revealed her soul. There was nowhere to hide under that gaze.

Florrie nodded, her heart thudding.

"And what did you think of my latest?"

Florrie hesitated, unease rippling through her. "This feels like a trap." She glanced at the men who waited, like the tricoteuses around the guillotine, watching for the blade to drop while they knitted caps and mittens.

Diana flashed a half smile and raised her champagne glass. "I'm surrounded by yes men, so I welcome the honest opinion of one of my readers."

Florrie cleared her throat. Well, she had hoped to talk about her writing once she realised who Diana was, so she should take this opportunity since it would never arise again. "I love the depth in your novels, how every word seems to work on so many levels and does so with a felicity of language that's truly lyrical. The longing and loss in *The Oratory* made me cry; it was so nuanced and emotional."

Diana's expression was unreadable, but she nodded slowly. Florrie flashed her a worried look to see how her truth had landed, but she didn't see anger or hurt in Diana's eyes.

"Thank you, but you avoided commentary about my latest, *Miss Brashwood Holds a Party*."

Florrie regretted her pale, freckled complexion that flushed with the merest hint of provocation. Of course Diana would have picked up on her omission.

Diana arched her smooth eyebrow. "Ah. I see you do not wish to share your thoughts—"

"No. I... Well, it's not my favourite. It was beautifully crafted, as expected, and the themes of death and loneliness were clear and deep, but for me, it lacked the same emotional connection to the character—"

"So she was a caricature?" Diana asked.

"No, I wouldn't say that. More that she was held aloof from the reader. On reflection, that may have been deliberate... And I have now embarrassed myself completely." She flapped at the neck of her dress, causing the string of beads to rattle. Who was she to critique such a talented writer? To her face, no less.

"On the contrary, I think you've hit the nail on the head. I've been struggling to write, staring at a blank page with my mind circulating around the myriad irritations of running a business, and I couldn't fathom why. Thank you for your insight and your honesty. I can't rely on these glorious sycophants to give me the truth." She waved at her entourage, then smiled. "Perhaps I *can* rely on them to fetch me another coupe of champagne? Thank you, Rex, darling."

Rex hurried off, and Nora charged towards them, a grim line of determination on her face: her *you disobeyed us* face, familiar to Florrie since she was little, but she wasn't sorry she'd spoken with this fascinating woman.

She gave Oscar her widest smile. "Oscar, let me introduce you to my sister, Mrs Nora Langley. Nora, this is Mr Oscar Harris, a Cambridge graduate who could be a potential tutor for Cam. And this is Diana." She didn't mention Oscar was a famous poet, knowing that would elicit an immediate refusal. Charles considered poetry a waste of time, and Nora echoed his thoughts without troubling her own brain cells between his mouth and hers.

Nora scowled at Florrie and barely shook hands with Oscar. She ignored Diana and Rex, who returned with a bottle he'd extracted from a waiter.

"How do you do? I'm Rex Taylor. Would you care for some of this fine champagne?"

"No, thank you." Nora said adopting a pinched expression.

Florrie's cheeks burned. Nora never used to be like this but had been influenced by Charles, who was little more than a snob. To him, people were separated into how useful they could be to him, either as a resource or to help secure advancement. Anyone else was tolerated or simply ignored. He had already made it clear that this group of brilliant authors were of little value, if he had any idea at all who they were. Nora, not a reader herself, had clearly adopted the same opinion.

Nora turned to Florrie. "I'm not sure what you're doing here. You were supposed to be circulating and trying to find yourself a job. Don't miss the golden opportunity Charles has bestowed on you."

If only the floor would open up and swallow her whole. Florrie had hoped to impress these people, not by writing but by reading and catching the coattails of their conversation. Now she was being shown as desperate and needing something. She hoped

Diana didn't think she'd come over here with the sole purpose of eliciting a job.

Diana stiffened and cleared her throat. "Actually, my publishing house is looking for someone to be a reader. We have so many manuscripts across our desk that we don't have time for other things. My writing is falling behind." She elegantly swung around to face Florrie with a warmth in her expression that took Florrie's breath. "Would you care for the job, Florence? It doesn't pay very well, I'm afraid, but you can do most of it from home. You would only need to come into the press about once a week. Would that suit you?"

Florrie ignored Nora's glare and allowed herself to be mesmerised by Diana's gaze. It was a look full of attention and understanding, one she would gladly receive daily. "Oh, gosh, yes. That would be wonderful." She would agree to anything from this woman.

"You could think about it, Florrie," Nora said, pulling at her arm. "Now. You should meet some *useful* people over here."

"Here's my card," Diana said, handing Florrie a gold embossed business card. "Come and see me tomorrow morning at ten o' clock."

Like some overzealous autograph hunter, Florrie almost felt like asking Diana to sign it. She stood with the card in her palms, prayer-like, and didn't move until her arm was tugged, bringing her out of her daze. As Nora dragged her off, Florrie gave her hurried thanks and farewells, wishing she could recapture and relive every minute of the interaction.

Florrie spent the rest of the evening pretending to listen to the boring conversations of the influential, while casting envious looks at Diana's entourage. She untethered her attention from the boasting and complaints and drifted towards the literary group, trying to catch wafts of their conversation and laughter. How strange that their amusement was so encompassing for those involved and so excluding to those outside. What she would give to be a moon circling that cluster of planets as they orbited around Diana's sun.

The following morning, Florence arrived at the address of the publishing house in North London, clinging to the hope that Diana's offer was genuine and not merely a ploy to rescue Florrie from Nora, so she could save face.

Florrie wasn't part of Diana's world, so to be invited, to have a peek behind the dusty covers of the literary giants had her wringing her rather sweaty hands. She should have worn gloves; it would have been more professional. Straightening her spine, she pushed open the door of the press.

A doorbell tinkled as she entered. She smiled at the older female receptionist at the front office, who looked like she'd stepped from the time of Queen Victoria, dressed all in black. "Good morning, I'm Florence Cooper, and I have a meeting with Diana Stratford."

From an inner room came the dull thump of a printing press. Even at this distance, it reverberated in Florrie's chest. It must be difficult to work in an environment like this, but Diana had said most of the work could be done at home.

The receptionist phoned through and relayed Florrie's presence. She replaced the receiver delicately in its cradle and gave a brief smile. "Come with me."

Florrie followed the woman as she wove through the printing presses, the relentless clattering pounding through her whole body. They ascended the back stairs, each step slapping on the worn stone, until they emerged into a corridor on the first floor. The receptionist closed the door behind them, mercifully muting the thumping of the presses. There were three doors off the short corridor. One had a brass plaque stating it was the office of Diana Stratford

Florrie's breath caught, and her heart pounded as loudly as the machines below them. After a knock, she was ushered into the inner sanctum. She was a little disappointed that books didn't line all the walls. Instead, there was a typewriter on a desk stacked high with papers. Manuscripts tied up with pink ribbon towered high on the chairs, spilling onto a small second desk, the filing cabinet, and in pillars of paper on the floor. Given how the paper yellowed and curled at the edges, they must have been there some time.

Diana rose from her desk like Venus rising from the shell. "Thank you, Jane. Can you take these letters to be posted?"

Jane accepted the packets with a bob and hurried out, closing the door with a soft click.

Diana shook Florrie's hand briefly, then gestured to a visitor chair, the only uncluttered surface. Diana wore a comfortable tweed skirt and turtleneck jumper, which seemed to be made of soft wool. Around her neck was a single string of pearls, and on her left breast, an enamel brooch that whispered luxury and refinement. Even though her outfit was simple, it looked more expensive than all of Florrie's dresses, best or otherwise. Florrie pulled at her collar.

Diana gave Florrie a warm smile, without a trace of superiority or condescension. Something loosened in Florrie's chest, and she relaxed into the chair, letting her shoulders drop a little. Maybe it had been a genuine offer.

Diana waved her hand. "I wasn't joking about being swamped by manuscripts, as you can see. I'd be grateful if you could weed out the complete non-starters. Despite having an eclectic mix of publications, one thing we insist on is that all manuscripts must be well written. We can edit, of course, but if a manuscript needs a huge amount of work, it will cost too much to fix it. Anthony is all about paring down the cost of production."

"That's understandable." Florrie nodded. "What are you looking for in a manuscript apart from it being well written?"

"Something different. Ideally, we're looking for books that touch your soul, or that take a different perspective, or are innovative." Diana sighed and settled back in her chair. "We also need more commercial works that will sell well, such as Rex's books. He never claims they're highbrow, but they bring in a lot of our income and keep the presses rolling."

Florrie struggled not to clap her hands together, although she felt like doing a little dance around the room. "This is so thrilling. I'd love to be involved. Do you need me to do a trial run first?"

Diana's eyes widened like she hadn't thought about such a thing. Perhaps the upper classes did everything on trust, but if she wasn't good enough, Florrie would prefer to know before she got too enrobed in excitement.

"Yes, I suppose that would be a good idea." Diana tapped her lip with her fountain pen.

Florrie prayed it wouldn't leak, but it was probably an expensive pen and would do no such thing.

"I'd like you to read the last five manuscripts I assessed, then you can give me your feedback and see how it compares to mine. To help you, of these five," she pushed a stack of papers towards Florrie, "we've taken one on for definite and another two are possibilities that would require a great deal of editing. The other two were a definite no. Could you come back in a week's time to discuss them?"

Florrie pulled the scripts towards her like she was hoarding dragon's gold; she didn't want a single page to slip away.

Diana shifted in her seat. "We haven't talked about money. We might need to do it per script rather than by time, being conscious some will take longer than others. All I ask is you read each one thoroughly, as novice writers pay more attention to the beginning, and their middles are often sluggish or muddled."

She wrote a figure down on a piece of personalised stationery and passed it across the desk. The skin on her delicate fingers was almost translucent, showing a hint of the blue veins beneath, and her nails were trimmed in a simple, practical style. She'd probably never done a day's labour in her life.

"That's the maximum I can allow for."

"Sorry?" Florrie had been so entranced by the woman's hands, she'd forgotten she was supposed to respond. Hurriedly, she glanced at the figure. Ten shillings was written in small, neat handwriting. Her heart sped up. What a thrill to earn her own money. But she had to be sensible and cover travel, and rent costs, and all the other items of expense for both her and Cam. "How many manuscripts a week would you expect? Five? If so, I could make that work when I've secured myself other lodgings."

Diana's eyes locked onto hers, sharp and probing, like a hawk. "You need lodgings? Will you still be able to attend weekly?"

Florrie stared at her own, less well-manicured fingers and wiped her rather sweaty palms on her skirt. She'd come in the most acceptable clothes she could muster at short notice. At least she had her new cloche hat to match her shorter hair style, which looked so much more professional. But was her precarious accommodation situation going to break the agreement? How should she answer? With the truth, of course. She nodded. She would find somewhere further out from London and secure somewhere big enough for Cam and herself, and they'd be okay. "Yes, for myself and my niece. I'm looking for somewhere out in the country and on a direct line into Euston, so I should be able to commute easily." She hadn't looked yet, but there were a few stations along the line that must be less expensive than the eye-wateringly high rents she'd reviewed in London.

"Will Oscar be your niece's tutor? If so, check out Bletchley. It's on a direct line from Cambridge on the Varsity line as well as the London Euston line. Oscar lives in Cambridge."

"I hope he will. Nora is worried about a man being around a vulnerable girl with only a maid and me."

Was that a curl of Diana's lip? It was difficult to tell because her expression flashed back to neutral in a breath. Florrie would love to know what Diana was thinking. She was so closed off, with those pinched lips and thoughtful expression, as if she weighed every word. A bit like her sparse writing, which was beautiful, haunting, and surprisingly passionate, given her rather aloof manner.

"You don't need to worry about Oscar. At least not with the girls. But I wouldn't say the last part to your sister."

Florrie nodded since she couldn't trust herself to speak. Was Diana saying what she thought she was implying? That was incredibly dangerous. But now she'd said it, Florrie could see it. She supposed that meant his poetry was to another man rather than a woman. The idea, which would shock and disgust society, intrigued her and her spine tingled. Diana had been so casual about it. How deliciously scandalous.

"Are you familiar with the works of Sigmund Freud?"

Florrie frowned. That came from nowhere. She suspected it would be ever thus: Diana making some enormous intellectual leap, and Florrie scrabbling to keep up. It was mind-expanding, discombobulating, and thrilling. "I've read *The Interpretation of Dreams*. In the English translation of course." She had no doubt that Diana would've read it in the original German and could discuss it in that language, slipping over the alternate vocabulary with ease. "But I can't say I understood it all."

Diana waved her hand. "There's a talk this afternoon. I have two tickets, but Anthony says he's too busy to go. Would you like to come?"

Florrie nearly bounced in her chair, but she caught herself and smoothed down her skirt. "I'd love to come. But I don't have anything suitable to wear."

Diana waved her dismissive hand gesture again. "Nobody cares about such middle-class sensibilities. That's settled."

Florrie burned up. She'd always aspired to rise above class and religion, which was difficult having been brought up in Belfast, where sectarianism ran as deep as the stripe in rock candy. She thought she'd left all that behind.

Diana checked the time on a men's large watch with a clear face and hands, so unlike Nora's feminine watch. It summed up their differences, and Florrie knew which she preferred.

It was all so exciting, to catch a cab to the venue, and see all the sights, and be in the company of such a brilliant and accomplished woman who held considered opinions and expressed them on such matters as recent scientific discoveries to the latest books and political thought. She was like a walking university dressed up in a stylish package. Florrie could see herself being offered a peep into the sweetshop of intellectual pursuits that London represented, through Diana's patronage.

By the following week, Florrie had devoured the five manuscripts and thought she'd worked out which of them Diana had chosen. There was one she was sure would be rejected; it was too different, although it had something about it that Florrie thought could be interesting. It had been written in the style of H.G. Wells and was set in a harsh world in which technology sought to dehumanise people. It was different and challenging, and she was unsure whether Diana would consider it. Florrie was determined to make a case for publishing it though.

She said hello to Jane, then bounded up the stairs, ignoring the deep throbbing of the presses and the industry of the printers, eagerly anticipating another thrilling conversation with Diana. But raised voices stopped her in the corridor.

"You can't keep on picking up every waif and stray you take a fancy to."

Florrie recognised the deep bass of Anthony's voice. She had the horrible feeling he was referring to her. She shrank against the wall, hoping the floorboards didn't creak.

"If she takes on some of my workload, it means I can spend time writing—"

"And when was the last time you finished something? You promised me three books a year to keep the presses running. Instead, I have to infill with all this non-commercial stuff. You're going to run out of money soon, and then you must comply with your side of the bargain."

"Was that a threat?"

Diana sounded less than composed, which was unsettling. Why didn't Anthony want her here? It looked like everything was going to work out; she didn't need him putting a stop to it before it had really begun.

Now Nora had agreed to let Cam stay with Florrie, Cam had relaxed a little. Their future balanced on a series of outcomes that interconnected, and one break in the sequence would bring everything crashing down.

Charles, in an unexpected turn of generosity, or guilt, had even offered to pay for Cam's tuition and part of the rent on a smallholding near Bletchley Park, which was mid-way between Cambridge and Oxford and about an hour's train ride from London. It was further out than she'd hoped, but Oscar had agreed to come by train from Cambridge, where he had "the choice of such sweet delights." Florrie didn't ask what he meant by that; she didn't need to.

She uncurled her fists, surprised how tightly she'd been clenching them, and expelled a deep breath. No more waiting. She stomped down the corridor, announcing her arrival. As she approached Diana's office, Anthony stormed out, slammed Diana's door, and rushed past Florrie into his own office. A picture of the book cover of Diana's first book rattled against the wall.

"Good morning," she called out to him. She was brought up to be polite, but clearly he had no such manners. So, he wasn't a fan, or maybe he knew she'd heard them. And what had he meant by "every waif and stray" Diana took a fancy to? Did he think she was a charity case? It stung a little that she *was* a charity case. This job was a lifeline and the final cog in the mechanism for her plan to work.

She strode to the office and took a breath before knocking softly.

There was a long pause before Diana cleared her throat.

"Come in."

Florrie entered.

Diana sat behind her desk, sucking on a cigarette. She puffed it out and ground the stub into the ashtray, her fingers trembling. "Disgusting habit. I presume you heard all that?"

Florrie cursed her pale colouring and freckles that were already halfway to a blush. She had no hope in disguising it and simply nodded.

"Because he's a businessman, what he doesn't appreciate is that the literary process takes more than squeezing in a couple of hours here and there. Some writers can do that. I can't. I need to feel my way in. I can only do that if there isn't constant interruption like there is here. I simply can't ignore the noise of the presses and the traffic in the street outside. I need to be at home in the country." Diana indicated Florrie should sit down, and she perched herself on the edge of the chair. "Tell me what you think of the manuscripts."

Florrie pulled out the tied paper bundles from her bag and placed them on Diana's desk. "I would say these two are a definite no, and these two are a definite yes with a varying degree of editing. This one," she placed it on the desk between them, "is not the usual offering and is nothing like I've read before. It reminds me of John Stuart Mill's analysis of the word, a *dystopian* novel much along the lines of H.G. Wells' *Time Machine* and *The War of the Worlds*. I suspect it will either fly or die. If the press is concerned about money, perhaps it should be rejected."

Diana seemed to concentrate on Florrie's every word, as though she was an expert. Her focused attention was daunting, unnerving...and thrilling.

"I agree with your analysis but disagree with your conclusion on the dystopian novel. This is exactly the challenging book we should be considering, otherwise we're like any other publishing house. Anthony be damned. He would make it so bland and beige. But it's not his choice, and it's not his money. It's mine.

Don't worry. You're exactly what we need. What *I* need."

Florrie puddled into a gooey mess of something she was loathe to acknowledge, though what else could it be but desire. She squirmed in her seat. She'd heard stories of women with such unnatural feelings, and Nora had been very clear what she thought about that. Surely, that didn't apply to Florrie, did it? That wasn't what she knew about herself, and yet... She closed her eyes. If she looked back over her life, all her excitement and interest had been stirred by the fairer sex. And Diana was such an appealing woman, with her superior intellect, control, and command of herself and all those around her. Florrie licked her lips. She shouldn't be thinking about her employer that way, nor drooling over her like she was a piece of bacon.

She hoped Diana couldn't see the impact she was having on Florrie. Perhaps it was safer to pack up her bag now and run away as fast as she could. She was a simple woman who merely loved to use her brain and loved her niece like her own daughter. This could be dangerous, and she'd need to keep herself in check. And this was such an opportunity. If Diana was happy with her work, then Florrie would do whatever she could to assist.

She blew out a breath and sat straighter. She could deal with this. She was grateful, that was all.

Diana checked her watch. "How about an early lunch? We can go to the Millicent Fawcett talk about expanding the franchise for women. It's ridiculous to restrict it to propertied married women over thirty. It should be equal rights with men. We should sign up to campaign for them."

That sounded exciting and terrifying in equal measure. "They won't throw us in prison, will they? I'm responsible for my niece. I can't—"

"Not for attending a discussion meeting, no. Let's go for lunch."

Florrie's face burned again. Red seemed to be the only colour it adopted around Diana. "I might need to join you after your lunch, because I've brought sandwiches."

"Nonsense." Diana steepled her fingers. "I need you there. I hate lunching alone."

Florrie twisted her fingers in her lap, wanting to swallow the words in her throat before she forced them out. "I can't afford it."

"Oh, darling, of course I'll pay. I invited you. Stop being so bourgeoise."

Florrie huffed out a breath. It was all right for Diana to say, she'd never had to worry about money. She'd probably never had to make a choice between eating or going on the bus, nor worn hand-me-down dresses. But those eyes were gazing at Florrie with an unblinking stare and, despite herself, she smiled. "Thank you, that would be lovely."

"Splendid. That's settled. I'll let Anthony know we won't be around this afternoon."

"Won't he be annoyed about that?"

"Let him. I'll tell him this is all research and thinking time. I'll get inspiration from the discussion this afternoon and the company of an intelligent woman." Diana waved toward Florrie,

She means me? Florrie grinned like Lewis Carroll's Cheshire Cat. "Thank you."

Diana rose and gathered her belongings into her capacious bag. She was about to add a bunch of manuscripts, then paused and handed them over to Florrie. "Do we have a deal? Get these back to me by next Thursday, and we'll discuss them."

Florrie took possession of the packets and cradled them to her chest as if holding a fragile truth, before she placed them reverently in her own large bag. The burden and excitement of responsibility zipped through her: she now held a duty of care to Diana, to the authors and of her own reputation.

Diana delved in her purse and withdrew five gold half-sovereign coins, which she passed to Florrie. Florrie rubbed them together like a talisman. They were warm and solid in her palm, and they were proof that she could make her own way in the world.

"Normally, Anthony deals with all the business matters, so I'm sure he has some tedious little forms he'll want you to complete, but this is for the scripts you've reviewed."

"Thank you." She fought the urge to bob in a mini curtsey. The train journey had cost more than she had budgeted this month, and she wanted to ensure there was sufficient cash set aside for her and Cam to settle into their new home.

Diana snapped her purse shut as if she loathed such unpleasant matters as money. "Tell me more about the manuscript you recommended. What captured your imagination?"

And as they walked to the dining hall, Florrie chatted happily about what she'd read and what she thought. It was so wonderful to be listened to, to be really heard, and to have her opinion thought of as worthy. She was already looking forward to that every time she visited.

Over lunch, Diana opined on everything from the previous week's Freud lecture to the state of publishing, from books she was looking forward to reading when she got the time, to the impact of the General Strike and the sudden disappearance of John Souter's painting *The Breakdown*, because "the stuffy idiots in the Colonial Office" couldn't cope with the depiction of a white nude dancer being serenaded by a Black jazz musician.

"It's always two steps forwards and one step back.' Diana sighed. "It's ridiculous and so hypocritical."

Her stream of curiosity and enquiry meandered like a river, and Florrie floated along with joy, absorbing the facts and Diana's opinions to mull over later. Being with Diana was expanding her mind, and she jumped into the details being laid out in front of her, questioning and inserting counter arguments at every turn. She'd never enjoyed such intellectual sparring in all her life.

"You're very good for my ego." Diana lifted Florrie's chin with her forefinger and stared into her eyes.

Florrie swallowed hard to stop herself from voicing how

that melted her inside. But did Diana mean that she was too obsequious, or could she tell Florrie was feeling things she shouldn't? She'd tried to hide her admiration and desire, but clearly Diana saw right through her.

Diana waved at the waiter. Immediately, Florrie's chin cooled at the loss of contact, then she chastised herself for being so silly.

"Thank you." Diana left sufficient coins on the table for the meal and a tip then rose. "Now, we need to get going if we're to attend this discussion."

During the taxi ride, Diana asked Florrie about the batch of manuscripts, challenging her assumptions, delving deeper, and pressing her to defend her opinions. Judging by the glint in her eye, Diana was enjoying the jousting as much as Florrie.

Diana gracefully alighted from the taxi, and Florrie clambered out after her. Florrie positively buzzed with excitement, picking up on Diana's mood.

"Before we go to the meeting, I want to give you a treat." Diana must have seen how wide Florrie's eyes went, as she laughed. "Nothing untoward, I promise."

Florrie had no choice but to follow Diana and her laughter down a small brick alleyway. They emerged into a courtyard, lined on either side by booksellers and antique dealers with enticing wares. One bowed window with thick crown glass prominently displayed Diana's books, but she didn't pause or look around until they arrived at a shop crammed with jars of sweets in the window.

"Instead of dessert," Diana said and flounced inside, the doorbell ringing frantically as she entered the shop.

An elderly man in a canvas apron bobbed his head as Diana strode to the counter. She pointed to a box filled with yellow cardboard cylinders and a liquorice stick poking out of the top of each one.

"Have you tried Sherbet Fountains? They're delicious. You suck through the liquorice straw, and it explodes and fizzes in your mouth."

Her enthusiasm was contagious. "No. But I love Liquorice Allsorts, so I'll probably enjoy them."

"You have to try one. And if you don't like it, I'll have yours."

Diana asked for two Sherbet Fountains and a quarter of Allsorts, and they left the shop like two excited children. The old man shook his head as he watched them go.

Diana led Florrie into a tiny park in one of the exclusive London squares with a bold sign stating in large letters that it was for residents only. She wasn't a resident.

Obviously seeing Florrie's hesitation, Diana waved her hand. "Don't be so bourgeoise. What's the worst they can do? Ask us to leave. I like this park as it has a fountain in the centre." She brushed a leaf off a bench, sat down, and opened up the sweet tube. "Now, taste that."

Florrie shuffled on her seat at Diana's intense scrutiny and put the straw to her mouth and sipped the powder. The lemony effervescence caused her to suck in her cheeks and smack her lips. "Mm, you're right! It *did* explode in my mouth. It's so tart and sweet simultaneously. It's delicious."

Diana flashed a triumphant smile. "See. I told you. Now you'll never want any other treat—"

"I still like my Allsorts."

Diana shook her head and handed over the paper bag. "Here you are then." A big fat raindrop splattered on the bag, then another. "We'd better go before we get drenched. It's only a few minutes' walk from here. Let's go."

Without waiting for a reply, Diana got up and strode towards the park gate, unfurling her umbrella as she went.

A few minutes later, they followed the crowd into an old church hall, where the air was thick with damp wool from the sodden coats steaming in the warmth. Diana mopped her brow before taking her reserved seat near the front. Her whole life seemed to revolve around people doing things for her and requiring her presence. Florrie took the seat beside Diana, acutely aware of the sidelong glares shooting her way, unsure she belonged here, in the best seats in the hall. She straightened her back and looked forward, faking a confidence she didn't feel.

The first speaker rose and laid out the current position with women's suffrage. Diana pulled at her coat sleeves, then grasped Florrie's hand. Florrie looked down at her hand-knitted gloves encased in Diana's silks. The warmth of her hands permeated through the layers of cloth and burned Florrie's own fingers. What was Diana doing, in full view of everyone?

"I call on our first key speaker, the world-renowned author and publisher, Diana Stratford, to speak."

Diana flashed a quick unsure smile at Florrie, who squeezed her hand. Now it was obvious why Diana had come, why she had a reserved seat, and she had gripped Florrie's hand—because she was nervous. The realisation that it meant nothing more hit Florrie with a crushing weight, and she had to breathe deeply to steady herself. Still, she would do what she could to support Diana, and if her companionship helped her in any small way, she was delighted. How silly that she'd thought there might be more.

By the time Diana had taken the stage, the uncertainty had slipped from her expression, and she became the confident, slightly haughty author once more. Diana began her speech by asking everyone to raise their hands. The audience obliged, flashing curious glances at each other. "I'm primarily addressing the women in the audience. Anyone younger than thirty, drop your hands, please. Will those who are unmarried also lower their hands."

More hands dropped, including Florrie's. Less than half the women still had their hands raised, probably a reflection of how many excess women there were after the gouging out of the male population in the Great War. Diana asked for those who were unpropertied to drop their hands. Of one hundred and fifty women in the hall, only about twenty held their hands up.

"Look around. Notice how few hands are still raised? We are told that women have the vote, but these few women before you are the only women eligible in this large group. Until we are awarded power on a basis equal to men, there will never be equality. The fight is still on. Do not be lulled into a false sense of security, whatever you read in the newspapers. They are but the mouthpiece of the establishment. We will continue the cause, the fight. Are you with us?"

The chorus of approval was loud, and Florrie's blood pulsed in her veins. She wanted to be part of this and to make something of herself, to take up the cause. It spoke to her. She would devote herself to it, and if her fervour gained her the approval of a certain tall, glamorous author, then all to the good.

She clapped so hard that her hands stung when Diana finally stepped down from the stage to a standing ovation. She threw a winning smile at all and reclaimed her seat next to Florrie while Millicent Fawcett took to the stage.

Diana leaned in and gave Florrie a smile so genuine that it warmed her to her toes.

"Did the warm-up act do all right?"

Florrie caught her hands mid-clap, her heart fluttering. "Perfect. You were perfect."

"Thank you, darling." Diana leaned in and feathered a kiss by Florrie's ear.

Florrie almost squeaked. It was so daring, so thrilling and stirring. Millicent Fawcett may have been talking, but Florrie heard nothing as what the kiss might mean flitted around her brain.

Diana had opened a whole new world up to her, and she wanted to run in and experience it all. *This* was living, and she loved it. Who would have thought she was a little spinster brought over from Belfast to care for her older sister's daughter? Now she was a woman employed in her own right, earning her own money, and attending discussions with a famous author, a woman who had kissed her on her cheek and had needed her hand for comfort before taking to the stage. Anyone else who had attended with Diana would have probably received the same treatment, but Diana had asked *her*, and she had shared this with her. Florrie brushed her glove against her own cheek, where she could still feel the imprint of Diana's lips, and smiled. The future lay before her like a promise, and she would dive into it headlong, pulling this moment with her, like an anchor for her hope.

CHAPTER THREE

WEEKS EXPANDED INTO MONTHS, with Florrie commuting every Thursday on an early train, leaving Cam with Mary, the maid, or Oscar, whom Cam more than tolerated now, especially as he taught her complex chess strategies.

She and Diana would spend a few hours discussing which books to publish, Florrie would do some organising in Diana's office, and then they'd break for lunch. Almost every time, they attended a talk or concert in the afternoon, and Florrie skipped from week to week, developing her understanding and critical thinking, and filling in the cracks in her education.

Florrie wasn't able to save much money, because she spent her extra cash on clothes from second hand shops and train tickets. By making a detour to Knightsbridge or Kensington, she secured quality clothes at a fraction of the cost at the charity shops. Fortunately, Diana paid for all their lunches, so Florrie saved on meals for herself and eked out the rest of her income, so she could put aside a little for a rainy day. It was enough, and she'd make it work to stay in Diana's close orbit.

The only sore spot was Anthony's presence. He loomed over her happiness with his judgement and disdain, and she became adept at avoiding him, speaking to him only when she needed to justify her time and expenses.

Today though, he'd called her into his office, which was pristine, his desk clear, and bookshelves around the walls lined with ledger books all neatly labelled. She had no doubt he was efficient, but it was soulless. There was no indication this was the office of a director of such a creative, radical company, pushing the boundaries of thought and literature, and challenging the rigid expectations of the past.

"Why are you claiming for ten scripts this week?" Anthony asked as she entered, dispensing with the niceties of a salutation or asking her to sit down.

His superior attitude irritated her. "Good morning, Anthony. I'm very well, thank you for asking. I've claimed for ten manuscripts because that's what I've worked very hard on this week to meet the deadline I believe you set. I've left the manuscripts with Diana with my recommendations, if you'd like to check my notes."

He peered over his glasses and down his long nose at her and sniffed significantly. "That's impossible."

Florrie gritted her teeth. "I worked very late at night. It helped that four were clearly not suitable—"

"So why should you be paid for those?" he asked, the faintest uptick on his smug lips.

She stood taller. "Because that's the agreement made with Diana. I don't like the implication that I'm not doing the work. I am. I've also been organising Diana's paperwork to help her, and she's started writing again, which is what you wanted."

His nostrils flared, signalling she'd gone too far, but she would never claim for something she hadn't done, whatever he thought, and she was merely defending herself.

"You're very close to being insubordinate. Do you know how easy it is to pick up some ex-grammar schoolgirl who can read?" As if he hadn't been clear enough, he snapped his fingers.

Now *wasn't* the time to inform him she'd never been to grammar school. "Nevertheless, Diana relies on my services—"

Anthony snorted. "Oh, I see. Your 'services.' I wonder what they may entail." He leaned forward. "Don't get too comfortable. She'll drop you as fast as she picked you up when she gets bored."

She tried to control her reaction but damn her face for betraying her; he may as well have set her on fire. What was he implying? He couldn't know how she felt about Diana; she'd been hiding it so well. And his tone was little short of salacious. She and Diana had been completely professional, and Diana genuinely seemed to enjoy her contribution and company. But if Anthony was about to fire her, would Diana stand up for her? If Florrie lost this position, she'd need to maximise her income. She couldn't afford to miss out on the salary she'd already earned. "Please pay me for all the work I completed. Now, I'm going to get back to it."

Florrie wasn't sure how she held her nerve as she turned around and marched down to the small water closet at the end of the corridor, but it left her the moment she locked the door and slumped on the toilet seat. Her hands trembled uncontrollably, and she leaned her head against the cool tiles until the emotions subsided, and she could face Diana again with her usual poise. She couldn't afford to lose this job.

The words Anthony had thrown at her churned around her head. What had he meant by Diana getting bored? He'd made it very clear her position was precarious at best, reliant on the favour of Diana. Florrie huffed out a breath. Perhaps she ought to look for another job, or talk to Diana about the conversation she'd had with Anthony, even though that went against her wish not to be a snitch.

There was a tap on the door. "Florence, are you in there? Are you ready for lunch and the science talk? Anthony's just gone out, so I assume you've finished your meeting."

"Give me a minute." Florrie used the facilities and pulled the chain before washing her hands, hoping she was sufficiently sanguine when she emerged.

A vertical frown line between Diana's eyes blemished her perfect face. "Is everything all right?"

It was the first time Diana had ever asked a personal question, and Florrie couldn't help basking in it. She flashed a smile. "Of course. I'll collect my coat and bag."

As they travelled by cab, Diana was engrossed in a pamphlet

about the lecture they were going to this afternoon, so Florrie stared out of the window at the passing sights, no longer with the same enthusiasm she originally had for the magnificent edifices of London. She'd discovered that, quite often, they were all façade with tiny miserable offices inside—a bit like Anthony and the rest of the upper classes, all external glamour but mean and dark internally. Maybe not *all* the upper class. She cast a glance at Diana, but her stare was focused on the print in front of her. The silence wasn't awkward so much as unusual, so devoid of their habitual spark of conversation.

It wasn't until they were settled at a table and Diana had ordered a glass of wine for herself and water for Florrie that Diana finally looked up. Her gaze was cool, and Florrie shifted in her seat.

"Anthony informed me you've claimed for more than you worked."

The skin on the back of Florrie's neck tingled, and she shivered. She swallowed to give herself a second before replying. So, this was it. She was about to be fired. "You gave me ten manuscripts to read, and I assessed them. I claimed for ten manuscripts, and no more."

Diana raised her hand. "I didn't say I agreed with him. I've been so angry with him that I've been trying to calm down before speaking to you." She snatched at the cloth table napkin and spread it over her knees before catching Florrie's gaze. "I believe you. It must have been quite a week to get through so much work. Thank you. I didn't realise there were that many in the pile. I wanted to complete them this week."

The waiter brought over their drinks, and they thanked him as he placed them on the tablecloth. Diana had a sip of her wine, appearing to wait until he was out of earshot. She closed her eyes momentarily before giving her attention to Florrie. "I informed Anthony that I'm basing myself in my home in the country as soon as possible. I wondered if you would pick up some papers on your way through and join me down there next week."

So her job was safe. Florrie exhaled noisily and allowed the rest of Diana's comments to filter through the relief. "Join you down where?"

"At Mead House, my cottage in Sussex. It's where I go to write," Diana said. "It will involve staying overnight, and you can return home the following day. Will that be convenient for you, with your niece?"

Florrie's heart did a little skip, but she held onto her professional expression. "Really? Mary, our maid, will almost certainly be happy for any overtime pay, and Cam's so independent that she doesn't require much attention, only a reminder to eat and to go to bed rather than be sidetracked by whatever science or mathematics problem she's dealing with. I'll insist she practices her cello and piano to give me a concert when I return." Oh no, she'd rattled on again. Diana didn't need all her boring life details.

Diana's eyes glistened, and she smiled. "Splendid. That's settled then."

The trip required a Tube journey across London and another train journey to the heart of Sussex, but Florrie would do it weekly if needed to accept this precious invitation into Diana's inner sanctum. Her inside tingled at being thought worthy to be allowed in *and* to stay. "Does this mean you're writing again in earnest?"

"I guess it does." Diana inclined her head. "Don't ask me about it. I don't share my work until I'm happy with it. Knowing someone is looking over my shoulder critiquing every sentence blocks my ability to write at all."

"Understood. I'll do whatever I can to help."

"You are," Diana said. "More than you can know."

The words hung between them, charged with a subtle tension Florrie didn't dare examine. Diana's gaze lingered a moment too long and traced a path down Florrie's body, like she was mapping her with her thoughts. Then, just as Florrie started to squirm under the scrutiny, Diana regained eye contact.

"I was reading about the lecture this afternoon. There's clearly a lot more we've yet to discover about the atom."

More than you can know. For once, Florrie wasn't listening to every word that passed Diana's lips. She was busy attempting to untangle the meaning behind the cryptic comment. Whatever it was, she warmed under the cloak of approval. She swallowed hard, her pulse quickening at the thought of sharing time with Diana, of discovering the unspoken hint of promise hidden in that look.

CHAPTER FOUR

The following week Florrie's bag held seven manuscripts she'd reviewed plus various letters for discussion with Diana when she arrived. The weight of all that paper hung heavy on her shoulder. She wiped her brow and switched the bag to the other side before approaching the cottage, which was really a large brick and flint house, far bigger than Florrie's in Bletchley. The gate squeaked on opening, and the doorbell elicited no response. Florrie sighed. She didn't want to disturb Diana; perhaps she was at a critical point in her script. Florrie didn't want to ruin her flow of concentration.

Florrie looked around. The garden was a mass of yellows, reds, and purples. Bees hummed, and butterflies spiralled around the blooms, and Florrie inhaled deeply at the unmistakeable floral scent of an English garden in summer. Her house in Bletchley was in the country, but this had been a good forty-minute brisk walk from the station and was so much more remote.

Florrie followed the stone path around the back of the house and spotted a wooden building halfway down the garden. She gasped at the expansive view towards the South Downs. If she worked here, she'd never want to leave. Though she probably wouldn't get any work done at all because she'd stare out of the window the whole time.

Florrie approached the garden room and through the French windows saw Diana, her long neck gracefully bowed over her writing. Florrie could imagine the small, neat script being scratched on small scraps of paper. Diana was so beautiful, so absorbed in her task, that it took Florrie's breath away. For a few minutes, she absorbed the sight, wanting to imprint it on her memory.

The edge of Diana's desk was caught by sunlight streaming in, and the reflection from the brilliant white paper lit up Diana's face from below. Not wishing to break her concentration, Florrie waited until Diana raised her head to stare out at the golden corn that gave way to the chalky grasslands of the downs stretching in front of her. Florrie gently tapped on the door.

Diana turned her head quite slowly, and her gaze shifted to focus on Florrie. A smile washed over her face. "Florence, come in. Don't wait outside, although it *is* the most glorious day."

There was something about the way Diana said her name, all soft and sibilant, that had Florrie melting, and it wasn't because of the warm sunshine and the walk from the station with a heavy bag. "What a beautiful location."

"It is," Diana said, capping the pen and stretching her fingers out with a small sigh. "Here, I can concentrate so much better than in London. At long last, I feel inspired to write, and the muse is upon me, urging me on." Her hand drifted in a restless gesture, before catching Florrie's gaze. She cleared her throat. "It's because of you. Thank you for taking on so much of the tedious paperwork. Anthony was supposed to do all of that, but I was getting more and more embroiled in it, and I detest it. He knows it was squeezing the life out of me, yet he insists I do it. But you..." She leaned in slightly. "You've been doing so much more than simply reading through scripts."

Florrie swallowed hard. "I don't mind."

"Nonsense. You should be paid for all the work you do, and you must charge your travel expenses to the press. I hope you took a cab from the station."

Florrie shook her head.

Diana stood. "Poor darling. You must be very hot and thirsty. Let me fix you a lemonade. I think Alice left some in the cold room." She stretched her back like a pedigree cat that hadn't moved for hours. "Come through and give me everything I need to sign, and much more importantly, tell me what you thought of the last manuscripts you've been through." She started up the path towards the house and called over her shoulder. "You brought enough to stay overnight, didn't you?"

"I did." Florrie removed the work papers and manuscripts from her bag and placed them on the garden table. She wedged a heavy ornament on top to stop them blowing away, then hurried to catch up with Diana, who strode quickly and with purpose.

Inside the house, books lined every wall in the hall and the dining room. Even the kitchen had a few recipe books lined up underneath the span of copper pans. Off to one side was a wooden door, which Diana entered. On a stone settle covered in a crocheted doily was a pitcher of freshly crushed lemonade.

Diana picked it up and re-entered the kitchen. She nodded towards the back of the house. "Your room is upstairs, third on the right, and the bathroom is next door if you want to freshen up. I'll take the tray outside, and you can join me there when you're ready."

Florrie went upstairs as instructed. It would have been thrilling to peep inside the various rooms, but she resisted the temptation and passed the door labelled bathroom before she came to her allotted room. The window was open, and the curtains billowed outwards like flags flapping in celebration of the glorious day. From here, she had a view down to the garden and writing room.

Diana emerged and placed a tray on the table. She settled herself on the garden chair and picked up Florrie's notes on the manuscripts. Diana stroked the paper as she read with an unexpected tenderness. Did that signify something or nothing at all?

Florrie shook her head at herself. What was she thinking, fawning after her employer? But Diana was more than her employer. In the last few months, they had become friends. She hoped so, anyway.

She had been gawking too long. Hurriedly, she freshened up in the bathroom then rejoined Diana outside at the table. Diana sat back in her chair, decorated in dappled light, with her glasses perched at the end of her nose, the very picture of poise and perfection. Florrie didn't dare acknowledge to herself what stirred in her heart as she observed her. Her crush on her mentor was growing stronger with each week that passed, and it was getting harder to hide and ignore.

"Tell me what I need to know and show me where I have to sign," Diana said, pointing at the correspondence.

Florrie went through her list and carefully marked them off as each item was dealt with. After they finished with the administration, she returned to her notes to go through the manuscripts in detail. Florrie had come up with a set of criteria to assess each submission, and Diana had asked her to use that basis to explain why she'd rejected the manuscript. Over the months, Florrie had been completing more of the correspondence with the applicants. They had received a few thank you letters in reply and promises to resubmit once they'd addressed the issues.

Diana waved a manuscript. "Anthony says we need to fill the presses with more commercial projects, so I think this one you'd dismissed may need to be revived. Leave it with me, and I'll take a look at it." She slapped it on the possible pile with a finality that felt like a personal rebuke.

"It'll need a lot of editing." Had Florrie made her recommendations on the wrong criteria? She should have known that the pressure was on. More recently, she'd been recommending the more innovative novels.

Her concern must have shown on her face as Diana raised Florrie's chin with her index finger. It was so cool against Florrie's hot skin, her arms raised in goosebumps. Surely it was only the cold touch.

Diana waited until Florrie met her gaze. "That isn't a criticism. I couldn't do what I'm doing without you. Thank you. I don't know if you know how much I rely on you." She traced her fingers along Florrie's cheeks.

Florrie held her breath and tried to imagine herself fixed into place, despite her overwhelming desire to move forward, to lean into Diana's touch.

"Perfect," Diana said and cupped Florrie's face.

Florrie could no longer resist and leaned into Diana's palm. This close, she could smell the flowery, earthy scent Diana used. She wanted to bury herself in Diana's essence, snuggle into her, trace her lips up Diana's bare arms. She wanted to whisper sweet nothings to Diana, nibble her ear lobe and suck hard. Florrie closed her eyes tight; it was too much, too intoxicating, too revealing. One breath, and her secret attraction would be laid bare.

Diana seemed closer, her breath warm on her face. Some external force was drawing them together, like a thread being pulled taut. Florrie opened her eyes to meet Diana's intense gaze, dark and unrelenting, unmasking her deepest fantasy.

"May I?" Diana whispered, making fantasy real.

"Please."

Diana kissed her, and Florrie's thoughts scattered in a breathless whirl. Diana Stratford was kissing her, *and* she had initiated it. Diana had closed the space between them, and Diana had begun it. Florrie kissed her back with an enthusiasm she didn't know she had, her heart doing double time. Diana gripped the back of her neck and pulled her closer, kissing to devour Florrie, to be devoured in turn. She arched up to meet Diana's embrace as much as she could from her position. Her body was twisted uncomfortably but she didn't want to break the kiss, risk losing this moment. This was straight from the fever of her recent dreams, and she didn't want to wake up. Diana licked Florrie's bottom lip, demanding entrance. Melting a little inside, Florrie responded, and their kiss deepened.

Some pages fluttered away with the slight breeze and littered the path and garden. Florrie forced herself to break from the kiss and glare at the wayward pages. "I'd better get those."

"Mm." Diana trailed her hand along Florrie's thigh.

Florrie wanted this so badly, wanted something more. But more papers lifted in the breeze. Reluctantly, Florrie rose, and Diana's hand fell away.

One page was caught in the rose bush, while a few others had scattered amongst the flowers and were flapping and floating on the breeze. Wretched pages had destroyed her slice of heaven. She rescued them all and ensured they were in sequence. "Shall I put the manuscript in your writing room?" she asked, trying to calm the rush of emotions coursing through her body.

"Thank you," Diana whispered. "Leave it on the side table away from the rest of my pages. I suppose I should show you the rest of the gardens. Anthony has started a vegetable garden in the orangery."

His name was a splash of icy water. Something magical had happened between them, but now reality intruded. Of course Anthony visited; he was Diana's business partner, and if the rumours were true, he was also her suitor, but so far, she'd rejected him. Florrie couldn't bear to see Diana with him. He made her skin crawl. Rex would be more in tune with what Diana needed, a true equal on her fragile literary level, not the dour businessman, full of himself and his own importance because he dealt with money, a man with not an ounce of creativity or sensitivity to beauty in the world.

Florrie busied herself in the writing room, not wanting to face Diana again after the salutary reminder of her nemesis. She was no match to any of them. She was a nobody. Perhaps they could just forget the kiss.

But how could she? She traced her fingers over her swollen lips, where Diana had laid her own. *Happy lips.* She scoffed. If she read that in one of the manuscripts, she would strike a red pen through it and say it was sappy nonsense. It didn't feel like that though. But it couldn't happen again. It *shouldn't* happen again, no matter how much she wanted it. She couldn't put her job in jeopardy. If it all went wrong, she would lose everything.

A chill ran down her spine. She had everything at stake, not only for her but also for Cam. Charles had made it very clear that if it didn't work out, he would send Cam to boarding school.

Florrie flung her hand at her chest that couldn't suck in enough air. Would Diana want her to leave? She couldn't lose Diana's debate and encouragement, nor the visits to the talks and their discussions and appraisals of the latest books. Diana and her business had become her whole life, her purpose, her source of joy and intellectual challenge.

"Are you all right?" Diana asked as she came into the writing room. "Have I shocked you? I hope you're okay with what we did. You seemed to enjoy it, and yet you've secreted yourself in here when it would only take a second to drop off the papers."

Diana gnawed at her bottom lip, clearly not her usual poised, confident self. Was she as unsettled as Florrie?

"Have I overstepped? I'd hate to be the kind of person who abused their position. I'd never forgive myself if I'd completely misread you."

Diana's voice trembled slightly, indicating a vulnerable side Florrie had never witnessed before. That this proud, self-contained woman would trust her enough to let the mask slip moved Florrie. But Diana had asked a question she hadn't answered, and Florrie needed to meet that raw concern with honesty. "No. Yes, I mean, that was more than okay. I can't believe it. I never knew you felt anything for me. I've nothing to offer you. I'm just a middle-class woman with virtually no money and no prospects—"

Diana placed her index finger on Florrie's lips. Something possessed her to nip the top of Diana's finger. Diana laughed, something so rare and delicate that Florrie wanted to hear it repeatedly and forever.

"I've been battling for weeks and weeks to get you out of my head," Diana said. "So much so I had to start writing to expunge my feelings. Florence, how could I not be captivated by you? You are a kind soul with a phenomenal brain, straining to be unleashed."

Diana caressed Florrie's face and she nuzzled into it, struggling to focus on the profundity of Diana's words as they washed over her.

"Sometimes I catch you watching me with such desire in your eyes, I can't help but be flattered. And I wonder about you when you're not here, what your opinion is of something or someone. I'm obsessed." Diana lowered her hand and placed it in her lap. "You've made me inarticulate. Florence, I wanted you here so I could spend time with you, to have you by my side." She swallowed hard like she was about to confess her sins. "You are my muse. It's because of you and my feelings for you that I've started writing again. I was dried up and empty, dying inside, and you've made me come alive. You've revitalised every creative nerve in my body."

Florrie stood stock still by the papers, her breath coming in short, shallow gasps as she assimilated Diana's words into something she could understand and believe.

Diana raised her eyebrow higher. By the curl of her lip and the quirk of her eyebrow, she displayed an entire category of judgements and opinions, and Florrie delighted in understanding them. Her favourite was when Diana's face softened, and her lips tweaked upwards, and her eyes glinted with pleasure. That made her want to purr and do whatever she could to elicit that look again.

"I can see you don't believe me." Diana sighed. "Come. Perhaps you'd like to read what I've written and give me your honest opinion. Although if you say you can't stand it, I'm not sure what I'll do." She hurried back to her desk and gathered a stack of small, neat pages.

Florrie leaned against the side table, her knees buckling and her head spinning at the torrent of emotion spilling from Diana. She wasn't able to grasp it, never mind believe it, even as her heart ached to accept it. "You'd let me be the first to read your latest work?"

"Of course." Diana reached for her hand, her thumb brushing across Florrie's knuckles, her gaze unwavering. "It's rough at the moment, but you need to understand that you've affected me in a way I haven't felt for a very long time. You've awakened something in me I thought I'd lost forever. It seems fitting you should see it first." She withdrew her hand and shuffled the papers into a large stack then passed them over with a wry smile. "Hopefully it's in order and you can decipher my scrawl. Let's head back outside. I'll read the other manuscript while you go through that."

"I'm honoured," Florrie said, then she clamped her mouth shut. She didn't want to come over as too eager, too naïve, a neophyte. She wanted to live up to Diana's view of her, even if she didn't see it in herself. She almost floated into the chair next to Diana, rubbed her hands and flexed her fingers, and then she picked up the first page.

Diana pointed at Florrie. "You see, that's one of the things that makes you unique. You're always wringing your hands in a particular way. It's quite beguiling."

"I'm afraid it's nothing so romantic," Florrie said and stretched out her fingers. "My hands and feet ache. My doctor says I have early onset rheumatoid arthritis, but there's nothing they can do about it, so I'll become an old lady before my time."

"Nothing?"

Florrie shook her head. "I've even tried the bee sting remedy, but that was just unpleasant, waiting for the next bee to sting me then die."

Diana placed her hands over Florrie's. "I'm so sorry. Perhaps you should move to the South of France where the climate is warmer and drier."

"That would be lovely, but I can't leave Cam. She needs me, and she doesn't like change. She's brilliant, and with Oscar's help, she should do well."

"Ah, yes, the niece. Oscar was raving about her. He said he'd never seen anyone so young so phenomenal at mathematics. He's already mentioned it to one of the professors at Cambridge and thinks she can be given a place early, perhaps in a few years' time."

Florrie instantly recalled the look of panic on Cam's face at the thought of having more children at her birthday party. In the end, it had been Cam, Florrie, Oscar, and Mary who sat down for a cup of tea and cake. How would she fare in a much bigger establishment such as Cambridge university? "But she's only twelve. I don't think she'd cope emotionally."

"So I gather. If you ask me, I think talking to the professor has as much to do with Oscar being infatuated as anything else."

Florrie chuckled. "He is a rule unto himself, isn't he?"

"He is. But I'm very fond of him. Thank you for giving him this opportunity."

"That's nothing to the one you've given me. And it was my sister Nora who gave Oscar a chance."

Diana flicked her hand in the dismissive way she had. "Get on with reading the script. I'm anxious you'll hate it. You may see a few of your tics in there, but I'm not going to apologise for that. It's all part of this homage to you. You've inspired me."

Florrie didn't need another invitation and picked up the pages with anticipation and trepidation. She was engrossed from the first sentence, although she cringed a little at the description of a rather plainly dressed woman being the main character, who rubbed and flexed her hands regularly and had a delicate little cough to clear her throat when she was anxious. She'd never seen those things in herself and became instantly self-conscious about them.

However, she soon forgot the manuscript was inspired by her as she got involved in the intrigue, and the raw emotions, and conflict as the main character fell in love with a remote, jaded man who had lost his way. It didn't take a genius to work out the man was Diana. Florrie coloured at some of the characterisation: "the longing, the barely disguised desire." Had she really been so obvious? She looked up to catch Diana watching her intensely, her mouth slightly open.

"Well?"

"I love it." Florrie stroked the pages tenderly as if they were Diana's skin. "What I've seen so far anyway. But you're flattering me... The characterisation seems very removed from the reality."

"Not at all. That's how I see you." Diana curled a strand of hair behind Florrie's ear. "This feels like such a treat to have you here in my sanctuary, where I can watch you reading my words inspired by you. It's magical."

Florrie swallowed. What could she say to such a sentiment? How could she respond to the beautiful words inspired by her? If this was all she ever had, she'd be happy.

"Say when you're hungry," Diana said. "I often forget to eat when I'm writing. Alice leaves me cold meats and bread. She's fed up with leaving hot food that congeals and burns, so for the summer, we agreed salads and cold compilations would be fine. Do you mind reading the rest of the manuscript rather than being entertained? I hate leaving the cottage when I'm here. It's not like the distraction of London. And do have the run of the house and garden. I never showed it to you, did I?"

Diana was so rarely out of sorts that Florrie wanted to reach out and calm her, like settling a thoroughbred horse that had been spooked. She didn't care what they ate or when they ate. She was just grateful to be in Diana's orbit. "Salad and cold meats are fine."

"I have cheese, I'm sure. Do you like cheese?"

"I'm fine with whatever's at hand, and I'm honoured to sit

and be the first person to read your new manuscript. It's all so intriguing, and lyrical, and flattering, and disconcerting at the same time. I love it."

Diana's shoulders lowered slightly, and she nestled back into her chair after picking up a script.

The next few hours passed in silence. Occasionally, Florrie would look up to see Diana watching her as if she was bracing herself for the judgement. Every time, Florrie smiled. Being permitted to witness Diana being vulnerable was an honour and was like observing a bird hovering over the nest as the hatchling attempted to fly.

Finally, the sun passed behind the house and the wind stirred with more of a nip in the air. The special moment had passed, and Florrie put down the last of the pages.

Diana rose and stretched, shaking the submitted script she'd been reading. "Anthony would prefer we use this manuscript, I think. It will probably appeal to the masses, but please continue with sifting out the gold in the pile. Would you mind sending an acceptance letter to this agent? Let's go inside, and you can tell me more about your genuine thoughts on my book so far."

How did she sum up the whole experience, which was laying her bare and flattering her in a way she didn't think she deserved? Though it wasn't her but rather her essence distilled into pure form. And Diana was so judgemental about the male character. If Diana actually thought that represented her, so flawed and unapproachable and damaged, it was disturbing, and Florrie wanted to fold her in her arms.

She was still collecting her thoughts, examining and assessing them, while they uncovered the meats and sat down at the rough-hewn kitchen table. No exquisite dining here, but it could have been a banquet by the way Florrie's mouth watered. It was long past the time she and Cam normally ate.

"Please start. There are no airs or graces here. I love being able to slough off all the demands and expectations of London.

This is where I can breathe, and be myself, and enjoy the simplicity of weaving words while being answerable to no one."

Florrie bit her lip. "I hope my being here doesn't destroy that peace for you."

"You needed to bring down the papers," Diana said and smiled. "And I'm waiting for your opinion on my writing."

The answer was too quick, and Diana didn't deny Florrie was upsetting her routine. The kiss earlier was not going to be mentioned then, even though it had left Florrie breathless and wanting more. Perhaps Diana regretted it. "I'll be out of your way first thing in the morning. And I'm still mulling over your manuscript. It's beautifully written even in its raw state, but you know that. There are the usual themes of loss, social critique, and longing, but there's something more I haven't quite put my finger on yet."

Florrie cast a glance at Diana, still watching her ferociously, her arms clasped on her opposite elbows like a taut bow. Florrie smiled to set her at ease. How could this phenomenal writer be seeking the appraisal of Florrie, who should be nowhere near her social or intellectual circle? There must be another reason for asking her to read it. Something didn't add up, or rather Florrie didn't want to believe, but on reflection, she was sure she was reading it correctly. There was one explanation that kept bubbling to the surface, and no matter how she looked at it, the truth was there for Florrie to acknowledge and name. What if she was reading only her own wishes? She would look a fool. Yet the meaning for Diana was there etched in the neat script. "At its essence, it's a love letter, isn't it?"

Diana speared a chunk of cold meat. Florrie missed her intense stare, no longer able to see inside Diana's soul. Had she got it so wrong, and Diana was too scared to let her down gently? Florrie put down her cutlery and straightened them to give herself something to do with her hands.

Diana cleared her throat. "You're so sharp. Of course you

would see it. It's something I was trying to avoid acknowledging to myself." She drew in a breath, her shoulders rising, then let it out slowly. "But it's true. It's clear and obvious now it's out in the ether. I feel exposed and uncertain how we proceed."

She averted her eyes and placed her cutlery on her plate, then shook her head gently. "I can't. It would be inappropriate. You are my employee, I can't abuse that position. I shouldn't have kissed you earlier." She pressed her fingers to her temple as though she had a headache brewing. "Anthony would be furious if he knew."

"You seem scared of Anthony. What hold does he have over you?"

Diana's superior mask snapped back into place, and Florrie kicked herself for pushing where it didn't belong.

"Get some white wine out—or red, if you prefer—but in the summer, I prefer white or rose."

Diana pointed at a cabinet covered by papers, and Florrie accepted the deflection without comment. The air became thick with tension. How could she get back to the open easy communication they usually shared?

Florrie located a corkscrew and, as she twisted the pointed end into the cork, she screwed up her courage to say what she needed. "You aren't abusing your position. I enjoyed kissing you, but I'm scared of what happens from here." She realised with certainty that she would need to make any further moves, *if* there were any further moves to be made. The wine splashed against the glass and glugged as it filled. Diana's breathing was deep like she was preparing to build her courage, perhaps to let her down gently. Florrie passed the wine and sank into her seat.

Diana raised her glass. "Here's to finished manuscripts. I'm still not sure how the story ends. I suspect it won't be a happy ever after."

Florrie clinked her glass against Diana's, but her food sat leaden in her stomach. Her hunger and thirst deserted her.

Diana's words implied she should expect nothing more, and Florrie had to blink hard to maintain her composure. Maybe today had been a one-time-only chance. Maybe she wouldn't even be invited here again, amongst Anthony's vegetables and Diana's sanctuary of written words. It didn't pass her notice that the story was about a man and a woman, and the man was too damaged to commit to the relationship. Diana couldn't be clearer that this would go nowhere, and Florrie was foolish to think anything more could happen. Hope was far too dangerous a thing.

And yet...Diana had kissed her, and it was every bit as exquisite as Florrie had imagined. Not only for the act itself —the merging of breath and clashing of lips stirring desire—but also for Diana breaking the barriers, paving the way for reciprocation, trust, and openness. This was probably Florrie's one opportunity while emotions were high following a blissful summer's afternoon, until reason and reality slapped her down. If there would ever be one chance to explore, to be who she'd always known to be her true self, to shrug off her good girl mantle and shatter the taboo, this was the moment, *here*, with the woman she admired on so many levels.

Diana seemed to be waiting for Florrie's reaction.

"I'd like to kiss you again," Florrie said without even considering tempering her response. "To see what happens, irrespective of being scared." Where she got the courage, she didn't know, but she needed to propel this forward, or it would wither here and now. She laid her hand palm up on the table. Diana examined it before placing her own over the top, and Florrie squeezed it.

"Let's finish our supper, then sit by the fire," Diana said. "It's getting a bit chilly. This is quite a nice bottle; you obviously have good taste in wine."

Diana seemed to be playing for time, to decide what she should do. Florrie played along. "I know you like French, so I chose a bottle I thought you would like."

"Actually, it's Anthony's." Diana grasped Florrie's hand tighter when she began to move. "No, don't pull away. He's my business partner, so of course he comes here. It doesn't mean I don't want you here. I do. I meant what I said earlier; it feels magical having you at my cottage, even though a certain awkwardness has arisen between us."

Diana rose. Florrie followed suit and placed the empty plates into the bowl with a clatter, then opened the cupboard under the sink to search for the soap flakes to wash up.

"Leave that for Alice in the morning. I'll put the rest of this away."

Florrie washed her hands in the cold water and dried them hurriedly.

With a sigh, Diana turned around, then bustled around, replacing the meats and bread back into the cold room. Florrie watched, trying to work out a way they could smooth out this awkwardness.

Diana stood by the door jamb, her arms crossed and her fingers drumming against her upper arms. "I don't know if you're jealous of Anthony, or if I'm not quite ready to admit my feelings to you." Her gaze darted to Florrie, then slipped away. "Yet you uncovered them anyway, through your reading of the script." She pressed her hand to her chest as if it was painful and gave a shaky laugh. "I'm feeling a little raw. I'm not sure I can give you what you want in the long term."

Diana took a couple of steps, then stopped abruptly, gripping the backrest of one of the chairs. "I need space, and I'm a hermit when I write. This is my sanctuary, where I get no demands." She stared towards the window now looking out onto a darkening garden. Her eyes were wide with a mix of fear and regret. "I can't promise to meet any expectations you may have, and I didn't think about how I would be affected with you being here." Her voice dropped to a whisper as she finally met Florrie's gaze. "I'm sorry."

Panic fluttered in Florrie's heart. Would Diana cast her out tonight? Surely not. "I get it. No demands. We'll sit by the fire and finish our wine, then go to bed. But just so you know, if you change your mind, I'm willing."

Diana blinked slowly, revealing large dark pupils. She cleared her throat. "You're such a temptation."

Not sure if she should act or not, Florrie finished her wine and placed her glass on the kitchen table. The air seemed heavy with expectation and uncertainty. Perhaps she should avoid the awkwardness by retiring to bed.

She was about to leave when Diana said, "Let's go into the sitting room. Bring your glass." Was Diana changing her mind or merely her conflicting desires? It reminded her of the thoroughbred snuffling towards an apple held out on the palm of her hand, caution warring with desire.

Florrie picked up her wineglass. She would be as clear as she could. She was all in, if Diana was.

Two wingback chairs were arranged around the unlit but made-up fire; Alice had no doubt prepared it earlier in the day. Diana sank to her knees on the Persian rug and donned a pair of thick gloves. She picked up the box of matches and struck one, but by the time she had it next to the paper, it extinguished into a thin trail of smoke...a bit like the fire that had never started between them. She snapped the second match in half.

Diana flung the gloves onto the hearth. "Oh, for Gods' sake. Why can't I even light a simple fire?"

Florrie slipped beside her and struck a match. It flared and caught the paper spills. She stared into the flames until they started to roar and consume the logs on top. She turned slightly to find Diana much closer to her.

"You're driving me insane," Diana said. "I don't know what to do." She shook her head and closed her eyes briefly. "I *know* what I want to do but I don't know if it's fair to you."

Florrie dusted her hands on her skirt then pushed back

Diana's hair behind her ear. She had such exquisite ears. Florrie trailed her fingers across Diana's strong jaw. She needed to touch and take this moment before her courage failed her. "This is my answer. Is this okay?"

Diana pressed their lips together. Before, their kiss had been soft, almost tentative, but this was hard, passionate, and feral. Florrie growled quietly and responded with a ferocious need to connect, to consume and to surrender.

"Please," Diana said, all semblance of the haughty woman disappearing in the thick neediness of her plea. Lust laced her expression.

Florrie lay back onto the rug and pulled Diana towards her, giving her permission, demanding she lie on top of her. Diana leaned on her forearms and lowered her hips to meet Florrie's. The delicate weight was enough to set Florrie's hips rising to meet Diana's body. Excitement boiled inside her, in danger of flowing over. She clenched her thighs, caught between Diana's long, enveloping legs, and tried desperately to tether herself to reality.

Diana swept a hair off Florrie's face. Her dark gaze tinged with raw hunger mirrored Florrie's own desire. She tensed her body, every nerve alight and screaming at her as Diana shifted closer and subtly ground against her. She leaned forward, the movement an intimate prelude to a kiss.

"I love this moment," Diana said, her fingers tracing patterns along Florrie's arms, sending shivers down her spine. "The anticipation, teetering on the very edge of uncertainty, the will she, won't she?" Her thumb halted over Florrie's wrist. "There's also that frisson of fear: will she kiss and tell? Break the trust and honesty required."

Diana leaned even nearer, her breath coming in warm puffs of air against Florrie's cheek, her eyes searching. "I need to know if you still want to do this. You must say stop if you don't like anything or want anything to change—"

"I'm certain," Florrie said, hardly able to speak through the arousal coursing through her body. "It's what I've dreamed of. I want everything."

"Good." Diana pressed harder and Florrie shivered.

When she raised herself off Florrie, she almost moaned in annoyance and she arched to maintain contact.

Diana laughed as she rolled back onto her heels. "We need to get rid of these barriers." She drew down the straps of Florrie's dress, slowly.

"Both of us." Desperate to be naked, to meld, to be as one, Florrie tugged at the fastenings on her dress.

"Let me do that," Diana said. "I'd love to unwrap you and savour every second." She carefully unhooked the side opening.

"Faster, please."

Diana paused and tutted. "Patience. Enjoy the moment."

Florrie closed her eyes a second to still her racing heart. Of course, Diana would tease her; she had an irreverent streak when she relaxed. And she seemed very relaxed now, the remaining awkwardness slipping off with their clothes.

She succumbed to the moment and opened her eyes to gaze into Diana's eyes. She shuffled upright to let Diana remove her dress down to her simple cotton bra and panties, to be exposed.

"Beautiful," Diana whispered.

She smoothed her hands behind Florrie's back, causing goosebumps in her wake, and unclipped her underwear, releasing her large breasts, so unfashionable in this age of tubular androgynous forms. But Diana seemed mesmerised, if the lick of her bottom lip was to be believed.

"Gorgeous." Diana lowered her head between Florrie's breasts, inhaling deeply, and kissed the skin there.

Florrie burned deep in her chest. "Sorry, I'm probably sweaty from all the travel."

Diana hummed and inhaled. "You're delicious."

Diana sucked her nipple, eliciting a gasp from Florrie.

Diana raised her head and made eye contact. "Do you like that?"

"Yes... I... Yes." Should she admit no one had ever kissed or sucked her breasts, and that Diana's biting was causing an exquisite, pleasurable pain? Who would have thought that could be so arousing? Diana tweaked the other nipple and sent her soaring. "Please. I need to feel you now. Naked."

Diana laughed quietly, and the vibration wobbled Florrie's stomach. "Be my guest."

Florrie was torn between continuing what they were doing and seeing Diana, being with her. She wanted it all. Her fingers caught at the zipper at the side of Diana's dress—of course Diana would have a zipper—and tugged the fabric down to reveal a beautiful cream silk bra concealing a swell of small breasts. She swallowed. "May I?"

Diana smiled and observed her, as if she was making mental notes on how to describe the process in her book, in metaphor, of course, to avoid the censor. Was Diana only indulging in this to provide material for her book? Florrie blinked slowly. Even if that was the case, she was happy to fulfil that role, although she would love to be the cause of real emotions. Diana seemed to be waiting; she must have said something. "Sorry?"

Diana stroked Florrie's cheek. "I said, 'of course.' You seemed to have disengaged a little. Are you sure about this?"

"Yes, yes. I was wondering if you were mentally describing the scene in your beautiful words." Why did she have to blurt that out? But it must be better to speak the truth, even if she revealed all her insecurities.

"No. nothing so esoteric." She threaded her fingers through Florrie's hair, slowly and deliberately. "I was just thinking that I've wanted this since I met you."

A rush of giddiness flowed through Florrie as her blood thrummed in her ears. "You have?" She stifled a laugh and clapped her hand over her mouth.

Diana arched her perfectly shaped eyebrow. "You're curious and intelligent, and you're kind. Kindness is so underrated, but necessary."

Diana put her hand behind her back and unclipped her bra. The straps and material fell, revealing two dark nipples stiffening into peaks as Florrie stared. "You like what you see?"

Florrie nodded.

"Touch me. We're talking too much."

Florrie had never been so delighted to oblige, and she squeezed Diana's nipples. Diana pushed into the touch and stretched her head back to expose her long graceful neck, asking to be worshipped. Florrie feathered soft kisses along it, eliciting a moan.

This was exquisite torture: kissing and being kissed, touching and looking and still being half-dressed. "Can we get undressed now? I want to feel you against me."

Diana laughed again and pulled away completely. With no ceremony, she stepped out of her dress and underwear, matching silk, of course. Florrie paused to admire the slim form emerging like a goddess from the sea of cloth, then remembered herself and scrambled to remove her own clothes.

A log shifted in the fire, and as twilight had settled into night, the flickering reddish glow from the grate was their only light source, giving an other-worldly ambiance. Diana was cast half in shadow, but the light rested on her breasts and the glistening of sex at the meeting of her thighs. Diana was wet for her. To see evidence of Diana's arousal sparked a similar reaction in Florrie.

"Come on top of me," Diana whispered, her voice full of wonder and excitement.

The teasing had gone, replaced with lust, wild and desperate in Diana's eyes. And Florrie now understood what Diana meant by the edge of uncertainty, the anticipation and want, and a tinge of fear. She lay on top of Diana and skin met skin, breast to breast, and as she slipped down Diana's body, the evidence of their desire spread over their thighs. This close, the meeting of bodies was accompanied by the scent of sex, strong and alluring.

Diana pulled at Florrie's hand and placed it on her hot swollen flesh, then whimpered as Florrie trailed her fingers over Diana's smooth thighs and her sex. "You're so warm and wet." Florrie couldn't hide her amazement.

Diana gasped, a sharp catch in her breath. "Inside now. Please, I need you. Two fingers."

Florrie did as she was instructed. The moment she did, everything changed: angles shifted, sensations stretched, and it felt nothing like her own body. It was deeper, all-consuming, and intoxicating.

"Harder. Faster, please."

Florrie obeyed, setting up a fast rhythm that had Diana squirming. Both were breathing fast and shallowly, and when Florrie flicked Diana's nub with her thumb, Diana moaned.

"Yes. Don't stop."

Despite Florrie's fingers cramping and aching, she drove them faster until Diana stiffened, let out a wail of elation, and then shuddered.

Diana's half glazed gaze met Florrie's. "I didn't know what to expect. Incredible."

Florrie pushed sweat-dampened hair off Diana's face, revelling in seeing her unkempt for the first time. She'd turned this exquisite creature into an exhausted, exhilarated mess; my, how that made Florrie smile. "Are you certain now?"

Diana stretched and pulled Florrie close. "Definitely."

The intimacy was unexpected. She didn't think Diana would be physical afterwards, though she wasn't quite sure why. Everything today was a surprise: from being allowed in Diana's sanctum to being given the honour of reading her work, from sharing her precious space to the incredible intimacy that Florrie hadn't dared dream about or acknowledge. She snuggled up and played with Diana's hair. "That would make a great title for the book."

Diana turned her head to look at her, a slight frown creased her brow. "Definitely?"

"No. *On the Edge of Uncertainty*."

Diana inhaled deeply. "Yes, maybe. Remind me when I've regained my senses. But for now, I think I'm recovered sufficiently to reciprocate."

Florrie laughed. "Only you could sound so erudite post-intimacy."

Diana flipped Florrie onto her back with ease. "Ah, you'd prefer a little rough talk? Would you prefer to be deflowered, debauched, or just good old-fashioned fucked? Would that titillate you, Florence? Would you like that?"

Diana's use of such alien words was surprisingly arousing. Florrie's heart beat faster, and every part of her pooled with need: her blood, her brains, and her final shred of decorum. "Yes, please. I want it now. No teasing. I'm close already."

Diana smiled wickedly as she traced her fingers over Florrie's belly button, down through the wet hair as she parted her folds. Then, when Florrie was taut with anticipation, Diana retreated and trailed her fingers on the undulations of her thighs, her hips, and her belly. Florrie sparked alive and hot.

"Are you sure?" Diana whispered against Florrie's ear.

"I'm sure."

Diana slipped in her finger as smoothly as liquid butter. She pushed harder, and suddenly, Florrie wasn't thinking at all. She was reacting, writhing and following each movement. Every nerve end throbbed, and she pulled Diana closer, needing to be consumed completely. "Yes...like that... I... Oh, God." When she thought she couldn't take any more, she was pulled apart into her molecules and atoms, particles in random motion, until she disappeared into the essence of the stars before gradually drifting back to herself. A newer version of herself: clearer, brighter, more vital, and vibrating with joy.

Diana stared down at her, with soft eyes and a fond smile.

Florrie smiled back. "Please tell me we can do that again."

Diana laughed and her kiss sealed their connection. "I know you must go home tomorrow, but perhaps you could stay here regularly while I write. You are a most delectable distraction."

And for a few minutes, Florrie was no longer the responsible one, caring for her niece and worrying over finances or the pleasure and pressure of deciding on the fate of others' works. Right then, she was Diana Stratford's lover and muse. Distraction indeed, nothing more. No whispered promises, no long-term assurance. Florrie was certain in the knowledge of what loving Diana entailed, because she did love her, and she had done for months now. But she was left with the uncertainty of whether it was reciprocated or not, and she couldn't ask. She couldn't deal with that kind of rejection.

"The fire's going down, but the water should be hot now. Should we bathe before bed? Will you stay in my room tonight?"

Florrie's pulse quickened and she nodded. For tonight and for every night Diana wished, she would return, drawn to her warmth, the brush of her skin, and the intimacy of being close enough to feel every heartbeat.

CHAPTER FIVE

Some months later, on Florrie's visit to Mead House in Sussex, they had been intimate most of the night and hadn't bothered to draw the curtains The aroma of sex hung heavy in the room. Florrie rubbed her eyes and stretched like a cat, sated, and sleepy, and deliciously sore, a gentle reminder of their night's activities. Diana stood by the window, naked, every smooth stretch of skin highlighted by the sun streaming in, giving her an ethereal aura. Florrie seared the entrancing image into her brain to remind her she was in love with a beautiful woman, that she was alive, and every cell in her body hummed with energy.

"We need some fresh air in here." Diana flung open the window.

The heady aroma of summer flowers and the beautiful sound of early morning birdsong rushed in to fill the room in a wonderful intoxication of senses. The cool air stroked Florrie's skin, still hot with recent arousal. She chuckled at their hedonistic decadence. She had never felt so complete before, brimming with exultant joy and love. And it *was* love, even if neither of them had uttered the words. Diana had brought out the wild animalistic part of Florrie that she never knew existed, and she loved it.

Diana continued staring out of the window, silhouetted by sunshine. "I wish we could remain here all day, revelling in this delight, but I've been summoned to London for a meeting, and I simply can't escape it. So I may join you on the train. Did you say you were meeting Oscar?"

"Yes, he promised to take Cam into London. He said it was educational, but I suspect he may have other motives."

Diana raised her eyebrow, and her lips twitched upwards. "Certainly. It will be entertaining for sure."

Florrie's heart fluttered. "But he's trustworthy," she said, perhaps more trying to convince herself than Diana, "if a little flamboyant. Cam likes and trusts him, and he's become almost part of the family. He's even slept on the couch a few nights. I'm very fond of him too."

"That's good to hear." Diana looked wistful and turned back to the window. She raised her hand and waved. "Ah, here's Alice."

Florrie jumped out of bed. "What? You're naked. Aren't you worried she'll see you? She'll know what we've been doing."

A deep contralto laugh burst from Diana, and she turned to Florrie. "Oh, dearest heart, you're so bourgeois sometimes. Do you think she doesn't know what we do when you stay over and only rumple one set of sheets? When the smell of sex permeates every corner of the room, and both of us glow with the internal health of vigorous lovemaking?"

"I hadn't thought of it until now, no." Florrie tugged the sheet up over her body. "Won't she say something?"

"No, Alice is loyal and discreet. Your middle-class sensitivities can be allayed. I'm going to run a quick bath. Join me in a minute," Diana said and strode out of the room.

It was all right for her; she had the security and confidence of the upper classes and never had to deal with the consequences of society's judgement. They would write her off as eccentric, and she was wealthy enough not to worry about losing her house or job.

Florrie wished she could be more like Diana, but people talked. What would she do if it ever got back to Nora? Her sister would probably snatch Cam away from her. She shivered. She couldn't lose Cam. She was part of her life, her world, her family. And Cam needed her. A deep sense of foreboding rooted in her, an absolute certainty this wouldn't last. How could she fall from ecstasy to reality in the space of two heartbeats? She threw back the covers and took a robe from the back of a door to hurry into the bathroom.

Later, throughout their journey on a smoky, rattling train into London, Florrie couldn't settle to read the manuscripts. Diana stared out of the window at the passing countryside, and Florrie tried to avoid the overstuffed man who impinged upon her space as he dozed, his head at a sharp angle that would leave him with a crick in his neck. She shifted towards Diana to stave off his approach. Diana turned and flashed her a soft look, one exclusively for Florrie, and it made her heart stutter. They shared a smile that would've revealed too much had anyone seen it.

Diana coughed and twisted back towards the window and the view of fields morphing into tiny new houses the closer they got to London. She seemed uninvolved with Florrie and absorbed in her thoughts, but Florrie didn't mind. She was busy reliving this morning and last night, which had all been so perfect.

She would never forget Alice's slightly widened eyes as they greeted her this morning, and her cheeks burned a little at the thought. She picked up the manuscript to hide her blush and glanced at the other passengers, all engrossed in their newspapers or books. There was more space in first class, so she shuffled into the plush red seats and enjoyed the extra comfort compared to how she normally travelled.

A few minutes later, a cool hand landed on her thigh, and Diana stroked her gently, startling her then arousing her in equal measure. Florrie shot a glance at the other passengers, but they were in the normal commuter haze. She peeped a look at Diana, but her head was turned away, as if she had nothing to do with the caress reigniting Florrie's desire. This was too much. "Stop playing with fire," she whispered.

"I thought you like it hot," Diana said without shifting her gaze.

But she removed her hand, leaving Florrie bereft of the tingle of her touch.

All too soon, they pulled into the station. The doors banged open, and the travellers swarmed onto the platform. Diana hooked her arm through Florrie's as they strode towards the exit. Two familiar figures stood at the ticket barrier, grinning. Florrie pulled away from Diana. "Cam, Oscar, how lovely to see you. Cam, this is Diana. Diana, this is my niece, Cam."

Diana kissed Oscar on both cheeks in the continental way that was all the vogue, then stepped back to greet Cam.

Cam put out her hand to shake, making it very clear she didn't wish to be kissed even once. "How do you do, I'm Cam."

Diana shook Cam's hand very formally. "Lovely to meet you."

Cam swung around to Florrie. "We're going to play tennis at Oscar's uncle's place, and we'd love you to come."

"Will you join us too, Diana?" Oscar asked in the earnest, slightly fawning way he adopted when he was around Diana.

Diana looked disappointed. "I have a meeting with Anthony that I can't get out of this morning. I could join you this afternoon, perhaps."

Cam's shoulders sagged, probably thinking her expedition was about to be cancelled. "We're going to Oscar's tailor this afternoon. He promised me he can get me set up, and I've got the money Mother and Father sent."

"We could swap it around. Let's go to my tailor's this morning. I'm sure he won't mind changing the appointment." Oscar smiled.

Florrie was about to point out that Nora and Charles had sent the money for Cam to buy a new dress, but Cam was so excited that she didn't have the heart to say no, and really, why would she? If Cam wanted trousers, she should have them. "That's all right by me, as long as it doesn't put out your tailor."

Oscar waved his hand. "He won't mind; he charges enough."

Now Florrie's heart beat faster for a different reason. "I hope it's not too expensive. I'm not sure I have enough cash with me. I'd hate to waste the money, especially as Cam is growing so much now. She takes after her father in that respect." But not in other ways, thank God.

"Oh, it's all right. Cam and I have already discussed the funding. It will go on to my account, and she'll pay me back, plus interest, which she must calculate on a weekly basis. We're working on practical mathematics, and what could be more practical than this?" Oscar dabbed his forehead with his handkerchief and replaced it in his top pocket with a flourish. "It's still so warm. Let's grab a cab."

Diana frowned as they moved away from the barrier. "Oscar, I hope you are not being usurious and taking advantage of your young charge."

"Oh, no," Cam said, sidestepping a man rushing for a train. "He's charging the same as the Bank of England rate of 5%. If the economy comes off the gold standard though, the rate will drop, and he will reduce the rate he charges me."

Florrie fidgeted with her bag, debating on guiding Cam but not wishing to dampen her enthusiasm. "I'm not happy with any debt at all, Cam. I'd like to pay for your clothes outright, with the money you have as well."

Cam flashed a look at Oscar, who shrugged.

Florrie struggled to keep her voice even and tamp down the rush of anger. "I insist you learn how to budget properly, Cam. You only buy what you can afford—what *we* can afford. I've never borrowed a penny in my life, and I'm not starting now. And neither are you.'

Cam shrugged. "Okay, Aunty Florrie."

They arrived at the taxi stand. Oscar hailed it and turned to Diana. "You take the first one. We'll be at my uncle's at two thirty. You know where it is."

"Yes, thanks. Have fun." Diana laid her gloved hand on Florrie's arm. "See you later."

Diana's look made Florrie's heart sing. When she turned back, she found Oscar watching her—watching *them*—with a slightly puzzled look on his face, though it slowly melted into a mischievous grin. She prayed he didn't say anything, not with

Cam around.

Cam was holding out her hand to the next taxicab, buzzing with excitement and totally oblivious to the looks and head-shaking she was attracting for wearing slacks. Nora would be horrified if she knew where they were going and how Cam was dressed, but Cam deserved this. To see her engaged and being herself warmed Florrie to her core. Her heart swelled with love as Cam chatted happily throughout the taxi ride to Jermyn Street.

Half an hour later, Cam stood tall as she was being measured for her first proper pair of trousers. "I want a fastening at the front, like men have. I don't want the silly side opening."

The tailor checked to see how Florrie and Oscar reacted, but at their nod of approval, he smiled. "Of course. We can also fit the latest Lightning zip, which is more reliable and doesn't break. Have you decided what colour you would like?"

"I think she should have peacock blue, but she's set on black. Cam darling, you're going to look so dull in comparison to me." Oscar thrust his hand against his chest, revelling in the dandyism he normally kept under check.

Florrie suspected he was flirting with the tailor but couldn't be sure.

"It's okay," Cam said. "I prefer it that way."

"If you're on a budget, I have a pair of non-bespoke trousers that should fit with a little alteration. Would you like to try them on?" The tailor spun around to pull a pair of black trousers from the shelf. He handed them to Cam, who took them from him reverently and stroked the material. "There's a changing room through there." He pointed to an old, polished door beside the full-length mirror. "Take your time."

Cam disappeared rapidly, and Oscar beamed at the tailor. "Perhaps you could show me your pocket squares and cravats?"

"Of course, sir, come this way. I have some around the back."

Oscar winked as he followed the tailor, and Florrie had

the distinct impression he would be seeing more than pocket handkerchiefs. She shook her head and hoped that no one else came into the shop and discovered them.

A few minutes later, Cam emerged from the changing room. The trousers were too long and too baggy at the crotch, but her chest swelled, and she swaggered as she approached. "What do you think?" She looked around and frowned. "Oh, where are the others?"

"Checking for cravats." Florrie hid her amusement as it would sail over Cam's head.

The tailor emerged from behind a rack of suits, looking rather flushed, and clapped his hands together. "Yes, we can do something with you. Stay very still." He kneeled in front of Cam and expertly placed pins to give it more shape, then stepped back so Cam could admire herself in the mirror.

Oscar wandered back in, waving a peacock blue cravat at Florrie with a triumphant *I told you so*. She shook her head at him, but he grinned and stood back to look at Cam. "Wow, very suave, Cam."

Cam coloured up, although she also looked pleased.

"And would madam like a waistcoat?" the tailor asked, handing over a vest in the same material.

Cam turned her big eyes on Florrie. Cam's money was enough for jacket and trousers but nothing more. She asked the price and did some calculations in her head. If she used some of her savings, she could afford it, and it was too difficult to say no to Cam's pleading look. "Okay, we'll take the waistcoat too," she said and sighed.

Before Florrie could change her mind, Cam slipped on the waistcoat and rapidly buttoned it up.

The tailor pinned a couple of darts then nodded at the fit. "I'll also insert a buckle at the back in case it needs to be let out later."

Cam turned scarlet, and Florrie squeezed her shoulder briefly, before addressing the tailor. "Thanks, that's very considerate of you."

"How about a jacket in the same material?" He chewed at the couple of pins hanging from the corner of his mouth.

Florrie didn't want to startle him in case he swallowed them and just nodded.

"I might have something off the rack I can alter for you. Fortunately, you're tall and slim." Without waiting for a reply, he went to the huge rack of garments and fluttered his fingers from jacket to jacket. "Ah!" He pulled one off the hanger and handed it over.

Cam accepted it and pushed her hands into the sleeves with care before standing before him.

He carefully placed a few pins from his mouth into the suit then stood back to admire his wizardry. "Take a look." He nodded at an old mirror that reflected the racks of suits and jackets, giving the appearance that they went on forever.

Cam stared at herself. She frowned as she checked herself over, twisting to see all sides. The suit was structured by the pins, showing where it needed to be altered. Then a slow smile broke out as she appraised herself.

"That's really me," she whispered.

The awe in her voice made Florrie clutch her chest. "You look very dapper, dear." To see Cam blossom and stand taller was seeing her step into adulthood and her own true self.

After another few seconds admiring her reflection, Cam sighed. "I'll change back into my slacks." For a beat longer, she eyed herself wistfully, then removed the jacket and waistcoat and handed them back to the tailor like she was handing over the crown jewels. Cam strode towards the changing room with a confidence that belied her age.

"What are you thinking?" Oscar asked.

Florrie had to blink hard to stop the tears. "To see the transformation from a lost, scared child into that young woman is such a joy."

"Clothes make the man, or in this case, woman," Oscar said gently and squeezed her hand. "You've done right by her. She's coming into her own now. She'll thrive in Cambridge."

"She's got to pass the exams first."

"I have no doubt she'll do very well. You must be so proud of her."

"I am. I just wish her parents were," she whispered. "Nora will be furious when she finds out their money hasn't been spent on a ball gown for Cam to attract a man."

He laid his hand on her shoulder, and they shared a wistful look. Life would never be exactly as they wanted, but Florrie didn't regret agreeing to this or spending a big chunk of her savings on an outfit Cam would probably grow out of in a year. The delight and wonder on her face when she saw herself in the mirror was something Florrie would never forget, and if she had to fight with Nora about how she was bringing up Cam, she would do so willingly.

After Florrie handed over the deposit, they left the shop and re-entered the bustle of London streets. Wherever they went, they seemed to attract attention and disapproval, not that Cam noticed. Oscar played up to it, blowing a kiss at an old couple who scowled at them.

He clapped his hands. "Right, lunch is on me, and then we'll make our way to my uncle's house to play tennis. My cousin said you can borrow her tennis dress and canvas Oxfords, Florrie."

Later, they were dressed in the tennis clothes and waiting for Diana to arrive and Oscar to emerge from the other changing room.

Florrie sat beside Cam on a bench with their backs to the changing room and looked up at the four-storey townhouse.

"This place is fancy," Cam said.

"Yes, when Oscar invited us to play tennis, I didn't think he meant at his uncle's private tennis court in Chelsea, no less."

Oscar appeared in front of them in perfectly creased white

trousers and shirt and matching canvas shoes. "They've also got a swimming pool in the basement, although they keep the house closed up when they're away."

"Were you earwigging, Oscar? You do know that eavesdroppers never hear good things about themselves." Florrie wagged her finger at him but smiled.

He grinned. "But you weren't talking about me; you were suitably impressed by my contacts. Should we knock about until Diana arrives?" Without waiting for a reply, he strode across the immaculately mown lawn to the net and checked the height.

Florrie gulped as she took her position. This setup was all too professional. Cam slammed the ball over the net. She'd clearly inherited her father's strength. Florrie scrambled to return the shot. Cam grinned as she sent a shot slicing across the court, enjoying making Florrie run.

Panting, she failed to connect with the next ball, which Cam had lobbed high to the back of the court. "Are you trying to tire me out before we start?"

Cam's eyes sparkled with mischief. "Oscar and I have been discussing tactics. We're going to play against you and Diana, and Oscar says Diana is quite a whiz at tennis."

Oscar volleyed the tennis ball across the net. "It helps that she's so tall."

Florrie returned to Cam, although her shot was a little weak.

"Are you talking about me?" Diana asked.

Florrie turned to see Diana at the garden gate, already dressed in a white, midcalf tennis dress with green embroidered motifs. She was stunning. The ball streaked past Florrie.

Oscar laughed. "Stop gawping and pick it up."

Florrie rushed to scoop up the ball and returned to the centre of the court. She had to stop herself from kissing Diana with the same wild passion they'd explored last night.

Diana smiled and brushed Florrie's cheek with her lips. "It's lovely to see you too. I spent my meeting thinking about last night, but we might need to behave if we don't want tongues to wag," she whispered. Diana turned to their opponents. "Okay, I've only got time for one set. We'll let you serve first. Now Florence, would you like to play up front."

Florrie understood that was a statement, not a question. Given how serious Diana was, Florrie almost said she'd prefer to watch from the sidelines. "Of course I should say I haven't played for about thirteen years."

Diana flinched slightly. "At least you've played before."

"And I wasn't very good." Her hands and feet hadn't ached then either. The blush burned up her chest. She didn't want to humiliate herself in front of Diana.

"Are we actually going to play or are you two going to whisper for the whole time? Ready?"

Oscar didn't wait before serving to Diana, who scooped it across the net for Cam to smash in front of Florrie. She did a little skip and jump as Florrie retrieved the ball from under the high hedge.

"Not holding back I see," Diana said to Cam, who grinned at her.

They lost the first game to love, and it was Florrie's turn to serve. She threw the ball up a few times without hitting it.

"You're tense. Just relax," Diana said.

As though anyone could relax when they're ordered to do that. This was such a mistake. Florrie threw the ball up again.

"I know you can relax," Diana said.

The memories of the previous night flooded into Florrie's mind, when she had come undone at Diana's tongue and fingers. She huffed out a laugh, and her racquet contacted the ball. Surprisingly, it went over the net and into the service box. It must have surprised Oscar as he scrambled to return it and hit it into the net.

Florrie glared at Diana, who stared back with hardly contained glee.

"Whatever works, dearest heart."

Florrie's frown softened, and their gazes held, one, two seconds too long. She loved that term of endearment.

"Can we get on?" Cam asked.

Florrie picked up another tennis ball. "Sorry, Cam." She served, and Cam returned the ball too wide for Florrie to reach.

But Diana came from nowhere to whip the ball back across the net, and then she continued to give them all a lesson in how to manipulate the play. After little over an hour, she had cruised them to a 6–4 victory. Florrie had only won two points for them in the whole match.

"Well played," Oscar said, his shoulders drooping. "I'm going to change and lick my wounds."

"Never mind, we'll win next time," Cam said as he headed towards the men's changing room. "We'll just smash the ball at Aunty Florrie."

Florrie winced. "Sometimes your honesty is brutal, Cam. Do you want to get changed first?"

Cam nodded and headed into the second changing room.

"Where did you learn to play?" Diana asked when they were left alone on the court.

"In Belfast, when I had to chaperone my elder sister on her quest to find a husband. The tennis club was a rich goldmine of eligible bachelors. It worked: she bagged herself a junior diplomat who was destined for higher things."

"Do you ever go back?"

Florrie shuddered involuntarily. "No. I don't want to be married off to a cabbage farmer. Charles was worried that the troubles in Dublin would spill over into Belfast and didn't want his child brought up there. I couldn't wait to escape, so was quite happy to accompany Nora and look after Cam when she was born. I've devoted my life to her. She needs me."

Diana touched her hand, and goosebumps raced up Florrie's arm. If only they were alone. Playing tennis with Diana and watching her skill had been arousing but also frustrating because she could do nothing about it. "Sorry I was so terrible at tennis," Florrie said.

Diana lifted her chin with her fingertip and stared into Florrie's eyes. "You weren't terrible. Perhaps a little rusty, but you improved as the match went on. I enjoyed playing with you. I'd love to do it again. However, I must go back to work." She cradled Florrie's face in her palm and gave her a chaste kiss. "Until next week. I can't wait."

"I hope you're not going to include my terrible tennis playing in one of your books."

Diana laughed as she walked away and waved over her shoulder before she banged on the changing room doors. "I'm off. Thanks for the game."

Diana continued walking as Cam and Oscar replied from their respective changing rooms. She must have known Florrie was watching her, because she slinked away with sass, sexiness, and a sway to her hips. When she reached the side gate, she turned and blew a kiss.

I'm doomed. I'm completely smitten with her. Florrie sagged onto the bench, letting her head rest against the cool wall behind her, a smile tugging at her lips. There was no hope for her.

Yet, she wouldn't want it any other way.

CHAPTER SIX

London, October 1929

"IT'S HERE!" FLORRIE RUSHED into Diana's office flapping the proof sheet. Diana rose and stood beside her, so close Florrie could inhale her now familiar and intoxicating scent, one Florrie associated with passion and intimacy. They studied the final draft covers of Diana's "love letter" to Florrie, now *On the Edge of Uncertainty*. The cover art, by the Polish-American Art Deco artist, Tamara De Limpicka, was of a tall thin woman in a cloche hat with her arm outstretched towards someone or something off-screen. Her expression was one of desire. It was a portrait of Diana, intriguing and risqué, much like the author herself. Florrie stroked the image, as if she was caressing Diana in person. She looked up and caught Diana's gaze.

"Yes, this works," Diana murmured. She then turned to Florrie, her expression reflecting that of the book cover and stroked Florrie's cheek. "So does this."

They'd promised themselves they wouldn't be openly affectionate in the office, but they were so drawn to each other, standing too close, brushing hands in passing, and sharing knowing smiles. They had only slipped up the once at work, after the exhilaration of the Equal Franchise Act of 1928 being passed. They both agreed it was too risky to repeat the tryst, especially after Anthony had banged on the door of the flat above the printing press as they were rearranging petticoats.

Instead, they shared their hidden intimacy in the depths of the countryside when Florrie stayed over, as often as they could arrange it. Every time Florrie left the cottage, it was like leaving a part of her behind, and she immediately calculated the time until her return.

Anthony knocked and without waiting for a reply, barged in, waving another copy of the proof around. "You can*not* have this as the cover. It's too provocative. Not after all the backlash, and the *Sunday Express* got *The Well Of Loneliness* banned last year. We can't afford to pulp lots of copies, not to mention court bad publicity, just because you want to flaunt your picture on the front looking lustful."

Diana's mouth tightened, and her eyes narrowed. "Anthony, don't be so dramatic. It's merely a portrait of a stylish woman, even if I say so myself."

"I forbid it."

Florrie half-expected him to stamp his foot like a truculent toddler. The tension in the room raised at the stand-off.

Diana raised her eyebrow. "Fortunately, it's not up to you. It's my creative choice, and the ignorant editor of the *Sunday Express* can take his toxic opinions elsewhere. This is perfect, and it sums up the themes of the book, of loss, longing, and wanting what you can't have."

Florrie didn't dare catch Diana's eye.

Anthony looked from Diana to Florrie and back again. Scowling, he glared at Florrie. "I need the expenses in pronto. I want to finalise the accounts." Without waiting for a reply, he turned and marched out of the room, letting the door bang behind him.

"Of course, Anthony." His animosity had increased over the past few months, and Florrie shivered. Fortunately, she worked for Diana, not him, so he couldn't fire her. She hoped.

"Shall we get on with it, then we can take a late lunch?"

Florrie nodded, and they worked for another hour, going through various correspondences and manuscripts, with Florrie taking copious notes.

The telephone rang, and Diana flapped her hand at it in obvious irritation. "Ignore that. It's probably someone asking a banal question they could resolve for themselves if they applied any mental acuity to it"

Florrie frowned. A direct phone call was unusual. Mostly people knocked and entered. Anthony was supposed to field the more complex business queries to free up Diana, but it never seemed to work like that, because he demanded attention from Diana mostly, Florrie was sure, to interrupt their time together. He seemed to sense their attraction, so whenever he had the opportunity, he asked Florrie to perform some menial task that would take her out of the office and away from Diana.

"Ignore it," Diana said again.

She trailed her fingers over Florrie's arms and up to her shoulders, stroking up her neck and along her jaw. She knew so well how to distract Florrie, and it was getting harder by the day to keep their hands to themselves.

Florrie curled into the touch, wanting more but sensitive to it being forbidden in this place, especially with Anthony sniffing around. "Stop it, we'll get caught," Florrie whispered, but they both knew there was no bite behind her request. She was intoxicated by Diana and was thrilled that her book was about to come to fruition. She felt almost as nervous as Diana at how it would be received by the critics and the readers.

As if she was reading her mind, Diana focused on the proof again. "Do you think they'll like it, or has it all been too long since last I published? Do you think readers will have gone onto the next young writer?"

"I'm sure your readers will love it. How could they not? It's beautiful, and haunting, and heart-breaking."

The telephone rang, and after they disregarded it another time, it rang once more.

The door banged open, and Anthony rushed in. "Answer your bloody telephone. It's your stockbroker, Robert Tyson. He's been desperately trying to call you. I hope you've been shorting your American stocks as Wall Street has just crashed."

"I don't even know what that means. I leave it all to Robert; that's what I pay him for."

"Wake up, Diana. This messing around has got to stop. "He waved his arms in Florrie's direction. "I hope to God you got out of the market, or you could be in real trouble—which means the press is in trouble." He caught sight of the cover, and it seemed to rile him up all over again. "And no, you absolutely cannot use that. Not now the stock market has crashed and the world is collapsing. If the press is to survive, we must sell the more popular works. We can't have any whiff of impropriety and you are not discreet." He shot a poisonous look at Florrie.

He knows. They thought they'd kept their affair hidden, but that look... A shiver went down Florrie's neck. Something deep in her gut told her the affair was over, and life would never be the same again. The premonition was so strong that it took her breath away.

She shot a glance at Diana, who was totally focused on Anthony, rage etched on her face and something else, something Florrie couldn't name. It looked close to fear. Was Diana worried about the money or was it something more? They'd discussed the worrying signs from across the Atlantic and the measures taken by some of the banks to stop the slide in the market, but it was clear Diana hadn't acted on the information. That was the thing about Diana: she was great at the intellectual discussion but wasn't brilliant at the practical follow through. It was probably why they worked so well together, with Florrie carrying out Diana's wishes and becoming her invaluable right-hand person.

"I forbid you to use this cover. There is enough potential scandal as it is, you carrying on these dalliances with all your women. It's time you put it all behind you and made good on your promise. We have a deal. You need to find out what's happened, and then we'll talk about saving the press."

Dalliances, plural? Florrie crumpled from her position of being special, of being certain. Of course Diana could be seeing other people, other women, and she would never know.

Diana slammed her hand down on the desk. "Get out, Anthony. The creative decision is mine and always has been, and the deal is off. You've known that for a long time, yet you persist. I'd prefer to lose the press than marry you." Her tone was not as firm as her words, and she trembled.

Marry? Florrie sagged onto the nearest chair and worked hard not to bring up her breakfast. That was the deal, the hold he had over her? And Diana hadn't denied other dalliances.

Anthony smirked at Florrie's reaction. He sneered at her. "Did you think all of this was real? Don't you know she sucks people dry then spits them out. Your job is done now. You've been her muse for the purposes of a novel, but you aren't needed anymore."

Florrie turned to Diana, but she held her head in her hands, denying nothing, and not standing up for Florrie. How stupid was she to think Diana meant what she'd said? Why had Florrie believed that what they'd shared was special, thinking Diana felt the same?

"Come and talk to Robert. He's still hanging on the line in my office. He probably has another dozen phone calls to make. Then we need to decide how to save the jobs of our employees." Anthony stormed out of the office but left the door open.

Diana stood unsteadily and meekly followed Anthony out. Where had her fire and confidence gone? She looked broken as she closed the door behind them and flashed a look of something akin to sorrow or regret as their eyes met. Florrie stared at the closed door. Surely Diana wouldn't throw her out now, would she? Florrie banged her hand on the table. How stupid to assume Diana would be monogamous, and she'd never said Florrie was ever more than a distraction. Yet the language in the book had been so beautiful, so loving, and longing, and the character was definitely based on Florrie. Or maybe it was just true at the time, and Anthony was right about Diana using and discarding people.

Florrie reached for her bag, but it slipped through her fingers as her hands shook so much. She tried again and pulled it onto her lap and cradled it to her stomach.

Did she mean nothing to Diana? Had she just been a passing infatuation? With that new knowledge, all the shared moments, the conversations, and the sex—Florrie cringed at how eager she'd been—were tainted with the shift in perspective. Although she'd never declared her love to Diana, she *had* loved her, loved her intelligence and kindness, and from the book and her looks and the time and attention Diana had devoted to Florrie, she thought it was reciprocated, a little bit at least.

How ironic that she found herself on the edge of uncertainty about Diana's feelings for her.

She supposed the immediate issue was her position. Had Anthony just fired her? Or had he been mocking her because he knew about them both? As if she conjured the devil by thinking of him, Anthony strode into the room.

"You may as well go. Diana is distraught. She's lost all of her investments in the stock market crash. I told her she should spread her portfolio, but she believed her stockbroker. When she's finished with him, she and I will need to decide what we can do to save the printing press and forty-seven jobs. That means we'll need to focus on the mainstream scripts, none of the more esoteric books you've been suggesting."

Florrie gaped.

"We're letting you go."

"I'd like to hear that from Diana, not you."

Anthony huffed out a sharp breath. "For heaven's sake, you're an employee, nothing more, whatever she made you think."

Florrie stretched out to capture the pile of pink ribbon bound reams of paper. "I'll take the manuscripts she asked me to look at this week."

Anthony stared at her, then his shoulders lowered a little. "Fine. Complete those and send them to me, and I'll make sure you get paid for them." He softened his gaze. "I'm sorry it hasn't worked out for you."

The pity in his eyes was almost more than she could bear. She preferred his arrogance, then she knew where she stood. *Don't cry at work, not in front of him.* There was going to be no reprieve, no happy ending. She looked up at the ceiling to stem the tears stinging the backs of her eyes and almost choked. "Will you provide me with a reference, please?"

Anthony blinked, then nodded. "Of course. Thank you for your work. Goodbye, Miss Cooper."

He pivoted and paced out of the office, his footsteps echoing down the hall. In the distance, Florrie thought she heard Diana sobbing, but that might have been her imagination. She wanted to comfort her, and hold her in her arms, and tell her it would be all right. But she couldn't. She didn't have the authority, and it wasn't true. Nothing was all right.

Half dazed, she scrabbled to gather the personal belongings she had in the office: spare shoes and a clean blouse for when they went to a discussion group, and the photo of her and Cam together at a picnic, taken by Nora on one of her increasingly rare visits to see her daughter. Altogether it didn't amount to much, but this had represented the very best of her and the ongoing joy in her life.

And now it was gone.

Florrie stared at her tiny desk, squeezed in beside Diana's volcano of papers. Out of habit, she smartened the manuscripts into a precise pile. Although gouged-out inside and slightly nauseous, she wouldn't let her professionalism slip. She couldn't leave without saying goodbye, so she scribbled a note, spidery and uneven, unlike her normal copperplate handwriting.

Please call me when you can. I've taken the eight manuscripts we agreed for me to look at and will return them with notes.

Thank you for the opportunity and everything. Yours truly, Florence.

She couldn't take the risk of anything more personal, lest anyone else read it, even though she wanted to say how much Diana meant to her and how Florrie would have done anything for her. But now Diana needed to concentrate on saving her press, and Florrie understood that. Maybe they could meet up when it had all calmed down...though the resignation on Diana's face when Anthony mentioned marriage didn't fill Florrie with hope. How had Diana defined hope once? The delusion of desire above expectation. It all felt like a delusion now.

She must have caught the next train and checked off the stations as they passed by, but she didn't recall it. And she must have bought a local newspaper at the Bletchley station stand to look for local jobs, but it hadn't been a conscious thought. With nothing better to do, she set about making supper.

A week later, as the shock faded and the initial anger subsided, all that remained was a deep, lingering sadness. With each passing day, the likelihood of Diana apologising or calling her diminished. She'd allowed herself a week to wish it wasn't so, just one week before she accepted they were truly over. The week ended today, and still, there had been nothing from Diana. Despite being angry with herself for vainly holding on to hope, Florrie wiped at her eyes as she stirred the stew. This week had seen so much extra salt added to the food, and she had burned a cake the other day, a cake she had baked a hundred times before. Cam hadn't complained; she'd merely cut off the edges and eaten it with gusto, as normal.

Cam entered the kitchen after laying the table and cocked her head. "Aunty Florrie, your face looks sad. Am I right? Can I help?"

Florrie couldn't be doing a good job of hiding her upset very well if Cam could see it, so Florrie enveloped her in a huge hug—and Cam allowed it—and tried not to let her ever-present tears fall. "You always do help me, Cam. You're wonderful around the house, and I'm very grateful. I don't know what I'd do without you."

"Would you like to hear what I've been practising on the cello and piano?"

Florrie had already heard snippets as she'd worked over the same pieces until they were perfect, but for Cam to offer to perform was a gift that lifted her heart. "I'd love that. You're so talented, and you've a wonderful voice—"

"Isn't it too deep for a girl?"

"It's beautiful."

Cam flushed, reminding Florrie she was just fifteen. Because Cam was so serious and advanced mathematically, it was easy to forget she was so young. How could Nora and Charles not see what an exceptional person she was? Florrie returned to her stew. "I thought about getting some chickens to lay eggs for us. Would you give me a hand looking after them?"

Cam frowned. "I don't know anything about hens. I'll have to get Oscar to pick up a book from the library for me, and then I'll decide if I'm able to help."

Florrie tried to hide her smile, because she didn't want Cam to think she was laughing at her. "I'm not sure the Cambridge University library will have a book on practical poultry husbandry. Let's go to the local library and see what we can find. I also need to go to the post office. Should we go down this afternoon?" The stab of loss sliced into her heart. This would be the last set of manuscripts she sent back, and these were to go to Anthony, not Diana. It really was all over. "Can you just stir the stew for me, please, Cam? I need to go." Without waiting for a reply, she hurried to the bathroom and slumped onto the toilet seat.

What hurt the most was there had been nothing from Diana: no explanation, no fond wishes, no apparent regrets. Utter and complete silence. Perhaps Anthony had been right all along about Florrie meaning nothing to Diana. She had served her purpose as muse, and her usefulness had passed.

Logically, she knew she would never be good enough, not for someone like Diana. She was just a middle-class nobody. And yet, there had been something between them, she was certain of it. Something more than the sex. Closeness, laughter, and companionship. Diana had expanded Florrie's world view and filled it with colour and understanding. Now her mouth tasted of ash, and her heart felt empty like a cold grate, long burned out. All hope was gone.

Taking the train down to Diana's cottage and demanding to see her wouldn't change the facts, and Florrie couldn't bear to have the wonderful memories associated with that place being tainted by the truth. It was pointless. It was clear Diana didn't want her, didn't want to see her again. She swallowed hard so her sobs couldn't be heard, and she propped her head against the wall, which gave cool relief to her pounding head.

Once last week, she'd picked up the phone to swallow her pride and ask for her job back, even though it would crush her soul to stop assessing manuscripts for the bold, the intriguing, and the avant-garde. Anthony had made it very clear; he was only interested in the safe bets, the beige certainties. And there would be too many associations with Diana and the glorious time they'd had together. She couldn't bear it, so she'd put the phone back on the cradle.

She blew her nose and breathed through the tightness of her chest. She couldn't break down, not in earshot of Cam. Florrie shrugged her shoulders. She wasn't one to mope, which she must have been doing for Cam to notice. It was the end of the fantasy, and she'd always known there would be no happily ever after. Diana had indicated as much in the book, where the lovers parted ways at the end.

A gentle knock came on the door. "Aunty Florrie, are you all right?"

The poor girl. Florrie could almost hear the anxiety in her

tone. "I'm fine. I'm just finishing up." She pulled the chain, washed her hands and splashed her face, all the while trying to think of a way to explain her predicament to Cam in a way that wouldn't upset her balance.

She smiled when she emerged, even though her eyelids felt gummy and her throat scratchy. "I'm sorry, Cam. I'm upset because the job I loved in London has come to an end. I've been offered a job in the office of the local estate, which I'll accept tomorrow, although it doesn't pay as well. It means I'll be home more, and we'll make do by planting more vegetables in the garden and having hens. And maybe a pig."

"Does that I mean I have to go to boarding school?"

Florrie shook her head emphatically to put Cam at ease. "Definitely not. Your mother and father still pay for Oscar. If we're careful, we'll have enough, especially if you help me with the garden and the hens."

Cam twisted her handkerchief this way and that. "I'll get that book."

Florrie smiled. "Good idea. Let's go into town now, and we can get an ice cream at the café and go to the post office and library afterwards. We can have the stew later. Who says we can't have dessert before the main course. What do you think?"

Cam's eyes sparkled. "Shall we find a book on growing vegetables too?"

They shared a shaky grin, like co-conspirators or explorers facing an uncertain world. Together, they would be all right. They would do more than survive; they would thrive.

The following day was thrown into turmoil when a letter came through the post with Diana's confident handwriting on the front. Nausea and hope went at each other, and Florrie just stared at the envelope for a while, wanting to know what was inside but also not wanting to uncover a true finale to their adventure.

Her fingers shook as she opened the envelope, and her breath caught in her throat. Thank God Oscar had taken Cam to a museum in London today. Her stomach lurched, a wave of dread rising as her legs buckled beneath her. She collapsed onto the nearest chair, clutching at the envelope.

It was thin—too thin. That couldn't be good news. With a slow, calming breath, she slid out two pieces of expensive monogrammed paper.

My dearest Florence, I am sorry, this isn't how I wanted it to be. Anthony told you I lost everything in the stock market crash, and I can't tell you how devastating that's been, emotionally as well as financially. He said you've left and won't be returning, and I think that is for the best. I couldn't cope seeing you and not being with you.

Anthony has come up with a rescue plan for the printing press, which will save most of the jobs and thus keep the families with a livelihood. He's taking over the press completely and has plans for how to change direction of the publishing company, which I may not agree with, but it means I can concentrate on my writing—if I can write.

There is a condition to him saving the press; he insists I marry him, just as our families agreed when we were younger. I'd managed to avoid it so far, but I now see no way out. I did seek alternatives, including approaching my bank for a loan, but they say there's no collateral, and my credit has collapsed. So, with deep heartache, I must do the right thing to save the press, however wrong it feels. I will forever think of our time together with much fondness, and I wish you every happiness. I'll send you a copy of the book when it's finally published. Yours, Diana."

Florrie slumped forward, her head pressing on her palms, empty and hollowed-out, like a jack o' lantern at Halloween, with nothing behind the mask. But she didn't cry. Not this time. She'd seen this coming and even if it wasn't sincere, Diana had expressed regret. It didn't solve anything though. If it meant Diana could write again and Florrie had contributed to that, it was some comfort. But why did it have to hurt so much?

The dismissal, with the formality and faint praise of "much fondness," made Diana's true thoughts clear. She hadn't felt the same depth of emotion as Florrie had. Anthony had been right, damn him. She rammed the paper into the envelope and, though she was tempted to toss it in the fire, something stayed her hand. She clutched the missive to her breast as though she could hold Diana close and reconnect through something Diana had touched and written.

Florrie pressed her hand to her mouth to stop the guttural cry of grief bleeding from her lips. How delusional she'd been to think there could ever be anything long-term between them. And yet, a part of her had nurtured a tiny spark of hope in the huge blackness of reality. Now it guttered out. She could never open her heart again to be ripped to shreds in the same way; she couldn't bear it. Unrequited love was a luxury she couldn't afford.

Her selfishness had already risked her relationship with Cam, and it could unravel everything. If the truth about her and Diana ever came out, Nora would snatch Cam away without hesitation. No discussion and no second chances. Of that, Florrie was certain. As an aunt, she had no legal standing and no parental rights over Cam. She had nothing. And if that happened, she'd have no one.

No. From now on, she would devote her life to raising Cam, to protecting her and keeping her safe, and would gladly forgo any indulgences of her own. She would do whatever she could to make Cam's life safe and joyful. She would box away that part of herself and never look at it again...if only her throat wasn't choked, her vision blurred, and her heart crushed, making it hard to breathe.

Wiping her cheek with the back of her hand, Florrie staggered to her desk, her legs too heavy to support her. She stuffed the letter at the back of the top drawer, as though burying it deeply would make it all disappear. She snapped the drawer shut. If only she could lock away that side of herself as easily, dismiss her love, her joy, her intellectual passion.

But as she stood in the silence, her heart pounding and her breaths coming shallow and fast, she knew the wound inside her wouldn't heal quickly. If ever. Some scars were too deep to fade or soften. This one would mark her forever, and she would be changed in a way she hadn't chosen but would have to live with. There was no edge of uncertainty now, and Florrie was most certainly alone.

CHAPTER SEVEN

"She's late." Nora twisted her watch around, barely keeping the irritation off her face.

"No. You're an hour early." Florrie wiped her hands on her apron. "I've only just arrived home from work myself."

Charles rustled his paper and stretched out his feet, so he almost took up the entire room. He'd taken prime position by the stove in the kitchen—unsurprising—and it was difficult to work around him. Florrie scraped the carrot peelings into a bucket to be taken to the compost heap later, just discarded scraps like they seemed to want to do to Cam.

"She should be here to see her parents," Nora said.

"I did say today wasn't ideal." It had been fruitless trying to persuade them to come any other day. When they first arrived two weeks ago, they were tied up with "important debriefings." What could be more important than seeing their daughter? Everything and anything else, apparently. Florrie gave the carrot a forceful chop and a piece spun off the table and onto the floor. "Little bit of dirt never harmed anyone." She snatched it up and checked there was no fluff on it before adding it to the pile. "It was an open day for Cam to be shown around the college she'll be going to. Normally, she would have been here to greet you, but the timing was out of her hands."

"I don't understand why she wants to go up to Cambridge this early anyway," Charles said without bothering to lower his paper.

"You should ask her, but Oscar has got as far as he can teaching her maths, and she'll be getting regular maths homework set by her professor until she joins a year this October. It seemed like a good compromise. She'll be challenged mentally but will have time to catch up socially and be able to cope more in a year's time."

"So why did she need to go there *today*, when we're home between postings?"

Florrie smiled to ease the tension and took great pleasure in lopping off the top of the carrot, imagining it was Charles' foot. "She was being introduced to her professor of mathematics and allotted a female mentor, who will show her around so she knows where to go when she visits."

"Why wasn't her tutor with her? And why didn't he show her around?"

Florrie poured the last of the chopped carrots into the water and put them on the range to simmer. Her breath caught sharply in her ribs. The knowledge she'd been trying in vain to push away all day came hurtling back and threatened to overwhelm her. The final shred of hope that Diana would find an alternative solution to her arrangement and be with Florrie had been snuffed out. It was stupid to have had such a fanciful thought. Life didn't happen like it did in romance books, and Diana's own novel had warned Florrie they wouldn't get a happy ending. She inhaled to steel herself, then turned around. "Oscar's at a wedding today, and even if he wasn't, he couldn't show her the women's college."

"Doesn't she realise how precious our time is?" Nora asked. "Charles is a very important man now. This will be his first deputy ambassador role."

"You said." About twenty times in the space of ten minutes. "I've made stew for this evening, and all the vegetables have come from the garden, so they couldn't be fresher." Having the produce from plants she'd nurtured was like a little miracle, and she'd loved spending yesterday in the garden, digging up the carrots and cutting the kale, chitting the potatoes ready for early summer harvest, and glorying in a warm spring day. She sat outside for half an hour listening to the birds singing, and a robin had been almost at her feet in its quest to find worms. It was soul-nurturing work, and this time of year, she never quite got the soil from under her fingernails. She looked up to Nora scowling at her. Florrie flashed her sister a smile. "What did you say?"

"I said when do you think she'll be here?"

"She should be here any minute. The Cambridge train might be late. I'm sure she'll get here as soon as she can, she's been so looking forward to seeing you again." If you could count ripping up three napkins at breakfast as excitement. It seemed Florrie's lot was to mediate between people and smooth the path at work and at home.

Right on cue was the telltale tick and purr of the bicycle as Cam placed it in the shed. Then silence. A couple of minutes passed with no sign of her.

"What's she doing? Hiding?" Nora asked, turning her watch around and around her narrow wrist.

Probably building up her courage to see you again. "Wiping down her bike, I expect. She likes things just so."

Florrie was about to go and check when the kitchen latch opened quietly, and Cam slipped in. Her eyes shone, but she bit her bottom lip. She stood to attention by the door. "Hello, Mother. Father."

Nora faltered with her arms wide open. "What on earth are you wearing?"

Both Florrie and Cam checked out her clothes. She looked particularly dashing in the three-piece suit they'd bought in London, which had been altered as she grew. "What do you mean, Nora?"

"You went out in trousers? To a university, no less?"

"It's so much more practical for travelling, Nora. Aren't you going to greet Cam properly?" How had Nora become this harridan, all judgement and no love?

Nora coloured slightly. They both shared the delicate Irish skin, after all. Then she crushed Cam in a bear hug. "Of course, it's lovely to see you, Camilla. It seems ages since I've seen my little girl."

"It's been one hundred and sixty-five days since we met in London. And I'm no longer a little girl."

She was taller than either of them now and only about six inches shorter than Charles. Cam was all spikes and sharp points, and Florrie wanted to calm her down and reassure her.

"Really, that long? Nearly half a year? Goodness, how time flies. Did you realise it was so long, Charles?" Nora had all but eradicated her Irish accent and now sounded more English than the English. With it, she'd lost the softness she'd had as a child.

Finally, Charles rose and shook hands with Cam like she was one of his diplomatic colleagues, but Cam seemed more relaxed with her father's formality than the embrace from her mother.

From her handbag, Nora plucked a small box wrapped up in pink paper and ribbon. "We brought you a little present from Egypt. It's rather expensive, so I hope you'll look after it."

"Thank you, Mother. I always look after my things. Can I wash my hands first?"

"That's a good idea. Let's have a cup of tea, and I'll hurry supper along. Why don't you all go into the sitting room and catch up?" Florrie squeezed Cam's hand as she brushed by. The bathroom door closed with a rattle, which was the equivalent of a slam for Cam.

Florrie showed Nora and Charles into the sitting room before escaping back into the kitchen, wondering if Cam would barricade herself in. Only a couple of minutes later though, the bathroom door opened, and Cam hurried past to the sitting room. She didn't look at Florrie, but simply kept her lips tightly pressed together and her eyes focused on her target. That wasn't good.

Florrie hurried to make the tea. Normally, Cam would have offered to carry the tray in, but Florrie would manage, even if her hands ached. She hoped she wouldn't drop it, though that would certainly add a bit more drama to the proceedings, as if they didn't have enough.

The tray slipped from her hands as she placed it on the table and some of the tea sloshed over the edge.

Cam jumped up. "Sorry, Aunty, you should've let me do that. I'll get a cloth." She scampered from the room.

Nora turned on Florrie. "What are you doing, letting her wear trousers like some radical suffragette? And letting her go *out* like that? It doesn't reflect well on us."

Florrie gripped the teapot, tempted to point out Nora's own sin was much more scandalous: marrying and having to leave Belfast in a hurry when she was pregnant with Charles' child. "Trousers are more comfortable, and she's happier wearing them. She can wear what she likes."

Nora huffed. "Most girls I know would love to wear nice dresses."

Florrie poured the tea, attempting to disguise her shaking hands. "Cam isn't most girls. She's her own lovely, unique self. If you'd only try and get to know her a bit better, it would do her the world of good. Sugar?" *You need it.*

"No, Florrie," Nora said, "you mustn't let her run wild or allow her to get any silly notions in her head."

Florrie noted Charles wasn't bothering to contribute to the conversation. He didn't even say anything when Cam returned with a cloth and wiped down the tray.

Florrie rose and took the cloth back from Cam. "I'll go and see how the stew is doing."

Cam flashed a pleading look, clearly not wanting to be left alone with her parents.

"Would you come and lay the table for me, Cam?"

"No," Nora said. "Let Camilla stay and chat to us. We haven't seen her in months. We'd like to speak to her on her own."

"One hundred and sixty-five days, and I prefer Cam."

Good for Cam for sticking up for herself. Florrie smiled as she carried the empty tray out, then she deliberately left the door open a crack so she could hear if Cam needed her.

"How did you get on in Cambridge today?" Nora asked.

"It was wonderful."

Florrie stirred the stew and smiled at Cam's obvious enthusiasm. She couldn't make out all the words, but her tone was light and easy.

"Did you see my alma mater?" Charles asked.

Why did he always have to talk like he had a broom up his backside *and* make it all about him? Florrie picked up the cutlery and made her way back to the dining table in the lounge they used for best.

"Yes, I saw Trinity, and the Bridge of Sighs, and the punts. And my mentor, Susanna, showed me all around the college. She rows, and I want to learn too. She said I'd be good at it, because I run and I'm tall."

That was probably the longest speech Florrie had ever heard Cam make, and her joy bubbled over like a geyser. She polished the cutlery before laying it on the table and smiled encouragement at Cam.

"That's lovely, dear. I'm so glad you're looking forward to it."

Nora sounded genuine for once. Maybe the rest of this visit would be all right.

"And I met Professor Thomas, and he's going to set me mathematical problems to test me. I'll send the answers back with Oscar. I'll do the rest of my studies with him as well as helping Aunty Florrie while I learn how to get on with people."

Bless her guilelessness. Cam was nothing if not honest, though sometimes too honest for her own good. They'd need to work on that if she was going to navigate social situations. Florrie left the room to collect the stew and kept the door slightly ajar once again.

"Did you meet any nice boys?"

No, no, no. Florrie pulled the stew from the oven as quickly as she could.

"I like girls," Cam said.

Florrie groaned. *Too late.* She put the stew down on the hob and gripped the handles hard. She couldn't rescue Cam now.

"What do you mean, you like girls?" Nora asked.

"Do you mean, like friends?" Charles asked.

"That isn't what you meant, is it, Camilla?"

Florrie abandoned the food and hurried to the lounge door and leaned her head against it. Every instinct screamed at her to burst in, to shield Cam. But this had to be between Cam and her parents. *Save yourself, Cam. Don't be scrupulously honest.* Florrie imagined Cam's brow would be furrowed as she realised she'd said something wrong but couldn't understand what.

"I do want to make friends. I don't have any apart from Oscar. But I'll never marry a man. I want to go to Cambridge and use my brain."

Florrie's heart twisted. *Oh, brave, honest girl. Now you've put the cat among the pigeons.*

Nora gave an embarrassed little laugh and a teacup clattered in the saucer. "Don't be silly, Camilla, you don't mean that. You're still young. You just haven't met the right man yet. Eventually you will, especially if you start wearing pretty dresses, and perhaps apply a touch of makeup."

"No. I won't."

"Don't talk back to your mother. And get this Cambridge nonsense out of your head now. You need to marry a man to look after you."

Cam rushed out of the lounge and past Florrie into the kitchen.

"Cam—"

"Leave me alone."

The kitchen door slammed. Florrie wished she'd gone in. She should have stood beside Cam and not left her to face her parents alone. Guilt knotted in her chest. She'd never seen Cam so furious and shaken.

But there was no taking it back now. Cam needed space and time to cool down. If Florrie couldn't make it right with her now, she could face the people who had caused the damage.

Squaring her shoulders, Florrie stepped into the lounge.

Charles's face was beet red. "I blame you for this. You've twisted her mind with your radical views, hanging around with those literary types." Spittle shot from his lips.

Florrie blinked and tamped down her instinctive response, which was to tell him to leave, but she needed to rescue this, for Cam's sake. She glanced across at her sister. Nora stared ahead, ashen-faced and trembling. Charles was no more than a bully in a diplomat's mask, and he was used to ruling without question. No wonder Nora spouted his vitriol; she had to keep the peace at home.

But Florrie wasn't going to be cowed by him. This was too important. She put her hands up. "Let's sit down and talk about this rationally."

Nora nodded at Charles, who snatched up the discarded newspaper and took his seat, then she perched on the edge of her chair, tensed and poised, as if ready to fly the nest.

Florrie smiled, attempting a lightness she didn't feel. "All this talk of marriage is such a long way off. She's sixteen. You must be so proud that Cam's been offered a place at Cambridge, especially at such a young age. And to study mathematics too? How wonderful that she'll follow in your footsteps, Charles."

Charles gave the slightest inclination of his head, and his shoulders lowered a fraction. His face returned to his normal hue. Then he shook his head and muttered to himself.

Florrie cleared her throat. "Cam should focus on being ready to go to Cambridge next year—"

Charles pointed his finger at Florrie. "We knew she'd never be a diplomat's wife. She doesn't have the social niceties for that. But she needs to make a good marriage."

The headache that had been threatening all day from the swallowed words and suppressed emotions flared in Florrie's brain, sharp and relentless. She rubbed at her forehead and sighed. "She's got a brilliant mind, and she's been offered a place in one of the most prestigious universities in the world. It would be a travesty if she didn't get the chance to use her brain. She's young and should make the most of her gift."

The latch lifted, and Cam slunk into the room, her eyes red and puffy.

"Come and sit with me, Cam," Florrie said in as gentle a tone as possible.

Watching her parents warily, Cam lowered herself onto an arm of the wingback chair. Florrie placed her hand over Cam's burning, clenched one. She didn't pull away. *Good.*

"We've been thinking about your future, Camilla. We're not sure Cambridge is the best solution for you," Charles said in a tone a vicar would use in the pulpit.

The colour drained from Cam's face. "I need to do maths. It's the only thing I'm good at."

"We only agreed to you applying for Cambridge as you'd meet a better class of man there," Charles said.

"And you can leave when you get married, like I did," Nora said.

Cam stared at her parents like they were talking a different language. "I don't want to marry. I want to do maths."

Charles frowned. "Don't be ridiculous. Women can't graduate from Cambridge, so how could you support yourself?"

Florrie took a deep breath, ready to jump in.

"You can stop all this Cambridge nonsense now, today," Nora said. "You'll go to a Swiss finishing school, where they'll teach you how to be a proper woman: how to dress and behave like a woman, and they'll prepare you for marriage, to a *man*."

"No. I won't," Cam said.

She gripped Florrie's hand so hard it hurt, and Florrie had to put her other hand on top of Cam's to get her to stop.

Nora sighed. "Darling, I'm sorry. We obviously made a mistake letting your Aunty Florrie look after you. She's filled your head with nonsense and perverted your sense of self."

"No. Aunty Florrie has been wonderful."

Florrie's heart thumped hard against her chest. Even when distraught, Cam was trying to protect her, and Florrie's heart expanded with love for her. Cam tapped her thumb and index finger together, one of her signs of stress. Florrie's fingers twitched with an urge to mimic the action. They couldn't take Cam away. Losing her would destroy them both.

"I'm sure she meant to do what's best, but now it's time for you to grow up and become a woman." Nora leaned forward and touched Cam on the forearm, but she flinched and pulled back.

"I'm not doing that. I'm going to Cambridge. They said they want me."

Charles blinked slowly. "It seems to me, Camilla, that you have a choice. You come with us and attend a Swiss school to teach you deportment and all the things a woman needs to make a good wife, like your mother. Or you persist in this foolhardiness about attending Cambridge, and you'll never see us again. Perhaps you'd like to think about that."

Cam gripped Florrie's hand even harder. "I don't need to think about it. I'm not going with you. I'm staying here with Aunty Florrie, and I'm going to Cambridge next year. It's what I'm meant to do."

Florrie's stomach turned at the uneven tennis match playing out in front of her. "Charles, you don't mean that. Cam's your daughter, and she's a kind, clever, loving soul. She needs and deserves your love and support."

"She'll go to a Swiss finishing school. That's it. My final word."

He placed his hands on both sides of the chair, as if he were a king on his throne.

The back door opened with a crash. "Oops. Hello, my beautiful girls. I've come to see how you got on." Oscar hiccupped, and by his heavy, staggering footsteps as he approached the lounge, it was clear he'd imbibed too freely with the wedding champagne. "I hope you had a fablu...fal...fabulous time and met the wonderful Professor Richard Thomas." He clutched at the door jamb and peered in. "Ooh, hello, I didn't realiiish you had company. Don't care for the party vibes much judging by your cat's arse mouths."

Charles leaned forward in his seat. "Who the hell is this?"

Oscar tried to bow and then had to grab at the door to stop himself from falling. 'Osh Kar Harr ish, tutor to Cam Langley esh quire, and penniless poet at your sher vish."

"Oscar, you're drunk," Florrie said. "Go and lie down on the spare bed. You're not helping."

"Ooh, Florrie, you look so hot when you take command. Does Di—"

Florrie flung up her arm. "Stop! Go to bed and sleep it off. Cam, fetch him a glass of water."

Oscar released a loud burp. "Sorry about that. Okay, I think I might lie down for a few minutes. Toodaloo. Let your knickers down and have a bit of fun. You look like you need it." He lurched away, and Cam followed him out.

"That's the fellow we've entrusted with the education of our daughter?" Charles slammed his hands down on the chair.

"He's been to a wedding. Haven't you had a few too many drinks at a wedding? He's not normally like this, and he's done an excellent job coaching Cam through the entrance exam, which she passed, more than a year earlier than most people attempt it."

"In which case, his job's done, and he doesn't need to teach my daughter anymore. All funding for him will stop today."

Florrie had to close her eyes. It would always come to this.

Money and bullying them to do what he wanted. Her eyes snapped open. "Don't do this to Cam. She's happy and thriving, and I've never heard her so enthusiastic as she was today talking about Cambridge. It would be cruel to try to force her to be anything other than who she is—"

"How will she get on in society like she is, going around in slacks like some radical suffragette?" Nora said, clutching her hand to her chest. "She'll be mocked and banned like that awful Radclyffe Hall woman—if you can call her a woman. That's not what we want for our little girl. You've been a terrible influence on her. I can't believe my own sister would allow this to happen."

"Stop, Nora." Florrie shook her head. "This isn't helping. We don't know what will happen in the future. I suspect Cam will take to the academic life, and they'll respond to her brilliance. At some point, she will find her niche, but she isn't, and never will be, a girlie girl. You remember how she was growing up." Her voice wavered a little, but she cleared her throat. She had to make this count. "Trying to force her into that will make everyone unhappy. But she's happy here. Let her be. Let her develop as she will into the wonderful person I know she can become. Just love her for who she is."

Nora dabbed a handkerchief at her eyes. "It isn't normal. She needs a place that will teach her how to be a lady."

"I won't go. I can't go. I'd rather die first," Cam said, hard and firm like a slap.

Florrie turned sharply. Cam hovered inside the sitting room, pale and rigid. Her eyes shimmered, and she blinked rapidly, holding back tears, but her jaw was set, and her expression tight with determination. Florrie's stomach churned. Cam wouldn't make an idle threat. A chill ran through her. She couldn't let things spiral any further. She straightened up and pointed to her sister. "You need to go. Now. You've done enough damage." She searched their faces for a flicker of remorse, some sign they knew they were wrong, and that they would do what Cam deserved. Nothing. Their expressions were tight, determined, without a trace of compassion or warmth. "Please think about it. Look inside your hearts and find the love you have for your daughter. I know it's there. When you do, when you're ready to love her for who she is, you'll be welcome here." She wasn't sure if she was making it worse, or if they even heard her, but it was heartbreaking to see Cam struggling to stand up for herself against her own parents. No child should have to face that. She stood behind Cam and placed a hand on her shoulder, in solidarity and comfort.

Nora replaced the handkerchief and snapped her bag shut. "Oh, for heaven's sake." She rose. "Come on, Charles, we're getting nowhere here. Hopefully your driver's still outside. Goodbye, Camilla. Please think about what I've said. We'll look at schools in Switzerland for you." She leaned forward to give Cam a kiss on her cheek, but Cam pulled away.

"I won't go."

Nora withdrew and gathered her bag tight against her stomach, as if it were armour. "Don't make this mistake. You'll never be accepted in society if you insist on dressing like this and becoming some...blue stocking. Not everyone is as laissez-faire as your aunt. You'll be mocked and shunned and maybe even attacked for who you are. I don't want that for you. I want you to be safe. I love you. We love you."

Cam stiffened beside Florrie, her jaw tight. "Then I'll learn how to box."

"Goodbye, Camilla. I hope you come to your senses." Charles held out his hand, but Cam didn't shake it. She didn't move; she didn't blink. After a beat he slowly lowered it to his side. "Goodbye then," he repeated, and they walked out through the front door no one used.

"You didn't even have Aunty's stew. She grew all the vegetables herself," Cam said as the door snapped shut behind them.

"It doesn't matter, Cam. I don't feel hungry now anyway."

Cam turned without a word and buried herself into Florrie's shoulder, sobbing with gut-wrenching, snotty tears that drenched Florrie's blouse. Florrie wrapped her arms tightly around the girl she loved with all her heart. They stood there for a long time, until Cam's sobs softened into sniffs and uneven breaths.

"Did you hear everything?" Cam asked.

"Not everything—"

"They don't want me to go to Cambridge. I can't go to Switzerland."

Florrie kissed her hair. "Let them cool down a little and get used to the idea. They might come around."

"They won't," Cam said, without looking up from her tight grip on Florrie.

Florrie was sure Cam was right, but she needed to comfort her, even though she vowed never to lie to her. "We'll go and see them up in London in a few days' time."

"It won't make any difference. Please don't force me to go."

Cam's body was as taut as one of her cello strings, and every second of being with her parents had wound her tuning pegs tighter and tighter. Florrie stroked her back until Cam softened her stance a fraction.

"To London?" Florrie asked.

"To Switzerland. I'll run away."

The image of Cam having to deal with the noise and the crowds was all too clear and horrific. "I won't force you to go anywhere or do anything you can't or don't want, I promise. This is your home. You can stay here as long as you like. But perhaps they'll think differently when they've had time to consider the ramifications. We can invite them back here if that's easier."

Cam looked up at Florrie, her eyes red and glassy, but with the strength of conviction on her face. "They won't come unless I comply. It's like when I was little, and they forced me to fit into their idea of a dutiful daughter."

Florrie shook her head. Cam was already the perfect, dutiful child. If only they could see it.

"Will I ever be normal?" she asked, resting her head against Florrie's chest.

She patted Cam's back and pondered how to answer the impossible question. "If by normal, you mean average, then no, you'll never be normal. You'll always be extraordinary, brilliant, and kind. And I love you exactly the way you are." Florrie released her grip as Cam's breathing had become more even. "What matters most is that you're happy with who you are. And maybe one day, when you're a world-class mathematician, you'll find someone who sees you, *really* sees you, and loves you for who you are, and you'll love them in return."

Cam pulled away to blow her nose on her handkerchief. "Thank you, Aunty. I love you too. And I hope somebody loves you that way too."

Florrie clutched her hand to her chest to stop the churning emotions she'd been trying to dam all day. Her throat constricted, and she had to swallow hard. Her eyes stung, but she couldn't cry in front of Cam. She needed Florrie to be strong. She pulled Cam tight, pressing her face into Cam's hair, so she wouldn't cry. "I loved someone, and I thought they loved me. But they chose someone else."

"They're stupid." Cam's voice was muffled but fierce, like she was about to go into battle on Florrie's behalf.

The ache in Florrie's heart deepened. "No. Not stupid, just conflicted. Trapped. Doing their duty to others." Her throat tightened again. "They followed their head, not their heart."

Diana married today. It was the death knell of Florrie's previous life, the final snapping of her brittle hope that Diana would change her mind. But she hadn't. It was done. The undertow of grief tugged at her, threatening to drown her. She gasped a panicked breath of air, too shallow, too tight, then another, trying to force the life-giving oxygen into her lungs. She had to swim, to take control, to be in charge of herself. For Cam's sake.

Florrie tightened her arms around Cam, clinging on for dear life. She hugged her until the girl struggled. Immediately, Florrie released her hold. She had to be there for Cam, to support and love her, no matter what happened. "Should we have some of that stew now, if I can rescue it? Go and check on Oscar, and if he's awake, bring him down. If he's asleep, make sure he's on his side, so he can't drown in his vomit. Take the bucket from the scullery and put it on the side of his bed. I'll check on him again later," she said, hoping Cam wouldn't notice her shaky voice.

"Why do people drink to make themselves ill?"

"To take away the pain."

"I *hate* weddings."

Both Cam and Florrie jumped at the sound of Oscar's voice, still hoarse and thick with drink, but he seemed sober.

"All the couples merrily coupling, casting their smug superiority over you, and knowing I'll always be alone, and I'm never getting married." He carefully crossed the room and slouched on the chair then nodded towards the table. "Your guests have gone then?"

"They didn't even stay for supper, even though Aunty grew all the vegetables herself."

Cam fixating on that point wasn't a good sign. "If you feel able to eat at all, Oscar, it might do you good to have some stew and bread to soak it up."

He waved his hand, but it was unclear whether that was in agreement or dismissal.

Florrie turned to Cam. "Would you be a darling and bring the stew through, and the plates and bread. Thank you."

Cam nodded and left the room.

Oscar leaned forward. "Sorry about crashing the party, but I had to see how Cam got on, and to pass you on a message," he whispered hoarsely. "Diana says she's sorry, but she didn't have a choice."

Florrie's knees buckled, and she collapsed in on herself. She'd been doing so well, putting it all aside, focusing on Cam and her woes and maintaining her composure by a hair's thread. Now it all rushed up: grief, betrayal, and longing dragging her down into a breathless vortex of despair. She pressed her hands to her head, trying to contain the sob that threatened to explode.

To be rejected, even though she knew it was coming, was unbearable. She was left with heart-breaking, gut-gouging pain that left her hollow and shaken. She wanted to scream, to rage, to sob. But it was hopeless. She'd been the stupid one, holding out a tiny candle of hope that Diana would come to her senses, even as Florrie's rational mind knew the truth. Diana never would.

Oscar eyed her with compassion in his bloodshot eyes.

She couldn't bear his sympathy, so she inhaled to control her weakness. "Of course she had a choice. She chose someone else."

"You know why she did that. Be fair."

The words hit Florrie like a spark to dry tinder. All the emotions that had been bubbling up all day rose into pent up anger, and she snapped. "Fair? When is life *fair*? It's not fair that Cam's parents have turned their back on her, even though she's one of the most delightful people I know. Is it fair that Charles is pulling the plug on your funding?" Her clenched hands trembled at her sides. "I don't know how we're going to manage. I'll have to take on more work or rent out a room. We already scrimp and save, eat meals from the garden and count every penny... What more can we give? Is that fair? I'm trying every damn day, but I'm so tired of doing it alone. And the one person I've ever loved, has..."

He grabbed her hands, and she could smell the stale alcohol on his breath as he hugged her close.

"Listen, Florrie, my main role with Cam is done. I probably need to find another job anyway, but I'm still your friend—and Cam's. And I'd love to come here and see Cam when she reports to Cambridge each month, and if ever you need somewhere to stay there, you're always welcome." He hiccupped again, but he seemed completely sober. He pulled away at the sound of footsteps. "Ah, here comes supper. Thank you for the feast. More fool them for turning it down. For turning you down, Cam. We black sheep need to stick together."

"Baa," said Cam and gave a half smile as she placed the stew pot on the table mat.

"That's the spirit." Oscar clapped his hands. "Now tell me how you got on. What did you see? Who did you meet?"

It was the right thing to give Cam something positive to focus on. Florrie mouthed "thank you" at him as Cam described her day in detail, becoming more animated with each sentence. Florrie looked around at her little family and was grateful for them both. They would be all right, when she could get over her hurt about Diana. If she ever did.

The following day, she received a telegram from Nora summoning her to London the next day. *Just you* was stressed in the message.

For the whole of the train journey, she fidgeted with her handbag, not able to settle with her book. The replica of her previous commute with the association of Diana, plus the stress about whether they would send Cam away made her sick to her stomach. Florrie had no say over her future. She had to try and persuade Nora to let Cam stay with her. Her vision blurred as she stared out of the window, and she blinked hard. What would she do if she was entirely alone in the world?

The address was not one Florrie was familiar with, and she was shown into an impressive porticoed building, where every one of her footsteps echoed across shiny marble floors. Each step seemed to bring her closer to her doom. This was her future, but she would fight for Cam to stay with her with everything she had.

The maid knocked, and Florrie followed her into a formal sitting room, all sharp modern lines but devoid of any personality.

The only photograph on the mantelpiece was of Charles being presented to the king, with Nora by his side. Not one photo of Cam was evident, as though she'd been erased from their lives. Cam deserved more than this.

Nora rose when Florrie entered. No Charles. Was that a good or bad sign?

"Tea?" Nora asked. "How was your journey?"

So, they were going for small talk and niceties. Nora chatted about their travels and how well Charles was doing as they waited to be served. Florrie wanted to shout at her to stop the pretence, but she needed to play along with the farce until Nora deemed it appropriate to address the pressing matter.

The maid re-entered, carrying a silver tea service with porcelain cups and saucers in fashionable black and white with gold trim.

"Thank you, Wendy. You can go now, I'll pour," Nora said, with the ease of someone born to this life, not to the streets of Belfast.

No doubt Florrie had been summoned here to give Nora the advantage of being on her own territory. The rattling of the teacup in the saucer when she handed it to Florrie was the only sign that her sister was anxious about the conversation. Nora raised her own cup, took the daintiest of sips, and then replaced her cup with a clatter. She retrieved a handkerchief from her handbag and daintily dabbed her lips.

Get on with it, Florrie wanted to scream. She wasn't sure how long she could continue with this charade. But she had to, for Cam's sake. She closed her eyes and only opened them when Nora cleared her throat.

"You've been a terrible influence on our daughter. I should never have let you look after her. She was supposed to have a nice dress to wear to balls, to catch a man, not that, that travesty of an outfit she was wearing."

Nora twisted her handkerchief around in her fingers, winding the fabric tighter and tighter. Florrie hadn't seen her this agitated since they were young and Nora, pale and trembling, had announced she was pregnant and that she and Charles were going to flee to England to marry. She said she couldn't cope with a baby. So, she'd turned to Florrie and asked the impossible: *Will you come and help me?* And Florrie had abandoned her studies and come to England. She'd always thought she'd study again and use her brain somehow, but she didn't regret a second being an unpaid nursemaid and governess to Cam. "You asked me to look after Cam and bring her up. I've done that. She's a wonderful, intelligent, kind young woman who has a great opportunity ahead of her. She's happier now than she's ever been. Who cares if she has her own individual style—"

"She'll be a laughingstock. You're supposed to be helping her get on in the world. Instead, you hang around with all those people of loose morals and speak of nothing but the wonderful *Diana*."

Florrie definitely didn't do that now. Her stomach dropped, and a vice crushed her chest, making it difficult to breathe. She had to speak. "I was employed by Diana, but that's over now following the Wall Street crash. I've got an administrative job locally." She swallowed hard, forcing the words out. "I'll never see her again."

"Oh, God. Diana Stratford," Nora said. Something shifted, and understanding flickered over her face, then her lip curled in disgust. "You're in love with her, aren't you? Don't deny it. I'm your older sister, I can see it. You were always such a terrible liar. No, no. I can't have you corrupting my daughter with your perverted ways—"

Florrie slammed her cup down on the saucer, sending tea slopping over the side and onto the table. "Stop. Diana married a few days ago, and it's over. This is about what's best for Camilla." She hated to use Cam's full name, but at least she wasn't there to hear it. She dabbed at the spilled tea with her table napkin. The brown liquid soaked into the cloth, staining it beyond restoration. It was ruined, a bit like this family. "She's happy with me, working towards Cambridge. She would hate it in a finishing school, and the other girls would bully her. She'd run away or regress—"

Nora screwed up the handkerchief in her fist. "Do you think I don't know that? I can see she's happy with you. How do you think that makes me feel as her mother? That she doesn't want me, doesn't want to be with me? With us, her parents?"

Of course, Nora had to make it all about her. She hadn't changed in all these years, and she wouldn't change now. "But she wouldn't be with you, would she? You'd throw her to the wolves in some finishing school. She'd never cope. You can't do that to her."

Nora's mouth set in a thin line. They sat in angry silence for a few beats, then Nora nodded slightly. "I know. But what's the option? It's obvious she hero-worships you, and whether you intended it or not, she's followed in your footsteps."

Florrie bit down on the tiniest smile. Perversely, it was heartening to hear her role acknowledged.

"What a choice." Nora gripped her fist so tight her long nails must have dug into her palms. She inhaled sharply, then stretched out her fingers and smoothed her handkerchief, like she was trying to soothe herself. "If she stays with you, you must promise me that you'll never tell her about you or your wayward lifestyle. You must never act on it, and you must do everything you can to discourage that side of her. You must encourage her to find a man and marry. And as Camilla can't tell a lie to save her life, I'll only have to ask her to see if you haven't done as I've asked. If you promise you'll never tell her about you, I'll let her stay with you. Not because I approve, but because I think that's what is best for Camilla."

Florrie swallowed. Could she live a lie? She scoffed at herself. It wouldn't be a lie, since she didn't have anyone in her life, not anymore. Diana had abandoned her. In some ways, it could be the hardest thing to do, agreeing to be celibate like a nun. But if it meant Cam stayed with her and thrived... Well, it wasn't a difficult decision. "I promise." Her stomach roiled, as if battling with her choice. But having Cam happy was worth it.

If only it didn't feel like she was giving up a huge part of herself.

CHAPTER EIGHT

Cambridge, 1950

GLORIA WAVED AT THE bus driver to stop. She boarded the bus with a swirl of her cape, smiling at the attention. Women graduates were a rarity. By contrast, Cam helped Florrie on and paid for all three of them with the correct number of coins. Florrie lurched from bar to bar to progress down the bus.

"Sorry, Aunty, I should have helped you." Gloria stepped back to settle her down on one of the seats.

"Not at all, dear. Enjoy your moment; you deserve it."

"Thanks. Your support has been wonderful." Gloria sat in front.

Cam dusted down the seat beside Gloria with her handkerchief. She pinched at the crease in her trousers before she perched on the edge, ramrod straight. Gloria leaned into Cam, and her posture softened. Gloria was so good for her.

The bus pulled out into traffic. Despite Gloria's teasing, there was no way Florrie was going to discuss anything on the bus. She smiled and stared out of the window at the passing scene, familiar and yet changed, because *she* had changed. Yes, she was still the same late middle-aged woman, but she was also something more: a woman with a past, a woman who had loved and been loved.

Gloria leaned over the seat to face Florrie. "So...Diana is clearly much more than your old employer. Do I get a little frisson of something there?"

Florrie's cheeks burned. "It's complicated. And this is not the place—"

"Nay, it's not that complicated." Gloria pointed at her. "You had a crush on her. Unless you...ooh you did, didn't you? You must spill the beans when we get home. You're such a dark horse."

Cam frowned. "What are you talking about?"

"I'll tell you later, love."

Cam shot a quick look around the bus to see if anyone had overheard, but Gloria was not one to temper her affection.

"Don't worry, I'm Yorkshire. We call everyone love."

The look she gave Cam was not one to be misinterpreted though, and Cam scowled at her.

Gloria laughed and looked out of the window. "Oh, look, there's a Vivaldi concert at King's College next Saturday, should we go? Will you come, Aunty?"

Florrie shook her head. "No, I'll let you two go. You need to spend time alone together and have some fun."

Gloria's eyes twinkled. "So we can leave you to have a bit of fun of your own?"

"Gloria Edwards, you are too mischievous." But Florrie couldn't muster any real harshness in her tone as she knew Gloria wanted the best for her. Her fingers caught the card in her pocket. She was tempted to take it out to stare at the embossed letters and stroke the thick paper that had been in Diana's hands. Did she want to rake up all that hurt and anguish? She rubbed the edge of the calling card and stared out of the window as the town gave way to the flat, open countryside and the big skies.

The pain was still there, buried deep and dulled now, but if she allowed herself, the low throb of discomfort could rise to her consciousness. She turned her gaze back into the bus.

"Are you going to see her?" Gloria asked in a much gentler tone.

Florrie rubbed her hands. "I don't know. I'm not sure I want a reminder of what was never mine. I don't want to stir up old upset that has long been buried." Emotion swept up her throat, giving a catch to her words.

Gloria reached over the back of the bus seat and squeezed Florrie's hands, stilling them and giving her comfort. Her cheeky grin faded. "Don't go if it's upsetting."

Florrie looked down at their entwined hands. Her shoulders heaved and for a moment, the long-abandoned grief washed over her. "It's more I can't bear to hear about her perfect life." She couldn't believe it had been perfect with Anthony, but that's what Diana had chosen, and maybe they had mellowed into a mutual companionship. Florrie sucked in a breath, not wanting jealousy to corrupt her thoughts or twist her acceptance. She was loathe to dig deeper. Her heart had healed over the years, but the scar was still there, a perpetual reminder that she'd never fallen in love again. In all those years, she'd deluded herself that she couldn't be that vulnerable again, because her devotion to looking after Cam was everything, even though they'd long since reversed roles, and Cam—and now Gloria—cared for her.

"We used to have such deep and meaningful conversations on anything," Florrie said. "She was so widely read, and held opinions on everything, and challenged me to question it all and think for myself. She took me to various lectures and introduced me to writers, and artists, and a whole new way of life throwing off the austerity of the Edwardian times and the horror of the Great War. London in the twenties was about living each day to the fullest. It was exhilarating and intoxicating. But we're not who we were then. I might be a big disappointment."

Gloria smiled and stroked the back of Florrie's hand. "I doubt that. She seemed really pleased to see you. And you'd have so much to catch up on. I'm sure you'd end up having one of those meaningful conversations."

Would they have a real conversation? Or would her son come along? She should have had a look around earlier to see if he favoured Diana, tall and lean with long features, or followed

Anthony with his jowls and over-indulged, heavy-set frame.

"Aunty Florrie, we're here," Cam said immediately after they passed the penultimate stop.

Florrie smiled, knowing Cam had calculated to allow sufficient time to help Florrie to rise from her seat and shuffle to the front of the bus. That it took both Cam and Gloria to help her down when the bus stopped for them to alight was annoying; she hated being a burden, yet that's what she'd become.

Despite their care, she hissed a breath against the jolt of pain when she stepped onto the pavement. She took a moment before she shuffled towards their home. It was smaller than their place in Bletchley had been, but they had an inside toilet both upstairs and downstairs. Florrie's room was downstairs, which was so much better than stumbling downstairs in the cold in the middle of the night. Her room also had French windows opening onto a small garden stocked with vegetables and a hen house down one side, and flowers down the other in a miniature reproduction of Diana's garden in Sussex. It hadn't been conscious, but over the years, she had stocked the beds with a similar array of colours and flowers as if she'd been trying to recapture her happiest time through sight and scents.

She paused to lean against the front wall and admire the tidy front garden. There were so many blessings. Her life was too simple, and ordered, and safe to upset it by reconnecting with Diana, who would probably be impatient with an invalid, if she wanted anything more than a brief meeting.

Cam opened their gate, and Florrie breathed easier with the smooth passage to the house and her favourite wingback chair.

"Cup of tea?" Cam asked when she helped Florrie to her seat.

"No, thank you, dear. If I have any more, I'll burst."

Gloria plopped down beside Florrie and patted the seat next to her for Cam. "Now we can quiz you about your relationship with Diana Snooty Pants."

Trust Gloria to make such a snap judgement, causing Florrie

to want to leap to Diana's defence, but why should she? D ana had chosen Anthony over her and had not communicated except her brief letter of regret and a copy of the book when it was finally published—with a different cover, not the beautiful painting they had chosen. "That's not fair, dear."

Gloria had the grace to look bashful. "Sorry."

"Never mind. If you pop into my room, on the left end of my bookcase there's a book called *On the Edge of Uncertainty* by Diana Stratford."

"The author? That was her?"

"Who is this person? I don't understand," Cam said as she sat down carefully, pinching her trousers so they didn't crease.

"Hang on. Let me get the book and then you can tell us all about it, Aunty."

Gloria hurried down the hall to Florrie's room and returned within a minute, brandishing the book like the Holy Grail. She sat beside Cam and snuggled up to her. Cam leaned into Gloria and smiled. It heartened Florrie they were so comfortable that they could relax into each other and be themselves around her.

They both focused on her, and she squirmed in her seat a little. Now that she had to articulate what she felt for Diana, what she'd been to her, Florrie's heart began to race, and her throat went dry. She sketched the basics of their work together. "I used to go down to her cottage in the country, and we became close."

"Ooh, how close? Did you? Yes, you absolutely did.' Gloria clapped her hands together in glee. On seeing Cam's look of puzzlement, Gloria turned to her. "They had an affair."

There was no turning back now. "Do you remember a few years ago, when I told you I'd been in love once? With a woman. The woman was Diana."

"You were so mysterious about it, I thought it must be a right juicy scandal with a married woman. It is. You're such a dark horse." Gloria could hardly contain her glee.

Cam frowned. "How come you didn't tell us, tell me?"

The hurt was so obvious that Florrie wanted to hug Cam. "You met her once, a long time ago. We played tennis in Oscar's uncle's Chelsea townhouse."

Cam nodded thoughtfully. "That was so posh. We got my first man's suit from Oscar's tailor. It was such a happy day."

"It was." Florrie smiled at the memory: the brilliance of Diana's tennis skill, Oscar's pretend sulking, and Cam stepping into her true self as she tried on her clothes.

"But why didn't you tell me about you when I was growing up? It would have helped."

"Oh, Cam, I know," Florrie said. "But I made a promise to your mother that I would never tell you."

Cam frowned and inclined her head. "I don't understand why."

"Because she said that she'd take you away and send you to Switzerland if I did, and you would never have gone to Cambridge."

Cam held her head in her hands, and her shoulders shook. Gloria put her arm around her and whispered something in her ear.

"I'm sorry, Cam." Florrie's fingers trembled as she reached out, and she paused without touching, not sure it would be welcome. "I could have told you later, after you'd been to Cambridge and you were an adult, but I didn't want to hurt you. I didn't want to tell you about your mother, because, well..." She huffed out a breath. "I always hoped you'd come to a reconciliation."

Cam shook her head vigorously, as though such a notion was impossible.

Florrie sighed. "Besides, I've never had a real relationship like you and Gloria have. Yes, I had a crush on Diana, and we became intimate for a few years, but I never lived with her." She swallowed hard, and her jaw ached, it was so tight. This was harder than she imagined. "In the end, she chose Anthony as her husband, and I had nothing more to do with her...until today."

She rubbed her forehead as though she was trying to erase the memory. "I've never hidden it, but I didn't want to relive it all. Perhaps I should've said something, but you never wanted to talk about that awful day when you looked around Cambridge and came home to your parents. It's part of why I was so angry with them. They were so harsh and judgemental, and they should have loved you unconditionally."

Cam held her gaze, her eyes warm and unwavering. "I've always felt loved by you."

"And I do love you, so so much." Florrie's breath caught. "Thank you for saying that. It means so much to me, more than you'll ever know. I never knew if I was doing enough to help you."

Cam rose from her chair, stood over Florrie and patted her shoulders, then she placed a kiss on Florrie's forehead. It was something she would never have done before Gloria and her joyful, tactile influence.

Gloria squealed, the book open on her lap. "She's written in it. 'For Florence, thank you for everything.' Then signed it and added a kiss."

Florrie put her hand to her chest. It was strange, hearing those words again. At the time, she was so hurt and angry that she'd thought it was a brush off, nothing more. But now she could see Diana may have been thanking her genuinely but was constrained by the presence of Anthony hovering in the background, jealously monitoring everything she wrote. "Look at the dedication in the book itself."

Cam stood by Gloria as she flicked the pages and read aloud. "'To F, for being my muse and my delight, for listening and challenging and encouraging me to write again. D.' Oh, my giddy aunt, that's you? You have a dedication, a declaration of love almost, from a famous author, and we never knew. You have *got* to see her again. Please tell me you're going to meet her tomorrow. You can't let that go."

Florrie laughed, despite herself. "Don't get carried away,

Gloria. She was only thanking me for inspiring her and facilitating her writing."

"My muse? My delight? You need to find out if there's something there."

Florrie shook her head. "I don't *need* to do anything. I was so hurt and betrayed when she married Anthony."

Gloria virtually bounced in her seat. "Be her friend then. See if there is anything there, or if you can inspire her to write again. The world needs another Diana Stratford novel. Please, Aunty Florrie."

"She hasn't written anything since," Florrie said. "That I know of, anyway."

"Exactly. You'd be doing us all a service. Go and call her, now."

"You can be very bossy sometimes, Gloria, dear."

"I know. And you love it." Gloria stood and flung her arms around Florrie. "You may deny it, but I can see the spark in your eye. Why don't you phone her now?"

There was no denying Gloria's enthusiasm. Even Cam seemed to catch the same feeling and nodded encouragement. Florrie was pulled up by them both, then bustled out to the hall.

Her hands shook slightly as she dialled the number on the card. "Diana? It's Florence. Were you genuine about wanting to see me again?"

"Thank you for calling back," Diana said. "Yes, absolutely. Shall we meet tomorrow? At the same tearoom? How about morning coffee and lunch, then we could take in the talk about Charles Darwin at Christ's College, if you're free."

Florrie laughed. It was like stepping back twenty-odd years when she happily went along with whatever Diana suggested. "That would be lovely. But I should warn you that I can't walk very far, and I have to use a stick."

"Let me pick you up in my car and drive you around then. Where do you live?"

Florrie exhaled noisily. Getting on a bus on her own would have been difficult, and if she didn't have to ask Gloria and Cam to accompany her, all the better. "Thank you, that would be perfect." She gave her address and after they said their goodbyes, her grin was reflected in Cam and Gloria's expressions. "What are you smiling about? Don't you know it's rude to eavesdrop?"

"Not when we want the very best for you." Gloria clapped her hands together. "I enjoyed the graduation and the high tea, but this might actually be the highlight of my day."

Gloria was so genuine, Florrie couldn't pretend to be cross with her. But then anxiety washed over her. "What can I wear for morning coffee and a talk in one of the colleges?"

Gloria began gently dragging Florrie to her bedroom before she'd even finished speaking. "Let's go and check out your wardrobe."

And they spent the next couple of hours debating what was appropriate, voices overlapping and laughing as Gloria teased Florrie about needing date clothes. Florrie felt loved and young again, or at least not a frail old lady with only the graveyard beckoning. How exciting for a fifty-five-year-old woman to be going out with the woman she'd fallen for decades ago. Was she being silly getting swept up in Gloria and Cam's enthusiasm? She knew she was loved by them, but it was so different with Diana. The love they'd shared had been passionate and all-consuming, and ultimately, heartbreaking. But was she getting ahead of herself? Would she be disappointed with the reality? Diana probably only needed a companion for the meeting. But even if that was all she wanted, Florrie would step into that role again, gladly.

CHAPTER NINE

DIANA KNOCKED ON THEIR door five minutes early. Previously, she had flounced in a few minutes late, or on time, at best, demanding an audience for every entrance. "Ready to go? Rather than coffee, I thought we could go for an early lunch—my treat, of course—and then go along to the lecture. Does that suit you?"

"That sounds perfect." Diana offered her elbow as they made their way to her car, although Cam was hovering to assist. The old Diana would probably not have noticed Florrie needed assistance, not through malice, but because she was always taken up with whatever fascinating thing was going around her head, that she didn't always see the practicalities.

Florrie gritted her teeth as she swung her legs into a Jaguar saloon. Of course Diana would have an expensive car. Florrie couldn't imagine her in a little Morris Minor. Fortunately, it was high up and not a sports car, which the younger Diana might have chosen. She'd hardly slept last night, petrified Diana might turn up with the latest model so close to the ground Florrie would never get in, or worse, get out of the car. "Thank you, Diana. I'm afraid you find me much changed."

Diana handed Florrie her handbag. "Physically, yes. I'll be honest, I was a little shocked. Rheumatoid arthritis?"

"Yes. It's always worse in the mornings and on cold, wet days."

Diana walked around to the other side and got into the driver's side of the car. She didn't know Diana could drive; she'd always had drivers in the twenties.

"Why do you live here?" Diana asked. "Why don't you emigrate to the South of France?"

Florrie chuckled. "Oh, Diana, we don't all have huge estates and bolt-holes around Europe. I can't afford it, and I wouldn't be without Cam and Gloria. They do so much for me."

"I'm delighted you have them. I don't have bolt-holes everywhere either though. I lost everything in the Great Crash, you remember. I gave up everything to save the printing press: my independence, my joy, my writing...you."

The bitterness seeping through her tone took Florrie by surprise. Diana had always been so enthusiastic and vivacious. Now she had lost her air of superiority, which had always been more confidence than arrogance, she seemed a sadder, more subdued version of her former self.

So they were going to address the matter of the change. Diana could be very direct when it suited her. Florrie would do the same; this may be the only opportunity to ask questions and lay some old ghosts to rest. "But we talked about the difficulties in the banks in the previous weeks. I assumed you would do whatever you needed to secure them."

Diana flashed a frown and put the car into gear. It jerked slightly as they took off, and she accelerated down the bumpy road. Florrie gripped onto the leather strap handle for dear life as she was rolled around. They hurtled around a blind bend, and the hedge scraped the side of Florrie's window, making her jump.

"Yes, but I didn't think it would apply to me and my investments. Naturally, Anthony had known from some of his American chums that it was likely not to blow over and got out of his stocks in time. His smugness used to drive me wild."

Florrie gripped tighter as they shot over a crossroads without Diana pausing to check traffic. She would be covered in sweat by the time they got there if they continued like this. *If* they got there. "Why did you marry him?"

Diana looked at her so long Florrie indicated she should revert her gaze to the road. She wanted answers for questions she hadn't had for decades beforehand, but she didn't want to die for them.

Diana sighed and concentrated on the road for a few moments. "That wasn't my finest moment. And you deserve an answer."

All the posturing and superiority had disappeared along with a bike they overtook. Florrie waited for Diana to speak. She glanced across. Diana wiped her hand across her cheek. Was she crying? "Let's pull over to the side before you kill us both."

"What?" Diana swerved into a large gateway and slammed on the brakes.

Florrie shot forward, flinging her hand on the dashboard to stop herself from crashing into it. "Do you always drive like this? When did you learn?"

"I had to do something to help the war effort, so I drove ambulances in London. It was the first time for years I had any real purpose in my life."

Florrie released her death grip and flexed her fingers. "Did you kill many of your passengers?"

Diana gave her an arch look. "I'd forgotten your humour." She put the car into neutral. "Sorry, I'll drive more sedately."

"And I'd forgotten how you could avoid answering a direct question."

Diana's shoulders sagged, and her hands slipped off the steering wheel. "I think you know the upper classes don't marry for love. We have alliances to consolidate lineage or fortunes. Anthony and I had been promised to each other when we were still children. I refused to go along with an early wedding, saying that I wanted to write and start a publishing company first. We agreed I would have creative control, and he would run the business side. He was always more interested with the profit than sharing my vision, and he never understood my writing, much preferring non-fiction to silly little novels."

Diana slipped her gloved hand over Florrie's. Florrie stared at the silk; Diana's gloves were always so elegant and expensive, and the tradition had continued. At Diana's silence, Florrie met her gaze, facing the intense stare that stripped her every defence and searched inside her soul.

"I know you were hurt when he mentioned my previous dalliances. It was true. I did have affairs with other women before you, but when you came into my life, I didn't have eyes for anyone else. You inspired my last book for heaven's sake. Couldn't you see that?"

Diana's passion and imploring was all very well, and very flattering to be sure, but Florrie still struggled to get over one fact. "You chose him. You had a whole other life and a child—"

"We had a *deal*. The publishing house was only breaking even with regular capital injections from me, and after the crash, I couldn't make any more. Anthony took over the business and saved some of the jobs in the press. I couldn't let all those people become out of work—they had families to support, as I said in my note. His condition on saving the press was that I would concentrate on my writing, and we would marry as soon as possible. He also insisted I didn't contact you again. I think he knew you weren't like my previous affairs. I genuinely cared for you—"

Florrie scoffed, a bitter laugh that caught in her throat. She shook her head and narrowed her eyes. All these years, she'd convinced herself that Diana didn't care, couldn't care for her, and that she'd been no more than a useful distraction. And maybe she'd had to convince herself of that to survive, to protect her heart, so she could focus on Cam instead.

Diana's nostrils flared. "The alternative was that Anthony would close the business. I'd be free but penniless, and more than forty people would lose their jobs. And the other writers whom we'd encouraged and nurtured over the years wouldn't get paid. I couldn't do that to them. I gave up my happiness for their sake." Her tone was clipped, each word enunciated like a smack. She exhaled loudly, and her shoulders lowered a fraction. "I'm sorry you were a casualty. I always hoped you would forgive me, move on, and be happy with someone else."

Florrie snapped her eyes shut to unscramble her thoughts. She couldn't imagine having to make that choice. She'd always been so clear in what was right and wrong, and any compromises she'd made had been to her detriment alone. "Sorry," she whispered and opened her eyes.

Diana checked the mirrors and pulled out into the country lane, fortunately taking it slower this time. Florrie stared at the passing countryside, the endless fields, and the vast sky. She could never get over how flat it was around here and how tiny and isolated she felt. She'd been too harsh on Diana because she'd been hurting. Florrie cleared her throat as she continued to watch the cornfields blur past. "There's never been anyone else." Unsaid words weighed heavily between them, thickening the silence. "I always believed you'd continue to write," she said quietly. Her chest tightened, and she wanted to reach out, to close the years, misunderstanding, and distance between them. Yet, she couldn't quite let it go, whether because of pride or pain, she couldn't say. "But you didn't write anything else, as far as I know."

"You were following me then?" Diana gave a genuine smile, but it quickly faded. She changed down a gear to take a sharp corner. "I couldn't write again. I was too distraught." She flashed a wry twitch of her mouth, half smile, half pain. "I lost my muse."

Florrie squeezed Diana's hand on the gear stick then released it when Diana skirted another bend. The fields gave way to suburban houses, then to the church-like Gothic university buildings, built to impress and still impressive now, hundreds of years later.

Diana parked in a side street behind one of the buildings. "It's around the corner from here. Will you be able to manage it?"

"Thank you, yes, that should be fine. I'll just be a bit slow."

Diana didn't move. She stared straight ahead, gripping the

steering wheel like it might escape if she released it. She exhaled a slow, shaky breath. "We married in 1930, and Edward came along in 1931, but I couldn't bear to have him around me. I felt utterly trapped, and he cried so much." She paused, swallowing hard. "I couldn't handle it. He was cared for entirely by a nanny. I barely touched him." Her voice faltered, and she had to clear her throat. "After he was born, I went into a dark place of despair, so dark I didn't think I'd come out. I hid away in the cottage in the country and drank more than I should. I hardly know my son."

Diana must have caught the look of horror that crossed Florrie's face, despite her trying to hide it.

Diana shook her head. "I know. That sounds awful, doesn't it? And it was. Not my finest hour, as Churchill said, but you deserve the truth." She rubbed her hands over the steering wheel. "When Anthony was killed in the war, Edward wanted to stay at boarding school rather than come home to me. That told me everything. I lost my son too."

"How sad...for all of you." Florrie hesitated. She wanted to comfort Diana but was uncertain whether physical comfort would be welcome. Diana sat rigid, staring out of the windscreen. She was aloof and self-contained in her misery, brittle like a porcelain vase. Florrie kept her hands folded in her lap, torn between wanting to bridge the gap between them and respecting Diana's space.

Diana exhaled. "Since Anthony died, I've been trying to establish a relationship with Edward but, unsurprisingly, he hasn't been receptive. It's only recently, now that he's come up to Cambridge, at Anthony's old college, of course, that we seem to be civil to each other."

A tear trickled down Diana's cheek, but she didn't try to hide it. Florrie reached up and swooped it away. How could she take away the pain? She'd never seen Diana so crushed, and it broke her heart to witness it. Yet she had observed the impact on a child growing up with the rejection of a parent and wouldn't wish that on anyone. That Diana had been battling with depression for so long was unthinkable, and it had taken great courage to admit it. "Thank you for telling me."

Diana withdrew her hand and rifled in her handbag for a handkerchief. She blew her nose delicately, then flipped down the sun visor and checked herself in the mirror. She extracted a lipstick, but her hands shook as she attempted to apply it She snapped the top on and threw it in her bag.

"Diana. Look at me."

Diana focused her gaze on Florrie. Their dynamic had shifted, and Florrie now had the power. She'd been happy over the years, joyful in the simple pleasures of life: the first primroses in spring, the dawn chorus after a rough night of not sleeping, the fresh hope that sunrise brought, Cam and Gloria's laughter, their singing together, and the cup of tea Cam brought in every morning with a brief hug. And the pain in her joints was far preferable to the dark misery Diana had endured for many years. She gently wiped away a tear that fell from Diana's long eyelashes.

Diana swallowed hard. "Do you hate me? I wouldn't blame you if you did. There have been many days I've hated myself."

Florrie shook her head. "No. I don't hate you. I don't judge you either, not now. I can see what your choice cost you. I loved you once and would have done anything for you, and it hurt for a long time. But now I'm happy, and I've had a joyful life, being in my garden, watching my niece, Cam, thrive and then blossom when she found love. I count my blessings every day. I loved the time we spent together: the discussions, reading, and the sanctuary and beautiful intimacy in your cottage." Diana had been honest with her, and she deserved the same.

Their eyes met, and something stirred between them. An unbroken thread that resumed the connection of two decades ago, and an undeniable spark of arousal smouldered deep in her core. No one had ever moved her like this. That it still existed, dormant like a seed in winter waiting for the right conditions to grow and flower was a surprise—and a delight. Heat burned in her chest and bloomed in her cheeks.

She was alive.

Diana stroked Florrie's cheek, no longer the soft down of youth, but creased with age and pain. "Your colouring always gave you away. It's adorable."

Florrie cleared her throat. This was heading into dangerous waters. Did she want to step into the maelstrom that was Diana Stratford, or should she withdraw her toe and wish her well?

"Those years with you were the most wonderful in my life," Diana said. "I felt invincible, and my creativity flowed from the well of my love for you. I never told you explicitly, but I hoped you knew because of the dedication in the book and the inscription. I couldn't say more as Anthony read everything that came in or went out. And yes, I could have called, but I couldn't bear to hear your voice and acknowledge what I'd lost, what I'd given up. It would've stirred up my guilt that I had ruined your life, just as I had my own and my family. I still don't know if I'd make the same choice even knowing how it ended up, with a husband who despised me and a son who followed suit. I'm not saying I didn't deserve it, especially as I hurt you so badly—"

"You didn't deserve that. But maybe we could make up for lost time and become friends now."

Diana gasped and retreated slightly. "Friends? Is that what you want?"

Florrie inhaled deeply to settle into her own emotions. It was so hard with Diana looking at her, pleading. To avoid the intensity of her gaze, Florrie stared down at her hands, now gnarled, the constant reminder she wasn't in her thirties. Her life was settled and contented. Did she want to throw that all up in the air for the uncertainty of being around Diana? She wasn't the woman she had been, naïve and impressionable; now she was strong and certain with who she was. "Yes. I'm happy with my life. I don't think I can give anything else. I can't be vulnerable and open to any more than friendship. Let's see how that goes."

"I'm sorry to hear that, but I understand."

They sat in a heavy silence filled with twenty years of unspoken truths and unlived possibilities, weighty like the pause between heartbeats before a decision is made. One breath, two. Florrie exhaled, releasing a hurt she'd held on to for far too long.

Was it too late to reconnect again? Was this the closing down of the past? Or could it be the first fragile link between who they had become and what might be?

Diana glanced at her watch. It wasn't the same one Florrie had known, but it was still unmistakeably a man's watch, a Rolex with a clear dial. It had probably cost more than Florrie's annual income, and the leather strap had an extra hole punched in for Diana's slim wrist. It summed up how different their lives were.

"We need to go to the restaurant now. Let me help you out of the car." Diana got out of the car and gave Florrie her arm to lean on and lever herself upright.

The maître d' bowed slightly at Diana's entrance. The name and husband's title literally opened doors and secured the best table in the house. The walls of the restaurant were lined with dark wood. The rich red carpets muted conversations and muffled the sound of chairs scraping, though Florrie couldn't help but think they weren't very practical when food was inevitably dropped and wine spilled.

A waiter pushed her chair closer to the table, snapped up the cloth napkin from the place setting, and laid it on her lap with a flourish.

"Thank you," Florrie said. It was a long time since she'd been in a restaurant as highbrow as this, with its chandeliers, crisp white tablecloths, and waiters in waistcoats with white bow ties. It wasn't that she felt uncomfortable, just out of place, out of time.

The waiter handed over a leather-bound menu, and Florrie opened the book of delicacies. It was handwritten and all in

French. She gulped. Her French was rusty, but she saw a menu du jour. She couldn't go far wrong with that. She blew out a breath when she saw the prices. A main course cost as much as her weekly grocery budget. She waited until the waiter left. "This is too much," she whispered. "It seems too extravagant when we still have meat rationing."

A flicker of something, perhaps disappointment or bafflement crossed Diana's face before she rewarded her with a warm soft smile. "I want to spoil you."

Florrie shook her head. "You don't need to spoil me. I would've been quite happy with egg sandwiches from the tearoom. I haven't seen this much meat on a menu since before the war."

Diana's shoulders sagged and her smile slipped. "Have I misstepped?"

Florrie stared into Diana's eyes, which seemed to glisten with more than the reflection of the light bouncing off the chandeliers. "I'm not sure why you're trying so hard. Or maybe this is normal life for you. We live simply. We've had home-grown vegetable stew for the last few nights so we could save up our ration coupons to have a roast on Sunday. I don't normally come out for lunch and a talk during the day. I volunteer at the local WI and bake cakes. And I'm happy with that."

"How do you feed your soul?"

Florrie opened her mouth then snapped it shut as an ache in her chest and a weight on her tongue stopped her from replying. She hesitated, unable to answer truthfully, completely, before the waiter returned, giving her a reprieve.

"Do you trust me?" Diana asked, and at Florrie's nod, Diana turned to the waiter. "Steak Diane pour deux, s'il vous plaît." She ordered a red wine and water for the table. He bowed and left. "I love the whole performance of having food flambéed at the table, and they make a divine sauce."

Florrie shook her head. "Don't you need cognac for that? The last time we burned brandy was over the Christmas pudding."

Diana laughed as though that were quaint, but Florrie's hairs on the back of her neck began to prickle. Their lives had drifted so far apart that she wasn't sure there was any common ground between them anymore. "I don't live my life like this, where food or drink is wasted. Our lives have become so different." She sighed deeply. "I suppose they always were. I love the simplicity and joy in my life. I love being with Cam and Gloria, although I don't always understand their conversations. We laugh and tease, and my soul is full and nurtured. All of *this*," she said and gestured around the restaurant, "is too much."

She must have sounded defensive because Diana leaned back and placed her napkin on the side of her plate. "I'm sorry if I offended you. I can see I've got your hackles up. I envy you your life, and I'm not judging you. It seems I've got this wrong. I was trying to woo you, not antagonise you."

Woo me? Florrie opened her mouth and closed it again. Fortunately, a sommelier arrived at the table, giving Florrie time to master her emotions. He presented the bottle to Diana, who nodded, then he efficiently pulled the cork before high pouring a few drops into the bulbous wine glass. Diana swilled it, sipped it and thanked him in a ritual as old as agriculture itself.

"Very good, my lady."

He poured the wine with the panache of a magician at the seaside. On completion of his task, he nodded and departed.

Diana twisted the wine glass in her hands, and Florrie so wanted to stretch over and still the movement. "I'm sorry. You're being very generous, but we've been so short of food for so long that I'd forgotten the decadence of the life pre-war and pre-rations."

"I think that's what I love about this place. I can step back into my past, when I was happy, and life was full and fascinating. And when I think back to those times, the happiest were when I was with you." Diana raised her glass by the stem, and they clinked them together with the resonance of a clear bell.

Florrie's face heated. She was probably turning the same colour as the wine. "They were happy times for me too. I loved… our life. It was thrilling, and we thought we could change the world with our literature." She almost said she loved Diana but recovered in time, she hoped. Diana was observing her, no doubt assessing and taking notes. Or perhaps she didn't do that anymore.

Florrie sipped her wine, which was incredibly smooth and full-bodied. "What did you do with your time if you weren't writing?"

Diana set down her wine glass and sighed. "After you left, I tried very hard to get a bank loan to pay off the printing press debts, but they were all running scared. It's such a truism that a bank's willingness to lend depends on how little you need it. Meanwhile, Anthony was drawing up a legal agreement for the bailout, and one of the conditions was to marry him, as you know. Did Oscar ever give you my message?"

"He did. That's a story I'll tell you about later." Florrie indicated for Diana to continue.

"It was very busy in the press, and I became embroiled in all the work you'd taken off my hands. I missed you every day on a practical level too. Every evening, I tried to write, but the blank page mocked me. Nothing would come. My mind was so shredded with worry that it had no space for words. I know that sounds like an excuse, but I was upset, and I knew you were angry with me. And rightly so." She offered Florrie a wan smile and took another sip of wine. "This is good."

Diana seemed to be stalling for time, so Florrie waited. It reminded her of when Cam was little, and she'd sifted through her emotions, trying to name them.

"When Edward came along, I was so distraught, and I couldn't bear to touch him, to have him paw me. I couldn't produce milk, so I felt like a failure as a mother too. Anthony organised a wet nurse, then a series of nannies and finally, boarding school, because that's what he'd had as a child. I hated Anthony touching me too, and he chastised me for being a useless wife. With Edward at school, there was nothing to be in London for, so I stayed in Sussex when he was away and tried to write, out I ended up drinking earlier and earlier every day. I even failed at trying to end it all."

Florrie stared at her. "You tried to..."

"Yes. Alice found me on the floor and had me admitted into hospital. Mental hospital." She shuddered. "I don't wish to think about that time."

"Sorry, is this too painful?"

Diana drew in a long breath and nodded. "But I need to tell you."

The waiter arrived and laid down a small plate with one tiny circle of toast covered by smoked salmon, with a slice of lemon and dill.

"Did you order that?" Florrie asked, wondering if she'd missed the instructions when she followed along with her schoolgirl French.

Diana waved her hand in that slightly dismissive way she used to do. "Oh, they always bring it for me."

"Have you eaten here a lot?"

Diana squeezed the lemon over the salmon and wiped her hands on a napkin, before spiking the fish with a fork. "Whenever I came up to Cambridge with Anthony over the years, and more recently with Edward."

Florrie followed Diana's example and took a bite. The lemon exploded in Florrie's mouth, followed by the hint of bitter aniseed in the dill and the smoky saltiness of the salmon. She licked her lips. It was such a contrast to the bland food they had eaten since before the war, and a fitting reminder of how her life was in comparison to Diana's—superficially, anyway. "That tastes so fresh, like the salmon was smoked this morning and was splashing up a burn a week ago."

Diana laughed. "A little more than that I think, but I know what you mean." She took another bite. "Driving ambulances in the Blitz gave me a real sense of purpose. I was doing something that mattered for the first time in my life, although it was particularly harrowing seeing the children. I still have nightmares about it. There was one child who survived without a scratch on her when the rest of her family died in the blast. I often wondered what happened to her."

The waiter returned to remove the salmon starter and placed large, gold-rimmed dinner plates in front of them.

After he'd left, Diana took another sip of wine and carefully set down her glass. "After Anthony was killed, I tried to make amends and reconnect with Edward, but it was too late. He hated me by then. Not that I blame him, but it's very hard to face such vitriol and remain unaffected. I'm still trying to make amends, but how can you create a bond that should have been forged over nineteen years?"

Florrie encased Diana's hand in her own. "It sounds like you're grieving your own lost child too. How sad and lonely."

Diana met Florrie's gaze, her eyes shining with unshed tears. "I am. It is." Seeing something over Florrie's shoulder, she painted on a smile. "Ah, here's the trolley. Prepare for a presentation and the main reason for coming here."

The chef placed a pan containing two flattened steaks and a creamy sauce over a copper burner. He pulled the stopper from a bottle on the trolley and sloshed brandy over the steaks. Then he took the flame from the burner and set alight a spill of alcohol, which flared and lapped the steak before burning out. With long tongs, he placed the steaks on the plates and poured over the remainder of the sauce, then he arranged frites and green beans. "Voila! Enjoy your meal."

"Thank you," Diana said and smiled as he wheeled away the trolley. "Please start. It's usually done to perfection: seared on the outside, pink inside." She waited to watch Florrie take a bite.

"Mm, the meat melts in your mouth," Florrie said.

"You see? I told you it was good. Some New York hotels claimed they invented it, but the chef here learned this in a small restaurant in Belgium a few years back."

They ate and talked, covering a broad range of topics from politics to growing vegetables, and it seemed only a few minutes before Florrie placed her cutlery neatly on the plate and wiped her lips with her napkin. She didn't remember the last time she'd eaten so much in one sitting. "It was a wonderful performance, and the food is delicious. Thank you for treating me. I feel very special." She didn't add that she hadn't felt this way in years. If this was wooing, perhaps she could relax into it, just a little, and enjoy it for what it was.

"You *are* special." Diana looked up for a moment, and a waiter rapidly appeared, brandishing the menu.

"Would you like dessert?"

"What do you recommend?" Florrie asked without opening it. As a regular, Diana would know what to choose. Florrie was also enjoying Diana reinhabiting her confident, assured self after her breakdown in the car. It was comforting watching her reclaim her poise, as if the world was tilting back to the way it should be. "The crêpe suzettes are divine," Diana said, "but their crème parfaits are perfect too."

"I've had enough flambéed food today, so crème parfait for me."

"Good choice. And me. Thank you."

The waiter took the menus and stepped away.

Diana drained her glass and cleared her throat. "Don't you want to escape this awful weather and the drudgery of rationing?"

Florrie chuckled. "Well, I didn't think we'd still have rations five years after the war ended. Not that you could tell, looking around here." She waved her hand at the decadence around them. "What are you suggesting?"

"Would you come with me to Anthony's house in the south of France for a month? Officially, it belongs to Edward now, but he won't mind. He's more interested in spending time with his Cambridge friends, and he said I can use it whenever I want. Or if not there, we could rent somewhere—not in August, of course. It's too hot and full as Paris empties out. Perhaps in September?"

This was all too much, like facing a tidal wave of expectation. Should Florrie upset her ordered, controlled life, even for a short time? And yet, her heart fluttered with excitement, and she could imagine the warmth on her aching hands and feet. It would be nice after the damp summer they were having, which swelled her joints. "I'll think about it. Now, what about this lecture? Tell me more about the speaker."

Diana's expression lightened, and her face glowed with the same animated eagerness Florrie remembered. Who knew Charles Darwin's study could elicit such a passion in Diana, in herself? The truth was that it was the company and conversation; it always had been.

They arrived at the lecture with seats reserved at the front, of course, mere seconds before the professor took to the podium. As she sat next to Diana, with the words washing over her, a tide of joy seeped into her soul, reawakening her curiosity, her libido, and her heart. Her younger self stared through the blurry eyes of late middle age, and she inhaled the excitement of possibility. She was alive. They had survived separation, yet another world war, and in Diana's case, depression and a child, and faltering health in hers. Yet here they were, attending a lecture at one of the world's most prestigious universities, an event she could never have imagined sharing with Diana again.

As the professor's voice echoed around the lecture hall, something in Florrie shifted. The seal she'd placed over her heart a long time ago began to crack. With every word, the hot magma of love long-buried surged up and warmed her heart.

Florrie glanced across at Diana, who was looking ahead, ostensibly enthralled, and her gloved little finger caught Florrie's own. That connection, however slight, was like a promise of more. Florrie responded by entangling her fingers with Diana's. Diana glanced sideways and arched her eyebrow, giving Florrie a slight smile as her eyes sparkled. How that expression curled Florrie's toes. She returned the smile and, with the slightest inclination of her head, indicated they should pay attention.

Diana nodded and faced forward. Perhaps she too was remembering how Florrie could occasionally be bossy in bed. Heat rushed up Florrie's face as other bedroom exploits flooded her memory.

"Concentrate," Diana whispered, but her smile belied her admonition.

Florrie sighed lightly and pretended to be listening. When she got lost in the rather academic pontificating, she glanced at Diana, who looked entranced, as if she were absorbing every detail to pick over later. Her profile, with her aquiline nose and regal bearing, was still the same. The old feelings came bubbling from under the surface, where they'd been hidden away, unacknowledged for so long. They hadn't changed but merely settled under the detritus of years of leavings. Like a seedling buried in the soil for a long time, spreading roots and gaining strength, love burst out in a rush, all heady blossom and vibrant colour, announcing its presence.

How ridiculous, at her age, to be thinking about falling in love again. But was it the old brilliant Diana she pined for, or this new complex and jaded version who revealed glimpses of her previous self? Perhaps they had both changed too much to recapture what they once had.

Either way, Florrie couldn't ignore it any longer. She decided to get to know Diana better and find out who she was now, and to discover if the fragile seed of their connection could take root, and whether there was any future for love to bloom or wither.

CHAPTER TEN

LATER THAT AFTERNOON, DIANA dropped Florrie off and declined a cup of tea. Cam helped remove Florrie's coat, while Gloria seemed to vibrate with anticipation.

Well?" Gloria asked.

How to put into words the entire roller coaster of emotions Florrie had experienced during the day. She settled for blandness. "I had a lovely time, thank you."

Cam returned from hanging up her jacket. "Would you like tea, Aunty Florrie?"

"I would love a cuppa, thank you, dear."

Cam strode off to put the kettle on, and Florrie and Gloria followed her more slowly. Florrie sagged into the kitchen chair, unable to control her turbulent emotions. It was as if she'd been untethered, like something deep inside her had been set adrift. She'd squashed down her feelings of admiration, love, and hurt over the years, and now she shook them out, they no longer resembled the same shape. Did they fit for who they were now? The uncertainty left her aching.

"What do you mean by a 'lovely time'?" Gloria grinned, clearly expecting something salacious.

Florrie rubbed her thumb, something she'd originally started to ease her aching hands, but it had become a habit, more emotionally soothing than physical. "We had a wonderful, expensive meal of real steak and Scottish salmon, and we went to a fascinating talk about Charles Darwin, which included an exclusive peep into Christ's College. And then Diana brought me home, so here I am." She smiled at the obvious frustration on

Gloria's face.

Gloria extracted the cups and saucers from the cupboard and looked at Florrie. "Aye, that's all grand and everything, but how was it between you? How do you feel about her? Have you arranged to see her again?"

"Oh," Florrie said and stopped rubbing her thumb. They hadn't made arrangements, and she had no idea how long Diana was staying in Cambridge. She might be driving back to London or Sussex now, or even be on a train to France. Her shoulders sagged, and the heaviness in her chest was a strong reminder how she felt. She yearned to meet Diana again, to find out who she really was now. Yet a pang of anxiety settled in her stomach. "We haven't arranged to meet again. I'd like to, I think, but it stirred up a lot of emotions, and we're both much changed. She hasn't had an easy life since we parted and hasn't written anything since either. I'm not sure if what I'm feeling is me now, or I'm conflating it with how I felt then. And if I see her again, I don't know if it's even possible to recapture the joy of our past."

Gloria's grin slipped, and she cast a sympathetic smile as she paused from cutting the cake. "The only way to find out is to meet up and see if you still feel the same."

It was typical of Gloria to make it sound so simple. The kettle whistled, and Cam bustled around warming the pot and adding hot water, before checking her watch. Doubtless she would time it to the second before she poured the tea.

Afterwards, Cam linked arms with Gloria in the comfortable way they had at home, seeming to fit together so perfectly. However much Florrie had fantasised about it when she was younger, she and Diana would never have had this same simple domestic life, circling around the kitchen with efficiency as they made tea and cut the cake. Diana was more of a thoroughbred, meant to be free and galloping amongst the literati, not yoked and reined to the solid carthorse like Florrie.

She looked up to face Cam and Gloria watching her intently.

Florrie cleared her throat. "Diana's asked me to go to her son's house in Southern France in September. For a month." She glanced at Cam to see her reaction. Her face was neutral, indicating she was thinking it over.

"Wow. Look at you, hobnobbing with the nation's elite," Gloria said. "Next you'll have an invitation to Buckingham Palace to meet the king."

"Don't be ridiculous, dear."

"You absolutely have to go," Gloria said. "What an opportunity. Even if it doesn't work out, you'll have a grand holiday. I'd love to visit the south of France. I'm right envious."

"For a whole month? How will I cope with the journey? However we travelled, it would be a struggle to get in and out, and I can't sit for hours without seizing up. I can't imagine Diana would want to burden herself looking after an invalid." Florrie raised her hand to stop Gloria disagreeing with the term, as she usually did. "I don't want to be weak—or dependent. And I don't know if I can recapture the lost love and the unlived years. We're so unalike, with massive differences in our lives. She drives a Jaguar and lives in a wonderful house in the country, she's wealthy, accomplished, and well connected, and I'm none of those things. I can't see her sitting in this living room in her worn slippers and drinking tea out of a saucer because it cools quicker." She indicated her own threadbare footwear. "It's a fantasy, and the reality will be a huge disappointment."

"Does that matter though?" Gloria asked. "She obviously enjoys your company, or she wouldn't invite you down to France. You both enjoy literature and reading, and you're intelligent. Love doesn't care about wealth or background. Look at me. I worked in a factory and am from Yorkshire. You couldn't get more down to earth than that, yet this wonderful person fell in love with me.' She nuzzled against Cam, who smiled and kissed the top of her head. "Now, is that cuppa ready yet?"

Cam checked her watch. "Three seconds." She counted it

with her index finger, then extricated herself from Gloria to pour the tea.

Florrie decanted some tea into her saucer. "I'm scared of being a disappointment, of not being good enough, of not being able to love Diana as she is now, as opposed to how she was then." She took a sip of her tea. "Nice cuppa, thanks, Cam. Besides, my body is older and uncared for, but she's still as tall and slim as ever."

Gloria shook her head. "No, it won't be the same. That's exactly why you need to get to know her better. Sometimes the person who was perfect for us in our thirties isn't the one for us in a different stage of life—"

Cam set her cup down with a clunk, her eyes wide.

Gloria laughed. "Don't look so horrified, sweetheart. I don't mean us." She nudged Cam and grinned. "What I was going to say is that sometimes people grow closer over time, like we have." She turned back to Florrie. "You won't know how you feel unless you meet her again. A month in France will be lots of time to work that out. If it's awful, I volunteer to come down and rescue you. Or better still, take your place."

Gloria squealed as Cam tickled her ribs, and they both laughed, collapsing into each other, their gazes entwined with such love and joy as they sat to drink their tea.

Had Diana ever looked at her like that? Florrie couldn't remember, and she couldn't imagine Diana would now that Florrie was post-menopausal, with all the chin hair-sprouting, waist-thickening years ahead of her. It wasn't romantic or sexy. She picked up the teaspoon and scraped it against the china. "I'm being ridiculous, even thinking of chasing this dream. Maybe she's only seeking companionship because she's lonely. Of course she is. She wouldn't want someone like me. Not as I am now."

Gloria stilled Florrie's hands from stirring the spoon in the teacup. "Maybe she does want companionship, or maybe she wants more. But unless you go, you'll never find out."

Florrie chewed at her bottom lip. "You've been very quiet. What do you think, Cam?" She was sure that Cam would hate the change in arrangements; it would upset their carefully crafted routines.

Cam ran her finger around the rim of her cup. "You should go."

Florrie almost spurted out her tea. "Really? How will you cope?"

"We'll be fine." Cam patted Gloria's knee. "I'd like reassurance that Diana will care for you properly while you're there, and perhaps you should meet up in the meantime to see how you get on, but Gloria's right. If you don't go, you'll never know, and you could be missing out on something special. You've always put everyone else before yourself. Now's the time to put yourself first."

Florrie clutched her chest. Sometimes Cam's honesty and sincerity took her breath away. "Thank you. That's incredibly thoughtful of you. I appreciate it."

Gloria grinned. "Besides, I've always wanted to be intimate with Cam on the rug in front of the fire, and if you're away we can do that—What? Don't look so horrified, both of you. We're all grown-ups here."

"You can't say that," Cam said, her cheeks taking on a pink glow.

"Fine." Gloria shrugged. "Pretend I didn't say that, but you thought it too. Do you have Diana's telephone number?" she asked quickly when it looked like Cam was about to reprimand her again.

"I have her Cambridge number, if she's still there."

"No time like the present. Phone her before it's too late."

Florrie made her way to the telephone, thinking that it may well be too late to have a physical relationship with Diana, but maybe that wasn't the point. Perhaps love in older age didn't burn with such passion, filled with need and hot desire. Perhaps love became gentler with age, wiser. Perhaps they could take delight in simple things and settle for the joy of companionship. And maybe that would be enough.

CHAPTER ELEVEN

September, 1950

"I CAN'T BELIEVE HOW luxurious it is," Florrie said as she stroked the plush leather seats in the saloon bar carriage before settling back. "Are you sure you wouldn't have preferred to drive?"

Diana raised her gin and tonic. "And battle the traffic jams on route de la mort down to the Cote d'Azur? I don't think so. We can share a drink here, and you can move around if you need to."

"But it must have cost a small fortune," Florrie whispered, so the other passengers couldn't hear.

"It's a small price to pay to have you here."

In the times they'd met before their trip, mainly to discuss logistics, Diana had surprised her with kind words, holding such genuine emotion that they'd made Florrie's heart stutter. She wasn't sure she could get used to gentle sentiments coming from anyone but Cam or Gloria.

The whistle blew, dragging her back to the present. Doors slammed shut, and the steam hissed. With a shudder and a chuff, a jerk and the all-pervading smell of smoke, the train pulled out of the Gare de Calais-Maritime and through the town of Calais.

Florrie patted her bag, which contained her newly acquired passport, and stared out at the different landscape. Instead of seeing medieval cottages and ornate stone churches, blackened skeletons of buildings, gouged-out rows of houses, and huge heaps of rubble lined the sides of the train track. "I didn't think it would still be as devastated as this five years after the war."

Diana's hands trembled. "It reminds me of the Blitz. There are parts of the East End that are still flattened." She tipped her head back and drained her glass. "Another one?"

"I'm fine, thank you." Florrie indicated her almost full glass of gin and tonic.

"Okay, dearest heart. I'll pop up to the bar then."

That name threw Florrie back to her thirties, when she was giddy and in love. There was something about the way Diana said it in her deep contralto that made Florrie's toes curl and her heart swoop. As Diana waited for her turn to be served, Florrie observed her and how beautiful she was, still arresting and magnetic, even if she still had a darkness clouded about her sometimes.

"Diana Packard Smith, how the devil are you?" a loud voice called out, breaking the low murmur of conversation.

A middle-aged man took Diana's hand and kissed it. Florrie had no idea who he was.

"Wilf, darling, it's been years." Her smile seemed brittle though, and her polished tone was laced with false humour.

"You must let me buy you a drink."

Wilf put his hand on Diana's back, propelling her to the front of the queue and snapping his fingers at the steward behind the bar. Florrie gritted her teeth. He reminded her of Anthony, with his upper-class entitlement. Of course Diana would know people in this exulted company, where Florrie didn't belong. She couldn't bear witnessing it anymore, so she twisted in her seat to look out at the countryside once again.

Where she'd expected to see fields was more destruction: bomb crater holes and carcasses of abandoned buildings with faded signs announcing businesses long since closed. In Britain, it was grim and grey, and the ongoing shortages were frustrating for ordinary people, but this was a complete obliteration of communities and a wasteland. Perhaps people had left rather than try to rebuild. Looking back into the carriage where passengers were untouched and oblivious to the scenes outside,

Florrie couldn't bear to witness the contrast. She closed her eyes until the seat beside her dipped slightly.

"Sorry about Wilf crashing the party. He was a big friend of Anthony's. I hadn't seen him since before the war. He bought us both a drink and said he'll see us later at tea."

Florrie eyed the glass as though it was poisoned. "I'll take it in the cabin."

"Truly? Part of the serendipity of a journey like this is who you meet along the way."

"Who you meet? They'll all be the same upper class wealthy socialites—"

Diana arched her eyebrow and gave Florrie the look that made her squirm. "Darling, are you jealous of Wilf?"

"I... No. Yes. I don't know. It seems obscene to be travelling in such style while we're surrounded by the aftermath of war," Florrie whispered and pushed her spare drink across the table to Diana. "I'm not sure this is going to work. Our financial differences couldn't be more obvious. You would have all the power in any friendship—"

Diana leaned forward, her amused expression vanished, her gaze becoming earnest and intense. "Dearest heart, I don't care about that. And I want more than friendship. Surely you know that. I'm trying to woo you, not turn you off. I want to treat you to everything, to give you all the pleasures you desire."

Florrie frowned. "You do?"

"Of course. Do you still want to go back to our cabin where we won't bump into anyone else?"

The certainty with which Diana spoke made Florrie's heart flutter. She sounded sincere and looked so earnest. The little spark of hope exploded into a puff of flame. Yet Diana was so at home in this company, with the gilded carriages and white-gloved servants, and she'd paid an inordinate amount of money for the privilege, so Florrie shook her head. "No, I don't want to spoil your fun."

"You're not. The thing I was looking forward to most on this journey, as well as staying with Oscar and his beau in Paris, was to spend time with you, to discuss the latest books you've read, to read aloud to each other, and talk about places we see and people we meet, and perhaps to reconnect intimately if it feels right. I'm sorry if you're unsettled."

Florrie stretched out her fingers and stared at them, not daring to catch Diana's gaze. The thought of revisiting their intimacy was both thrilling and terrifying, and she couldn't decide which took precedence. "No, I'm sorry. You've gone to all this trouble and expense, and I'm being ungrateful."

"Let's finish our drinks and then return to the cabin. In the meantime, I think we need to work out who's the spy."

Florrie smiled at the memory. It was a game they had played when they were younger and were in company. They concocted stories about passersby and had to convince the other that one person in the restaurant or meeting was a spy. If the person caught them watching, they were dead. It was silly and fun and gave Florrie an opportunity to observe Diana's creativity at work. She could always weave the most incredibly authentic stories about people.

"The young man who's pretending to read the newspaper, two tables down," Diana said. "It's his first assignment, and he's terrified he's going to be caught by the Soviets. He defected in Lossiemouth, and they're closing in on him."

Florrie scanned the room pretending she wasn't looking. After taking in the occupants of the carriage, she shook her head. "No, it's the middle-aged woman in the back, writing in a notebook and wearing that rather awful brown tweed suit. She's writing in a cypher that would pass as normal sentences. It's always the older women, because they're invisible."

Diana sipped her gin and slowly turned to locate the potential spy. She half choked on her drink and laughed. "That's Agatha Christie. Perhaps she's writing a follow up to *Le Train Bleu*. Don't stare or she'll see you, then you'll be dead."

Florrie snapped her jaw shut, having established it really was Agatha Christie. "So she's the perfect cover to be a spy."

Diana laughed again and clinked her glass to Florrie's. "All right, I'll give you that round. Chin chin, then let's go to the cabin."

Their cabin was a double berth with a corner hand wash basin. There was a shared toilet at the end of the carriage, even in first. The compartment was configured for day use, with the bunks tucked away, revealing seats in black and tan geometric Art Deco designs. The walnut fittings were so shiny, Florrie could see the look of wonder on her own face reflected in the surface. She sat beside the window and stroked the soft seats. "Wow. This is stunning."

"I know, dearest heart, but we won't be sleeping on this one tonight, because we're getting off in Paris. I haven't seen Oscar in years."

"Me neither. I have a letter for him from Cam: some mathematical proof she's been working on that she insists he'll be fascinated by. I'll tell her he was, even if he isn't."

Diana took the seat beside Florrie and interlaced their fingers. "I envy the wonderful relationship you have with your niece. I wish mine with Edward was half as good."

Florrie smiled and traced circles on Diana's hand with her thumb. "It wasn't always easy, but I found time, patience, and genuine engagement helps."

"None of which I gave to Edward." Diana exhaled noisily. "It's too late to change his childhood, and I've been trying unsuccessfully to build a rapport with him since Anthony died, but it's so difficult when he seems to hate me."

Diana's stiff posture crumbled, and she sniffed and swallowed hard. Florrie clutched Diana's hand tight. "That's hard and sad. I can't give any suggestions, except to keep trying."

"Thank you." Diana looked out at the passing scenery. "Sorry. How maudlin. We're supposed to be on vacation, and all I've done is upset you with the company on board and the sights of the ravages of war, as if anyone needs to be reminded of those. And then I've cried all over you. I don't think I've ever cried so much in front of anyone in my entire life. This isn't how I envisaged this holiday."

Florrie wiped away a tear tracing a path on Diana's cheek. "Not at all. I appreciate your honesty, and I'm flattered you trust me enough to be vulnerable with me. It's not something I would ever have thought, but it feels more real."

Diana huffed a laugh and pulled away to draw a handkerchief from her bag. "A real mess, perhaps. Thank you for understanding. And I do trust you. I always have."

"Anyway, the scenery is becoming more spectacular now. Look at those fields and those ancient villages. It's all so different from England."

Diana studied the passing landscape then checked her watch. "Gosh, it's only a few hours until we arrive in Paris. Should we read Mervyn Peake's *Gormenghast*?" The book was already placed on the side table.

Florrie clapped her hands together. "Oh, yes. Will you read or shall I?"

"I'm happy to read so you can look out of the window as we come into Paris...although you'll have to ignore these." Diana pulled out a small leather case and unsnapped it. She removed a pair of wire-rimmed spectacles and placed them on her face.

They gave her a studious air, like a domineering headmistress. Florrie licked her lips. The temptation was too much. "You look adorable," she said before she could stop the words from leaving her mouth.

"Thank you," Diana said, taking the compliment easily.

She leaned towards Florrie and without hesitation, Florrie met her lips with her own. The kiss was tender and soft, more a tentative reconnection than the passionate devouring of their youth.

"I'd forgotten how you kiss, like the drape of silk: soft, sensuous and the promise of more. Very different from Anthony, for whom kissing was a mere forerunner to the main act.' She sighed deeply as she must have seen Florrie wince. "Sorry, you probably don't want me to mention him. But he was the only person I've kissed since you." She smiled and trailed her fingers through Florrie's hair.

Florrie flushed. "You were the last person to kiss me like this."

Diana's eyes widened. "Really?"

"I'm not proud of the fact. My sister, Nora, if you remember her, made me promise not to see anyone else if I wanted Cam to remain with me."

Diana frowned, the two lines between her brows more prevalent now. "Ah, yes. She was under her husband's thumb. But what about when Cam went to Cambridge, and afterwards?"

The heat in Florrie's cheeks could probably start a fire. "I was always happy with friends and being busy. It didn't seem important." *And no one would have ever compared to you.* "Besides, Gloria would never have stopped teasing me if I'd started dating." That was probably unfair; Gloria had been nothing but kind and encouraging.

"We'd better make up for lost time then." Diana leaned towards her, and they kissed again, as if the first time wasn't sufficient.

This one was more certain, more a stating of intentions and incredibly arousing. But not here. Florrie pulled back, and Diana followed her, trying to maintain contact.

"Mm, nice. Oops, I've left a trail of lipstick. Why are you blushing? Do you not want to do this in here, where anyone could walk in?" Diana wiped away the lipstick from Florrie's cheek with her hankie.

The door from the carriageway slid open, and the conductor entered, asking for their tickets.

Diana replied in rapid French and handed over the cards. He

punched a hole in each, bowed and departed.

Florrie sat back, creating a distance between them. "That was close."

Diana laughed. "I'm sure they've encountered many more scandalous sights. We're safe now—"

"Nevertheless, I don't feel comfortable, and I'm sure you'll accuse me of being bourgeoisie."

"Now who's being adorable?"

Florrie waved her hand, a gesture she must have picked up from Diana all those years ago. "Just read."

"Yes, your highness." Diana opened the spine of the hardback with a crack, making Florrie wince, and began to read aloud.

As they passed through Northern France, over rivers lined with poplars straight out of a Monet painting, and through to the more built-up suburbs, Florrie strained to catch a glimpse of Paris and the Eiffel Tower. Excitement bubbled up inside her, and she wanted to yell with glee.

"Are you listening?" Diana asked, but there was amusement in her tone.

Florrie looked back, sheepishly. "Yes, sorry. It's exciting. I've always wanted to see Paris, and here we are... Well, nearly."

"I know. That's why I arranged for us to stay over for a day, rather than continuing on to the coast overnight."

Florrie placed her hand over her heart. "Oh, thank you. You remembered. I don't know what to say." That Diana made the arrangements especially for her made her feel loved.

"You're very welcome," Diana said and rose. "Now I'll go and freshen up before we arrive."

Florrie wasted no time peering back outside as some archetypal architecture came into view, all tall windows, wrought iron balconies, and ornate cornices. Diana would probably know the name of the style and the architect and had doubtless attended a lecture about it, but for Florrie, it was simply quintessentially Paris. With the taller buildings though, the chances of seeing the

Eiffel Tower faded. As they approached the Gare Du Nord, the buildings became shabbier, the neon lights were still switched off, and beggars huddled in the street amongst the litter. It was probably the same in any major city, and Florrie was grateful for having a guide in Diana and Oscar.

Diana reappeared, looking glamourous as ever, and Florrie sighed deeply and smiled. "I'll do what I can to repair the damage of fifty-odd years."

Diana looked horrified. "Don't say that, dearest heart, you're beautiful."

Florrie snorted and hurried to rinse her face. It seemed only a few minutes before the train pulled up at the terminus, doors banged, and people called out in French. She was in Paris! Diana secured a porter, who carried out their luggage and helped Florrie down to the platform. They made their way to the barrier, which reminded Florrie of long ago in London because Oscar was there to greet them.

"Diana, Florrie, darlings, over here!"

He waved a bright blue umbrella, a perfect match for his striking suit. He seemed the very opposite of a dowdy English gentleman, making Florrie smile.

Diana gave him the traditional three kisses before turning to tip the porter.

Oscar flung his arms around Florrie and repeated the greeting with her. "Darling, how wonderful to see you. I can't tell you how thrilled I am you came. Bertrand, if you can take their valises, that would be perfect. Merci."

Bertrand was a middle-aged man dressed in a uniform that seemed a little snug. He nodded and pushed the trolley towards the exit.

Oscar gave both women the crooks of his elbows, and they promenaded across the concourse three abreast.

Oscar squeezed them both close. "Maurice is so sorry he can't be here to greet you. Important banking business I know nothing about, but I'm happy to reap the benefits of the spoils. Now, I've booked us a table at Les Deux Magots. It's a bit earlier than the French normally eat, but we still have lots of tourists taking snapshots, so I wanted to ensure we get a good table—the one they said Ernest Hemingway used to sit at."

"I'm sure Hemingway sat at all the tables as long as he had his favourite drink in front of him," Diana said and winked at Florrie.

"Don't be naughty, Diana, or I'll ask Bertrand to take us straight back home. I'm sure our Florrie here would love to sit where such famous novelists and playwrights have sat before. They've even taken a photo of my humble poet self and hung it up somewhere—in the toilet, probably."

They arrived at a limousine, and Bertrand opened the door for Florrie and Diana to enter first. Diana helped Florrie into her seat then took the place beside her. Oscar settled himself opposite them. Florrie had never been surrounded by so much walnut and leather as she had today.

Diana shook her head. "Don't be so humble, Oscar. Your early works have been reprinted many times."

"Only thanks to one snippet of one of my poems being quoted in a Hollywood film. Thank you, Alfred Hitchcock, you have paid for my lifestyle."

Diana raised an eyebrow. "I thought that was Maurice?"

Oscar flicked his hand at her, dismissively. "Well, yes, darling, but it's paid for my champagne. Who'd have thought little old me would have reprints. Now, Florrie, Bertrand will be driving us around the sites tomorrow, and if you need to stop at any time, please say. We want you to be as comfortable as possible."

"Thank you, Oscar. It's wonderful to see you so happy. It appears Paris is very kind to you."

Oscar patted his slight bulge of a tummy. "But not good for my waistline, sadly. Fortunately, Maurice says he loves me anyway." He must have caught Florrie's quick glance at Bertrand. "Don't worry, darling. Bertrand's family and lives with a very cute young artist called Michel. Although we have to be a bit discreet, living in Paris is such a breath of fresh air after the dowdiness of Britain."

Florrie laughed. "You, discreet? I've never seen you so flamboyant—or radiant."

"Why, thank you, darling. And how is my favourite brilliant mathematician?"

"Cam is thriving. She's given me a letter for you with some detailed mathematical formula she said you'd understand. She and her partner, Gloria, live with me, and they both work at the university."

"Cam's one of us? I can't say I'm flabbergasted. So we're all just a happy little band of queers. And when are you two going to make it official?"

Diana paused from applying her lipstick and waved it at him. "Oscar, you're going too far." But there was a slight uptick to her lips, and she leaned against Florrie's hips.

Florrie grinned, and he winked while raising his hands. "Fine, fine. Now you're making Florrie miss some of the splendid sights—"

"Me?" Diana shook her head then continued to apply her lipstick.

Florrie had to drag herself away from watching Diana pouting her lips. It was so sensual and the most splendid sight.

"If you've finished drooling, we're now approaching the Seine and the Notre Dame. We'll come back tomorrow, and you can see it properly."

Oscar chattered on about his adopted city, and Florrie obliged by following his entertaining commentary, all the while leaning into Diana, thrilled at the warmth of her body brushing against hers.

It seemed no time at all before Bertrand pulled up at the café restaurant.

"Can you return in two and a half hours, please?" Oscar asked as they clambered out onto the street.

Bertrand bowed again and slowly drove off.

Inside the large restaurant, which was filled with tourists as Oscar surmised, the proprietor led them to a quieter table.

"Madam Stratford, may I have your photo taken?" He nodded to photos of some of the famous patrons lining the walls.

Diana smiled, before shooting a glare at Oscar. "This is your doing."

He shrugged. "Darling, it's worth it to have this fabulous table. Maybe we could have one together, get the tongues wagging."

"I'm a respectable widow."

"Widow, yes. Respectable? The jury's out." He turned to the proprietor. "Where would you like Diana?"

"Over here, where it shows off the restaurant."

As they adjusted angles and positions to make best use of the light, Florrie admired Diana's poise and her professional smile. But when she caught Florrie looking at her, her whole face lit up, and her smile widened to brighten her eyes, the creases at the edges showing where the years had left their mark. It made her more appealing somehow, more real and intriguing. The flash went off with a puff of smoke. Whichever photograph they used, it was this moment, this expression that Florrie would remember and treasure forever.

"Take my photo too," Oscar said. "Before I lose all my golden tresses."

They laughed as he settled himself beside Diana and slung his arm around her shoulder. He had aged, evidenced by the greying and thinning of his hair and the softer outline, but he glowed with an inner happiness that had never inhabited him when she knew him before.

The food was delicious, and the wine flowed along with the banter. Florrie sat back and let the joy wash over her. She hardly got a word in edgeways as Oscar kept them entertained through supper and on the ride home, and she loved it. Some evenings were meant to savour forever, and she knew this would be one. "Where do you live?" Florrie asked as she peered out into famous boulevards.

"In some artist's garret in Montmartre."

They arrived at an apartment building beside the Sacre Coeur, and Oscar opened the door to a large room, all sleek marble and antique furniture. Florrie clapped her hands together. "This is hardly a garret. It's beautiful." She rushed to the open shutters, through which she could see the whole city laid out with shining jewels in the matt black, and it took her breath away. "My, what a view. And there's the Eiffel Tower. I never thought I'd see it in real life."

Oscar opened the French windows, and the dull background noise became more vibrant and immediate, rushing in to fill the space. "It's stunning, isn't it? Please make yourselves comfortable in my humble abode while I check the room's ready."

"You can see why it's called the City of Lights, can't you?" Florrie rested against the ironwork balcony, her neck stretched to catch the cooling air. People talked and laughed below them in a café, and the smell of cooking, garlic, and spices wafted up, along with a hint of drains. Somewhere, a harmonica played accordion music.

Diana's warm body rested beside her on the balcony, sending tingles through every nerve, and Florrie instinctively leaned into her.

"It's also known as the City of Love," Diana whispered, her deep sensual voice as soft as silk.

Her breath, warm and close, tickled against her cheek, and Florrie shivered and swallowed hard, her heart aching with how full it felt, at this moment, this place, and being with Diana. "I know," she whispered. "Thank you for arranging this. It's heaven."

Diana nudged against her, the heat of her body causing goosebumps and stirring something else in Florrie's belly.

"You're very welcome. You deserve it all."

Florrie turned her face slightly. "If I could hold one image in my head for the rest of time, it would be this, with you pressed beside me, whispering in my ear."

Diana gestured to the night sky. "It *is* heavenly, to experience the lights and stars, to listen to French music being played, and to inhale the delicious smell of cooking. To feel your body beside mine is something I yearned for in those dark and dreadful years. And here you are. It doesn't seem possible. I feel like I can breathe again, and I know you're not sure about us, about me, but I'll do whatever it takes to win you over."

Florrie looked up at Diana. "You're right; I'm not sure I believe it yet. I'm so grateful for everything you've done, and this is perfect, so romantic and wonderful. Thank you."

"Take your time. I'll be here. Waiting...*hoping* for you to come around."

The key sounded in the lock, and Oscar ran to the entrance hall at the back of the apartment. There was a whispered conversation in rapid French, and then Oscar burst into the room, arm in arm with a Clarke Gable look-a-like, all sardonic smile and expressive eyebrows with the same trim moustache. He looked about ten years older than Oscar, but he'd maintained a taut physique.

"Darlings, let me introduce my beau, my benefactor, my gorgeous Maurice. I see you're so impressed I've got the winning ticket that you can only stare and marvel at my good fortune."

Maurice tapped Oscar on the arm, like admonishing a naughty puppy. "Don't mind him. Enchanté, Diana, Florrie, I've heard a lot about you. Welcome to our home. Sorry I couldn't meet you, but I had a business meeting." He greeted them with the standard air kiss three times.

"A business dinner, he means, judging by the smell of alcohol and garlic on his breath. It's lucky I love you." Oscar gave him a quick kiss on the lips.

Seeing their intimacy thrilled Florrie, and it sparked something warm inside.

"Champagne is required to celebrate this evening," Oscar said. "Only the very best for the very best."

He scampered off in a blur of delight, and Florrie couldn't help but take up his enthusiasm for love and for life.

"Forgive Oscar, he's so excited about you coming that he's forgotten his manners. Please, sit down. Florrie, would you like to take the raised chair? It may look like a commode, but I promise you it is but an ancient seat. Oscar thought it might be easier for you to get in and out of, and there are a number of cushions to make you more comfortable."

"Thank you, Maurice, that's so thoughtful." Florrie would've managed the sofa but doubted she would have been able to extricate herself gracefully. But she shouldn't hide that. Diana had seen enough of her now to realise the reality of her life. Florrie wasn't who she had been, and her life had taken a very different path from Diana's, who seemed so haunted by her past. In her unguarded moments, her melancholy weighed heavily like the presence of a crow at a funeral. But then she would light up when she responded to Florrie, who'd decided she would do everything she could to elicit Diana's genuine smile again, as often as she could, and banish the crow.

Oscar returned and topped them up with panache, his good mood bubbling as much as the drink. Florrie accepted hers and raised her glass. "It's a joy to see you in your element. I remember you saying once you'd never be in a long-term relationship, yet here you are. Cam will be delighted too."

"I must write her a letter you can take back with you. To friendship."

There were many toasts and chatter until a few minutes before midnight, when Maurice excused himself as he had work early in the morning.

"So," Oscar said, filling Diana's glass and sitting beside her on the sofa, "how's it going with trying to win Edward around?"

Diana groaned. "It's not. He tolerates me, that's all. I don't blame him, but it makes it hard to connect."

Oscar grinned. "You ought to introduce him to Cam. She was rejected by her parents too. Sorry, darling, but it's true," he said when Diana physically winced and sat back. "Cam also went to Cambridge, rowed for her college, and is super bright."

Florrie frowned. "Cam? You do remember Cam doesn't like people? She has many wonderful qualities, and I'd lay down my life for her, but playing nice with people is not her greatest skill."

Oscar raised his glass. "Cam has overcome most of her difficulties with lots of strategies and your support, of course, over the years. She could be very useful to Edward. Darling, I think sometimes you forget Cam is now an adult."

Diana swatted his arm. "Oscar, are you trying to insult us both? Have you had too much of the bubbly?"

"Au contraire, Diana. I say what other people can't, and I want the best for you and yours."

Florrie took his hands in hers and squeezed them. "I'm delighted you've found yourself, and found love too. It's wonderful to see you so happy."

Oscar kissed her knuckles. "Thank you. I am. Now, before we get any sappier, do I need to freshen your glasses?"

"No, thanks. It's time for bed. Do you want to use the facilities first? You take longer than me." Florrie grinned. Diana couldn't deny it. She looked as if she was going to protest, then shook her head and left. "I really like Maurice, and he's good for you. Where did you two meet?" She immediately regretted the question as Oscar's joy dropped away, and his eyes filled with pain. He stood. At first, he didn't seem as though he would speak, and instead, he went through the ritual of turning off the lamps until only one remained lit.

"We were in the same resistance unit," he said, without looking at her. "I saw and did things I never want... If that whole horrible thing taught us anything, it's that we should cherish our freedom every day, be grateful for the ones we love, and live our fullest, glorious lives."

"You definitely seem to be living that."

His whole face lit up. "I am, darling, I am. You should too. I'm so thrilled you've found each other again." He smiled. 'If I'd thought you'd had any chance to reconcile, I would've put you in contact before, but after the war, I struggled mentally, and it's taken years to feel good and find myself again. Maurice has been my rock. And here's yours, if you let her."

The sight of Diana, devoid of makeup and in pyjamas and a robe made Florrie's heart flutter.

"Now, we need to discuss sleeping arrangements," Oscar said. "Even though this apartment is huge by Paris standards, it only has two bedrooms. I've made up the bed in the second bedroom. Are you sure you're happy to share a double, or I could put some sheets on this sofa? I think you'd need to take the sofa, Diana. You'd have a wonderful view in the morning but I can't promise how comfortable it will be."

"Diana shouldn't have to sleep on the sofa," Florrie said, "but I may struggle if it's very soft, so it's up to you whether you wish to share the bed. As a practicality, nothing more." Florrie's heart picked up pace. To share with Diana, to be that close and in the same bed after all this time was melting her resolve. But nothing could happen. Nothing *should* happen. They'd both had too much to drink, and she was self-conscious about her body, which was softer now than it once was.

Diana smiled. "I'm sure we'll manage, and I promise I'll be good."

Although her mischievous eyebrow raise and twitch of her lips didn't seem to match that promise. *Do you have to?* Florrie couldn't stop the thought.

"We normally close the shutters but leave them open if you want to enjoy the view. Goodnight, darlings. We're going to have a wonderful, exciting day tomorrow before I put you on a train to continue your adventures." Oscar blew them both a kiss and wandered down the hall to the master suite.

Florrie tried to quell her conflicting emotions by staring out at the city. Some lights had been extinguished now, but she could still trace constellations of boulevards and avenues. It settled her racing heart. Diana joined her at the balcony and without a word, they leaned into each other, sharing the view and a companionship she thought was long lost. "Did Oscar tell you he'd been in the French resistance in the war?"

"Not in so many words, but I assumed that's how he met Maurice. He never speaks of his experience, but it must have been horrible for someone as sensitive as he is. 'He who fights with monsters might take care lest he thereby become a monster. And if you gaze for long into an abyss, the abyss gazes also into you,' to quote Nietzsche."

"It does, or it can, but I think Oscar is right about living life fully now."

Diana arched her eyebrow, a flicker of challenge in her gaze. "And are you?"

Florrie held her breath. The question hung between them, the air suddenly charged, crackling with possibility. She looked down at her fingers gripping the balcony rail. "I thought I was living fully, and I was happy, contented. But you've come into my life, upended it, and expanded it—again, like when we were younger. And now I need to find the courage to step into that wider world."

Diana entwined their hands, her thumb gliding over Florrie's knuckles. "What can I do to give you courage, dearest heart?"

Florrie stared into Diana's face. "I don't know yet. Give me time."

"That I can do."

Their eyes met and the years slipped away, dissolving into the silence between them. There was no past, only this, now, lost in each other.

Diana broke into one of her rare, genuine smiles. "I can't

tell you what it means you agreed to come. I was dreading a month on my own, another month on my own, in a place that should be enjoyed and cherished in company." She stared out into the cooling air. "There are some experiences that demand communion between two people, and this is one of them. It's been such fun with Oscar, but he's sweeter for being in tiny morsels of time, and being with you..." She cleared her throat.

Florrie glanced at her. Diana gaze was fixed ahead but reflected by the lights was the glint of telltale tears slipping down her cheeks. Florrie tucked her arm into Diana's elbow, using touch to express all the comfort she couldn't say. "Diana, sweetheart."

Diana roughly brushed at the tears with the back of her hand. "Don't mind me, I've drunk too much. I know we've only just reconnected, and I know you're not ready for anything. I promise I'll be honourable."

Florrie wasn't convinced she *wanted* Diana to be honourable. Diana straightened up and shifted away slightly, leaving a small gap between them. Florrie missed the contact but respected the physical distance.

Diana inhaled deeply. "I can't believe it was only this morning when we left London. The city is so grey and dreary, decimated by the Blitz, but Paris is ostensibly intact, but the people are hollowed out, as though their psyche has been destroyed. Did you see the bullet holes in the square near the restaurant? They shot informers there, and the Nazis hung resistance fighters. Perhaps the country will reunite again, but the internal scars will never disappear. Sorry, I'm getting maudlin."

"It's like the aftermath of the Great War all over again. As a generation, we've seen the best of times and the worst of times."

Diana huffed out a chuckle. "Trust you to quote Dickens even though you know I'm ambivalent about his writing."

Florrie grinned. "It made you smile though."

"Thank you. You're so good for my soul. I can't believe you're here beside me." Diana stifled a yawn. "But we ought to get some sleep because tomorrow night will be difficult. However luxurious the carriages are, the train's noisy, the bunks are narrow, and the whole contraption vibrates as we pass over points. And there are a lot of points."

"And then we'll be in the South of France." Florrie couldn't keep the glee from her voice.

"We will. Do you need help with anything?"

"No. I'm fine." It wasn't quite true, but she didn't want Diana to see her so vulnerable. She'd manage. "I'll get myself ready for bed now. Thank you for a wonderful day."

"Thank you. I'll close these windows, then I'll slip into bed. Good night."

"Good night." Florrie padded down the hall and picked up her wash bag before making the way to the bathroom. When she finished, she tapped lightly at the door to the second bedroom before entering, but there was no reply. Slowly, she pushed it open, grateful it didn't squeak.

Diana had left on a Tiffany lamp by Florrie's side of the bed, its soft light casting a glow through stained glass. She lay turned away and was purring slightly. She had left Florrie's preferred side for her as they'd always had. The sense of déjà vu was so sharp, Florrie had to pause to steady her breath.

Then, it had been all passion and possibility. Now, it was only sleep. Maybe Diana wasn't attracted to her anymore; her body was too changed and unappealing. A quiet ache clamped around Florrie's heart, a mix of disappointment, shame, and unfulfilled hope. She sighed. She was being silly holding onto expectations she didn't fully understand, especially as she vacillated with her own feelings.

She crept into her side of the bed as quietly as she could and shuffled down to get comfortable. She faced away from the centre of the bed and tried to ignore the warmth of Diana beside her, a comfort they had once shared. This was chaste, and maybe that was for the best. They would simply become friends again without all the complications of passion.

Florrie fumbled for the switch and doused the lamp. She huffed out a breath, not wishing to disturb Diana but unable to stop her thoughts. They were a bit like the two cities. Florrie was damaged physically, like dour London, but stoically keeping on, and Diana was like Paris, exotic and appealing but broken internally. Maybe they could help each other mend and...maybe she'd taken the metaphor too far. She chuckled to herself.

"Night," Diana said. "It's comforting to be in bed with you again."

"Goodnight," Florrie whispered. The contrast with how they'd been before could not be sharper though. They often didn't make it to the bed, so desperate they'd been in their physical lovemaking.

Now Diana talked of comfort and drifted off to sleep once again. She'd said she wanted more than friendship, but her actions implied they'd be nothing more. And yet, the look she'd given her, the pull they'd had, the magnetism between them, and the blatant look of desire she'd seen in Diana's eyes—none of that was *nothing*.

She turned over, trying not to disturb the mattress too much, and settled her gaze on Diana's sleeping form. It was so tempting to stroke her cheek, feel the smoothness of her body against hers, but she stayed her hand. She felt the warmth of Diana's breath mingling with her own...intoxicating. And dangerous.

She couldn't risk everything on impulsive desire, not if it was only nostalgia and wishful thinking. She twisted onto her back and matched her breathing to Diana's, hoping the easy rhythm would lull her to sleep. Perhaps she wouldn't be able to sleep tonight, and maybe that didn't matter. They had a whole month to resolve what they felt for each other in this stage of their lives. Florrie would wait and watch and see how everything played out.

Later, when she woke in the middle of the night, they were

entwined together, exactly as they used to lie. Florrie's head rested on Diana's breast, which was, of course, covered in silk pyjamas. Florrie didn't dare move. She lay there and enjoyed the sensation: the steady beat of Diana's heart beneath her ear, the warmth of Diana's body, the softness of the silk against her cheek, the faintest hint of Diana's perfume and underneath it, Diana's own heady scent. Everything was the same, and yet everything had changed.

Florrie inhaled deeply. The sound of Diana's voice had faded over the years, and she had to strain to recall her youthful face, but she would always remember her aroma. How she'd missed this, being snuggled up together so interlaced that it had always been difficult to differentiate whose body was whose. It would be so easy to slip her hand under Diana's pyjama top and caress her breasts, feel the hardening of her nipples and the smoothness of her skin. Or perhaps it wasn't smooth anymore, not that it mattered. However much her rational mind told her to take it easy, her body was urging her to rush in regardless.

She lifted her head and pulled away.

Diana tugged her closer with the arm wrapped around Florrie's waist. "Don't go. Stay here."

Florrie did, cringing as she noticed a wet patch on Diana's top where she must have dribbled in her sleep. How unsexy. But this wasn't about sex, however much her libido had come out of hibernation. This was comfort and connection. Nothing more. She cuddled up to Diana and gradually, drifted off, physically safe but in emotional peril.

The next day with Oscar passed in a blur, seeing the sights, and laughing, and sharing stories. In a blink, he was seeing them off at the Gare du Lyon. When he blew his nose rather hard a few times before they waved goodbye, they pretended not to notice, and Florrie clung onto him tighter than was polite, even in tactile France.

This train was even more luxurious than the first, being le train bleu proper, with shiny blue and gold livery. Their cabin had two tiny bunks on each side of the compartment, already made up as beds. With a whistle, they were off.

"We should get as drunk as possible, so we sleep through the movement," Diana said and dug out a bottle of champagne Oscar had smuggled into her suitcase.

It was hardly glamorous to drink out of tooth mugs, but it seemed all the more special as they passed down the Rhône valley and through places whose names blurred at each station. They made their way to the restaurant car for a late dinner and to the saloon bar, but there was nobody who knew Diana. Florrie sighed with relief. All too soon, they were getting ready for bed. After the intimacy of sleeping in the same bed, ending up so entwined at Oscar's, it felt lonely to be in separate bunks.

Diana reached out her hand across the chasm of the compartment to take Florrie's. "Thank you for another wonderful day. Sleep well."

Florrie didn't think she would sleep, but it seemed like only minutes before the guard came along, shouting and banging doors to say they were arriving in Marseille in half an hour. Florrie checked her watch: 5:45 a.m. She groaned and turned over. The next time she awoke, Diana presented her with a warm croissant.

"A baker at the local station bakes these and sells them to passengers. He's probably making a killing on them."

"I'm beginning to love France." She bit into the buttery pastry, and it dissolved in her mouth. It was so light and fresh, she salivated.

Diana raised the blind and gazed out at the passing scenery. "It's not long until we get to Antibes now, and it's worth staying up to watch the seascape. We pass so close to the Med, it feels like you can touch it."

Florrie rubbed her eyes, blinking at the sudden brightness. Diana was right. The train crossed a many-arched viaduct skirting the edge of the coast. The morning sun glittered on the mild sea, scattering silver on the serene waves. It was a sunrise of new beginnings, and this was their new beginning, separate and distinct from what happened before.

"This is heaven," Florrie said softly, and she wasn't only referring to the view.

CHAPTER TWELVE

Antibes, France, September 1950

FLORRIE'S EYELIDS GLOWED RED from the September sun, and she held them closed tight, savouring the effect. She hummed as the warmth eased her bones. Below them, the sound of the Mediterranean Sea sloshed and sucked, lulling her to sleep. Birds chittered and a cicada buzzed in the late summer heat. She shuffled deeper into her deckchair and sighed. This was the life. A shadow fell over her face, and she opened her eyes and smiled. Diana stood over her in a form-fitting swimming costume, revealing far more flesh than Florrie would ever dare, but on Diana, it was perfect and effortless. She wore her lean figure with the same confidence she always had.

"I'm going for a swim." Diana brushed a dark strand of hair away from her cheek. "Join me?"

At one time, Diana would've simply assumed Florrie would follow her lead without question. But now she asked, and Florrie appreciated the consideration. It reflected how their relationship had shifted; she was no longer the neophyte, hanging on Diana's every word. Now they were more equal. "Later." She stretched like a cat toasting itself. "Right now, I'm enjoying not travelling, not moving, and not hurrying. Just soaking up the sun." She glanced up at Diana with a grin. "I'm also enjoying the view."

Diana laughed and leaned forward, giving Florrie an eyeful of luscious cleavage, before kissing her on the forehead. "Glad you approve. I chose it especially for you."

She turned and sashayed towards the pool in a deliberately

provocative manner designed to cause Florrie to lick her lips. After being dormant for many years and losing the last remnants in menopause, Florrie was rediscovering her lost libido. Diana looked back over her shoulder, noting where Florrie had been staring, then winked and plunged in. Of course her dive was clean and athletic like she was practicing for the Olympics.

A few seconds later, Diana emerged above the surface, and she gasped and coughed a little. "That was colder than I expected."

Florrie grinned. "I'm delighted with my choice then. Enjoy your swim."

"I will." Diana dunked her head below the water again.

She swam an efficient crawl up and down the pool. The gentle rhythm of splashing water had Florrie's eyelids closing again. Birds sang, and the sounds softly drifted away.

Cold water droplets shocked her awake, and she half squealed. Not very classy.

Diana laughed and towelled herself off. "Florence, if you're going to fall asleep, you might need to wear a hat, so your delicate skin doesn't burn."

"I was only dozing," Florrie said, then caught Diana's quirked eyebrow. God, she'd missed that expressiveness in such a tiny gesture. "Okay, I was. You're right."

Diana looked so mischievous and alluring when she wrapped her towel around her and tucked in the end. Almost without thought, Florrie tugged at the soft material, and the towel fell away, revealing Diana's glistening skin. She shrieked, laughing, then jumped on Florrie's upright deckchair. She straddled Florrie and rubbed her wet body against her, cold, salty, and arousing, causing goosebumps to appear down Florrie's arms. Diana smelled of sweat and chlorine, which should be repulsive, but Florrie inhaled deeper.

Suddenly, the laughter shifted. Diana's eyes darkened, and their breaths came in shallow pants. Diana slowed her scattering of water, and her cold nipples brushed hard against Florrie's, causing her to writhe in response. "Oh, you're making me wet... everywhere."

Diana pulled back and cleared her throat. "That's the idea. I want to take you to bed now, but we'll need to wait until Amelie leaves."

"Amelie?"

Diana stood up, leaving damp patches cooling on Florrie's body. "Anthony's, and now Edward's, housekeeper. She's a rather formidable woman who would not approve. Not that I care, but I'd prefer to tell Edward myself in my own time. He's likely to be judgemental of my bohemian lifestyle, but I don't think he can disapprove of or hate me any more than he does already."

That was a mood-dampener. They were in a borrowed house, with servants no less, and Diana had a son she needed to tell—or hide from. Florrie didn't want to hide. She wanted to shout it from the cliff tops, yet she feared leaping off the edge.

Diana rearranged Florrie's dress and covered her up before returning to the other seat. "You've gone very quiet. Is there something wrong?"

"It feels slightly weird being in a place that once belonged to your husband and is now your son's, with staff to judge, and a son whom you'll have to speak to about us. The journey down was so carefree and thrilling like Audrey Hepburn in *Roman Holiday*. It felt like I was thirty-two again, not late middle-aged. But now all the responsibilities and consequences have come thundering in, pushing more obstacles in the way."

"It was carefree, wasn't it? Sorry, sweetheart. This is supposed to be relaxing."

Sweetheart. How the word made Florrie's toes curl and warmed her heart.

"As for the other matter, Edward never comes here. He isn't interested, and it's good for a house to breathe with life. Anthony inherited it from his grandmother, and we rarely came down together. And we always slept in separate beds anyway, if that's your concern."

Florrie *hadn't* thought of that and really *didn't* want that image seared in her brain.

"Talking of Amelie, here she is now." Diana rose from her deckchair and strutted over to welcome her staff member with a formal handshake.

Florrie checked her clothes and fought off the blush creeping up her neck. She pushed herself up using the chair arms to give her leverage. When she'd got her balance back, she waved. "Bonjour." She had never seen a woman so at odds with her name, which she thought of as light and frivolous. Amelie was round, dour-looking, and dressed in black, which must be uncomfortable and positively unpleasant in the height of summer. Diana spoke to her in rapid French, and Amelie dipped her head slightly, the minimum possible without seeming discourteous.

Her stony gaze fixed on Florrie, who consciously had to retain her relaxed posture. She'd been invited here, and she was welcome, despite the offhand manner of this woman.

"Qu'est-ce que vous voulez boire?"

Florrie smiled. "Avez-vous de la limonade, s'il vous plaît?"

Amelie gave a slow blink as if Florrie had spoken in Japanese, and she didn't understand.

Diana repeated Florrie's order, and Amelie gave a half nod and padded back into the house. Florrie sat down again to cover her embarrassment. She wasn't used to people not liking her. "That's exactly what I said. She must have understood, despite the awful accent. I feel like the prioress in *Canterbury Tales* who learned French at the school at Stratford at Bowe, although in my case it was Miss Docherty in her strong Belfast accent."

Diana laughed again. "Sorry, sweetheart. She's punishing you because she adored Anthony. She couldn't do enough for him on the few occasions when he came here with me, or with his mistress."

Florrie could get used to being called that, and she tingled inside at the promise of more to come. "Wait... he had a mistress, and you knew? Didn't you care?"

Diana flopped down in the chair beside Florrie and waved her hand. "Melinda is the woman he was in love with for longer than we were married. If he was discreet, I didn't care. It meant he didn't pester me."

Florrie shuddered at the thought of Anthony with his meaty hands all over Diana. "How awful. I couldn't do with that."

"I know. In some ways, I envy you. No, in a lot of ways I envy you."

"You envy me?"

Diana picked at the wood on the arms of her chair. "Yes, you have a gentle joy about you that you cast around to everyone close by. I saw how your niece and her girlfriend looked at you—when they weren't ogling each other, that is. They're not subtle, are they?" She chuckled, as did Florrie. "What they do for you, they do out of love and not duty."

Florrie smiled at the thought of Cam and Gloria who had sent her off with best wishes and Gloria's instruction to be "as naughty as she liked."

Diana gestured to the house. "And the way you chat to waiters and staff. You care about them, and they know it. I'm tolerated and am called difficult and various toxic names I pretend not to hear." She gave a brittle laugh.

"I don't think Amelie would agree with you."

"Oh, she's being grumpy because she can't take it out on me. She has to be polite to me in case I complain to Edward, whom she also adores."

They lapsed into a comfortable silence for a few moments, and Florrie relaxed into the lulling of the gentle waves lapping at the cliff below them. "It's so restful here. A little slice of paradise. Thank you for inviting me."

"Thank you for saying yes. Even as we're sitting here at the start of our vacation, I'm dreading going back to England and the cottage. I already don't want to be apart from you. Mead House is a long way from Cambridge."

Was Diana really saying what Florrie thought she was? That she wanted to stay with her, maybe to share a life under the same roof? Florrie's heart raced, pounding so hard that she was sure Diana would hear it. A thrill surged through her, wild and dizzying, yet it was too sudden, too much. She didn't know what to do with the rush of feelings: to dive in like Diana or tentatively climb into the depths. "Why?"

Diana leaned forward and pushed her sunglasses up her head so she could look Florrie in the eye. "You radiate love and warmth in everything you do, and everyone responds to that. You're gentle and kind, and I want to step into that radiance, be warmed by it. Even if it means my shadow side stands in stark contrast to you. How could I not be drawn to you, or want to share the joy you beam around? I'm blessed by your attention and your affection."

Florrie was saved from replying when the door squeaked open, and Amelie stepped out, carrying a tray with a pitcher of lemonade and two glasses. The scene stirred a memory of the first summer afternoon when Florrie had visited Diana's house and how it had felt like stepping into a dream. The interruption was welcome, giving Florrie a moment to recover from Diana's revelation. She didn't know what to feel. It was all so real and happening so fast, she couldn't catch her breath.

"Thank you, Amelie. Leave the salad in the refrigerator before you go. We won't need you again until tomorrow. Thank you for opening the house."

Diana spoke in fluent French, and Florrie had to concentrate hard to follow what she was saying.

Amelie nodded. "À demain, Lady Packard Smith."

They watched her retreat towards the house.

"I hate the title, like I was some chattel of Anthony's, and she knows it. I can't remember how many times I've asked her to call me Diana. She says it deliberately to grate on my nerves," Diana whispered as she lowered her sunglasses over her eyes.

"She definitely doesn't approve." Florrie stood, moving with more grace than normal. She supposed the heat was proving a balm to her joints. She adjusted the position of her chair to sit deeper in the shade. Diana hurried to help and gently squeezed Florrie's shoulder. She stayed silent, waiting until Amelie was out of sight, although the woman seemed to take an unusually long time to cross the sun-baked stones back to the kitchen.

In her new position, Florrie lost her view of the sea but could fully focus on Diana, who perched on her seat as stiffly as Florrie usually felt in the morning.

Diana had always been so poised and in control before, where nothing could shake her confidence. Now she fidgeted with the pitcher and poured the drinks as they waited for Amelie to be gone. There was a long pause between the door pulling to and the final click, as though Amelie had been hoping to overhear their conversation.

"I think your Amelie understands more English than she lets on, and she was hoping to hear something juicy."

Diana's shoulders dropped a little as she handed over the lemonade. "She isn't *my* Amelie. She always tolerated me when Anthony wanted to play happy families. But I do have something juicy to say, or I hope it is."

Florrie inhaled sharply, stopping the glass halfway to her lips.

"I've missed you for so long, and I can't believe you're here with me now in this glorious setting. Those three years, when we shared discussions, and passion, and writing, were the best years of my life. *On the Edge of Uncertainty* was probably my best work, although not my most popular, and yet, I've written nothing since. Nothing I would publish anyway. As we travelled down here, sleeping together in the same room over the last few nights, I've been inspired to write again, but I don't want to waste my time here with you. It's too precious."

Florrie put down her glass, masking her disappointment. Diana didn't want her: she wanted a muse. She tilted Florrie's chin up with her fingertip. When had she come so close, their chairs nearly touching? Her eyes locked onto Florrie's, searching and steady. The dark, familiar intensity was always so entrancing, Florrie couldn't refuse whatever she asked.

"I'm not saying this to ask you to let me write. I want *you*. I want to be around you, to have your sharp mind challenging mine, to share the joy of reading and discussions about the world. I'd love your friendship and your companionship, but I want more than that."

Diana's eyes shimmered with unshed tears. What was causing her so much pain? Florrie couldn't quite believe what she was hearing, what she'd once longed for all those years ago. She'd never seen Diana so on edge, so unsure of herself, and Florrie didn't know how to respond. It was all too much. She rose slowly and wandered to the balcony overlooking the Mediterranean. Below them, waves crashed and roiled against the rocks, while seagulls swooped and soared, carried up on warm currents rising from the cliff faces. The wild motion of the sea and sky echoed the turmoil in her mind.

Footsteps sounded behind her, and she felt Diana lean against the balcony, close but not touching.

"Have I offended you? Or pushed too hard?"

Florrie turned toward Diana, who pushed her sunglasses onto her head. In the bright light, she squinted slightly, showing the lattice of lines etched with the life she'd endured and survived. They hadn't been there before but somehow made her more appealing. So much for Florrie's assumption Diana had had it easy. The more she had spoken about it over the last few days, the more Florrie pitied her being trapped in a loveless marriage without the solace of writing or the joy of parenthood.

Florrie pointed at the waves churning at their feet. "I can't run headlong into the sea of my emotions. It's too overwhelming, and I'm scared, and yet I'm pulled to you like a rising tide."

A seagull cried close to their heads, and they looked up as it was buffeted against the strong breeze. Wind whipped a strand of Diana's hair across her face, and she tucked it behind her ear. Her hairstyle was different now too, a short bob she'd claimed was easier to care for. So much had changed, and yet the reality was there: Florrie loved her. Could she deny that? *Should* she deny that?

Diana hadn't seemed to take a breath, so Florrie smiled to put her at ease. "Are we going to talk about the fact we've gone to bed together very chastely, each on our own side, then find ourselves entwined like rope in the morning?"

Diana arched her perfectly plucked eyebrow. "I'm sure our bodies were seeking each other for comfort."

Florrie shook her head. "My body is never completely comfortable now, but the warmth is helping."

Diana stroked Florrie's arm. "Oh, poor darling. You must let me know if anything hurts—"

"It all hurts. And not just physically," she said. Diana flinched as if stung and took a step back. Regret swelled in Florrie's chest, leaving her heart heavy and aching at all the years lost, all the wasted time and energy recovering from heartache. And if they didn't work out, if she was no more than Diana's muse and a distraction, would she be left on high tide to dry and wither? She wasn't strong enough to endure that heartbreak again. She expelled a frustrated breath. "Sorry. I didn't know how raw I felt. I thought I was over you and was living a contented life, and I was happy with that. Then you came crashing back like those waves, tossing me around. And now I don't know if I should cling onto the rocks for safety or plunge into the sea with you." She swallowed hard. "We have responsibilities. My head is screaming at me to cling on to my life as it is." She paused, her throat tight with emotion. "I don't know if I can trust you again," she whispered.

Diana said nothing. Her shoulders sagged, and she seemed to curl in on herself. The wind blew strands of her hair across her face, but she didn't flick them back. Instead, she stood, staring out to sea, as if searching for solace on the distant horizon.

Florrie bit her lip and tried not to fill the silence, to apologise or retract her words. She'd spoken her truth, and that had to be enough. She had nothing to lose by saying no but opportunity and the potential for a friendship—or more—with a woman she had loved for over twenty years. And yet, she had everything to lose.

"I'm very flattered. It feels like you're asking me to run away to the circus, and that's thrilling and exotic, but ultimately, I don't know if this is me and my life and if I can follow you there and believe you won't tire of me. I should be grateful and delighted, and I am, but...trust takes time to rebuild." A knot of doubt twisted in her chest. If she said no now, would she be making the biggest mistake of her life?

Diana finally turned and offered a small wry smile. "I understand," she said, though her voice wavered. "It makes my heart ache to hear it, but thank you for your honesty. Without trust, there can be no love. And yes, it stings that you don't trust me. I always tried to tell the truth, and my heart has never changed, even when I felt I had no choice but to accept the conditions Anthony set to save the press." She shivered and rubbed her arms. "I'm getting cold in the breeze. I'll take a shower and get dressed. I don't want to pressure you, one way or the other. Would you prefer to take the second bedroom? I'll move your bag across."

Florrie grasped Diana's hands. Her skin was still so soft and unmarred by old age spots, unlike Florrie's. The contrast tugged at something deep within her, how different they were now, how their lives had split apart. "I'm sorry," she said softly. "Can you give me some time? I need to go slowly, to let it all settle and seep in. I want to trust again, but I need to relearn how." She gave a mirthless chuckle. "At least you aren't sending me back on the next train."

"Of course not. You'd never manage the steps or your luggage."

Florrie smiled. "No, I wouldn't. Thank you. I know I'm blowing hot and cold, but could I stay in your bed—to sleep? It's been such a comfort and joy to lie beside you and snuggle up in the morning."

Diana's face lifted into a genuine smile that lit up her eyes. "I'd like that." Her features softened. "You're like the waves, surging forward then pulling back." She let out a small laugh. "I'll wait for high tide, even if the Med doesn't really have tides."

Florrie kissed Diana's hand. "Thank you. Please give me a bit of time to get used to the idea, to rebuild trust. We'll also need to tell the youngsters. Cam might struggle with any long-term changes. How do you think Edward will take it?"

Diana barked a bitter laugh. "If he's like his father, he'll hate it. I hope he has enough of me in him to accept it. I'm going in now, but please stay here and enjoy the view."

Diana squeezed Florrie's shoulder as she departed, leaving Florrie more confused and uncertain than ever. After a few minutes staring down to the sea, Florrie returned to her seat, opened her book and became absorbed in her reading.

"You look very beautiful and comfortable there."

Florrie looked up, and the sight almost took her breath away. Diana was dressed in a red and white polka dot summer dress, white floppy hat, and matching slingback shoes, and carried a tray. Florrie swallowed hard. "Wow. That's what you wear when you're on holiday? You're stunning."

"Thank you," Diana said. "So are you. Come and sit. I've collected up the food Amelie prepared earlier."

"I hope you have a poison-taster on standby."

The deep, rich sound of Diana's answering laughter enveloped

Florrie in warmth and comfort. She'd missed that laugh, missed the way it came from somewhere deep and real, somewhere Florrie had been treated to on occasion. It brought memories tumbling back of shared moments reading a manuscript, arguing over a discussion point of a lecture, of a stolen glance in the office... All moments so simple and filled with joy.

"I don't think she'd dare. Even if Amelie has poisoned the food, at least we'll have a nice bottle of wine to go with it." Diana placed the laden tray on the table.

A wax tablecloth had been attached to the table with huge clips, and a couple of twigs and flower petals had blown onto it. Florrie brushed them away and helped to set out the cutlery. It all felt so easy and natural.

Diana poured wine for them both and raised her glass. "To reconnection and a wonderful vacation."

They clinked glasses, and Diana held Florrie's gaze. She'd forgotten how intense Diana could be. Or rather, she'd put the memory away as it was too painful to hold.

Diana took a sip of wine. "I'm wearing this dress because I know you like me in red, and I wanted to impress you."

Florrie laughed. "Why would you need to impress me? You already know I love you. The issue is whether I can trust you again. Trust that you won't hurt me, trust that this is best for both of us at our different stages in life."

"Okay. Perhaps you can see it as trying to persuade you then." She smiled. "Nice wine. Now, what are you reading, and what do you think of it?"

And they settled into the easy conversation like they had before, with argument and counter-argument about the merits of different books they'd read, latest philosophical thoughts, and the state of the world.

Later in the evening, Diana switched on the patio lights and lit citronella candles. "They're supposed to repel mosquitoes. I'm not sure if it works, but the scent is quite pleasant."

Eventually though, Florrie yawned and twisted her shoulders to ease the discomfort.

"It's getting cool. Are you ready to turn in?" Diana gathered up the remains of their meal and they went indoors. "Would you like a douche this evening?" She placed the tray on the counter by the sink. "Did you know the modern shower was invented by a Frenchman to improve hygiene in a Rouen prison?"

"Of course you'd know such a quirky fact. Did you go to a lecture about it?"

"I did actually."

They both laughed.

Diana flung her hand to her head in faux offence. "If you're going to mock me, I may rescind the offer."

"Too late, I accept. That might be easier than a bath. Thank you."

Diana held out her hand to lead Florrie upstairs. "Tempting though it is to join you, I'll leave you to it. There's a spare towel in the cupboard."

"Thank you."

Diana closed the door behind her, and Florrie slowly undressed, feeling like she'd been abandoned, which was ridiculous. She was the one requesting the distance, and yet she resented Diana giving it to her. She turned on the water, which gurgled and banged before allowing a small stream to come through. It wasn't scalding, which was how Florrie took her baths, but it did its job of washing away the day's grime. The towel was huge, and soft, and felt very luxurious as she wrapped it around her. *Damn it.* She hadn't taken her pyjamas and slippers out of her case, so she padded across the creaky floorboards and knocked on Diana's door. "Is it safe to come in?"

"It depends on whether you want me to ravish you or not."

Florrie tentatively twisted the handle and entered. The room was lit only by a bedside lamp and another by a desk at which Diana sat. She was already in her robe and was slowly removing her earrings without a mirror, with the ease of someone who has done it hundreds of times. She smiled at Florrie. There was something very intimate about watching her preparing for bed. Florrie squeezed her legs together, trying to regain control of her body. "It would be too easy to be ravished, and I'd love it, but I think it would complicate everything."

Diana nodded, but a flicker of disappointment passed over her face. "I understand. I presume you're happy taking the side closest to the door again?"

"Yes. Thanks." As she wandered past the desk, she couldn't resist trailing her fingers across Diana's back.

Diana groaned. "You're not being fair."

"No, sorry. I'll get into bed and be a good girl." She snapped open the locks of her case and withdrew her nightwear and slippers. Florrie checked Diana wasn't looking before peeling off her towel. She placed it on a wooden chair at the side of the bed and was about to slip on her pyjama bottoms, but turned at a cough.

"Beautiful," Diana whispered.

Florrie snatched the pyjamas to cover herself but warmed at the praise. "You're only saying that."

"No, I mean it. Don't be ashamed. You're a strong, mature woman who has lived life, and you glow with the radiance of your personality."

"I...I... Thank you. But I'm still not ready."

"I know. You need to learn to trust."

Florrie nodded and slipped on her nightwear, trying to ignore the guilt and the disappointment she'd caught in Diana's expression. She shuffled into her side of the bed and closed her eyes. A few minutes later, she heard the padding of footsteps on the old floorboards and the light clicked off, dropping the room into darkness. The other side of the bed dipped as Diana crept in. Florrie turned to face Diana. "I'm sorry if I'm being hard."

Slits of moonlight through the shutters cast bright lines on

Diana's face. She smiled. "You're scared, and I understand that." She raised her hand and traced Florrie's jaw and face with her index finger. "Goodnight, sweetheart."

"Goodnight." Florrie closed her eyes as their lips met in a chaste kiss. She reached for Diana's much softer hand and entangled their fingers. "Thank you for waiting."

Diana squeezed her hand. Florrie kept her eyes shut tight, but sleep eluded her. It wasn't long before Diana purred softly, blowing light puffs of air on her cheeks. When her hands began to ache, she extricated her fingers from Diana's and turned over, trying not to rouse her. After a quick intake of breath, the gentle snoring continued. Florrie smiled. Diana was adamant she didn't snore, but how could she tell if she was asleep? If only Florrie had a way to record it.

She rubbed her hands to soothe them without jostling the mattress. Why was she holding back? It wasn't only her concern about being physically capable anymore. It was the letting go of everything she held dear: her life, her equilibrium, her security of living with Cam and Gloria, and everything familiar to take a chance with Diana. There were no guarantees.

Maybe it didn't have to be all or nothing. Perhaps there was a middle way, allowing the space for loving Diana and also living the life she already cherished. She wasn't there yet. Not quite. But she was getting closer with every breath.

Florrie awoke with a start after a disturbing but only half remembered dream about not finding something precious. She didn't need to be a genius to know where that had come from. The sheet was wrapped around her ankles, and she carefully untangled her feet. Diana slept soundly beside her, her hand resting on Florrie's hip.

She couldn't see her watch, but it must be early. She huffed out a breath. There was no way she would sleep again now. She carefully removed Diana's hand, slid off the bed, and straightened her stiff back. After grabbing her slippers and a robe en route, she shuffled downstairs and out to the balcony overlooking the sea.

To the east, a pale light split the indigo sky and gradually expanded as the glowing ball of the sun crescented the horizon. Beneath her, the waves lapped against the rocks, drawing her into the day. Morning rippled on the water, full of promise for a joyful day. There was something about this time; the slight breeze brushing against her cheek before the stifling heat set in, and the birds and bees hummed their welcome to a new beginning. She too was seeing the world anew.

The door creaked a little, and the sound of footsteps told her Diana was approaching, so it was no surprise when Diana slipped her arms around Florrie from behind.

"I missed you. Couldn't you sleep?"

Florrie sunk back into the warmth of Diana's body. "No. I needed to think, and it's beautiful out here at the start of a new day. So much hope of possibility."

"It is. It never fails to amaze me. Are you comfortable?" Diana asked, her warm breath tickling Florrie's ear.

She raised her head slightly to nuzzle into Diana. She was softer now, more approachable. Where once she'd been all sharp angles and sharper comments, now she was gentle consideration. "My neck's a bit stiff, but I'm fine. I'm enjoying being here with you."

"Let me massage your neck."

Diana kneaded and caressed firmly, causing Florrie's whole body to relax. "Mm, that's nice. You have wonderful hands, and I hope they'll be exploring elsewhere soon."

"Good. I'd like that." Diana feathered a kiss by Florrie's ear.

She shivered. It was getting harder to resist. "Are you sure you want to be hitched with me and my wrinkles grooved deep with pain and a body that seizes up?" she asked, still staring out to sea.

"It's me who should ask you the same question," Diana said

quietly. "Why would you want to be with me? I've been thinking about it, and I don't see it. I always thought you loved me for how I looked and because you hero worshipped me. But that's all gone now. Inevitably, love based on appearance falters as beauty fades. And love based on hero worship vanishes the moment the hero becomes human."

Florrie turned around, and Diana gave her a small, wry smile and stepped back. "Maybe," Florrie said, her voice hoarse with pent-up emotion. "Yet love based on a person's essence, their true self, grows and strengthens if you tend it, nurture it, and let it blossom."

Diana looked down before meeting Florrie's eyes again. "I'm more concerned whether you will still love me as we slip into old age and my looks have diminished. I'm all too human, with faults writ large, as my son is quick to remind me. I'm selfish, arrogant, and need to work on my relationship with Edward. Why would you take me on?" She blew out a shaky breath. "I'm honoured you've come here with me. You're right not to trust me after I rejected you. And I know I'm on trial, having nothing to show for the intervening years but a failed business, dark moods, and abandoned manuscripts."

Diana hunched in on herself. She looked so bereft that Florrie worried she might do something scary. This was a glimpse of the melancholy Diana alluded to, and her heart went out to her. She threaded her arm through Diana's and tugged until they were side by side against the railing. There was some truth in Diana's words. She wasn't easy to be with, and Florrie had to sift through how she felt, without Diana's influence and encouragement. "There is no trial, judge, or jury," Florrie said. "I'm enjoying reconnecting with you, rediscovering the same joy in similar things. I never loved you *just* for your looks, or status, or confidence, or because I loved your writing, although I did love all those things about you. But I loved you most for who you are and who I became around you. That's the essence I'm talking about." She chipped at the paint on the railing with her fingernail, searching for more words, for better words to put shape to her feelings and fears. "But I have a life I love, with family who love me, and it's a huge step to change it all. I need time to filter through my feelings. I know this isn't nostalgia. My heart still flutters when you're near, and I love spending time with you. I'd like to explore where this can go. But whether it's enough to throw up my sure and safe life, I don't know yet." Florrie smiled and stretched out her fingers. "I'd like to meet Edward, and for you to get to know Cam and Gloria. They're a huge part of our lives. This—" she gestured around them, "this is blissful, but we have real lives waiting."

Diana nodded. "I agree. Thank you for being open to the possibility." She waved at the sun, now warming their faces, and the cicadas started their buzzing for the day. "It's fully light now. We should have breakfast outside. And music. I'm sure there's a portable wind-up gramophone somewhere. What do you think?"

Florrie had to laugh as Diana seemed to suddenly wind up herself into enthusiasm for the idea. "I'd love that."

"Wait here."

Her footsteps receded, and while she waited, Florrie absorbed the fresh quiet of the day before the bustle of the world intruded.

Within a few minutes, a beaming Diana carefully handled a large box onto the patio. This was a side to her that Florrie hadn't seen before: the practical one, who lifted, and carried, and was attentive to Florrie's needs. And she loved it.

"I'll put this on the table, and I'll let you choose the music. There's lots of jazz and Glenn Miller. And more Glenn Miller."

"I can take a hint. Should we have Glenn Miller then?"

Diana let out a huff as she placed the record player on the dining table at the side of the villa. "Now for the records." She returned a few minutes later carefully carrying a box of precious vinyl records. "How about this one?" she called from around the corner.

Florrie laughed "I don't have X-ray eyesight." There was the telltale drop of the needle and hiss before the music started with a big band song she didn't recognise.

Diana reemerged around the corner, her eyes shining. "Would you care for a dance?"

"I don't know if I can."

"Lean against me." Diana held out her arms. "I'll hold you. It's only a slow social foxtrot."

Florrie did as instructed. Diana was a superb dancer, light on her feet and leading her with clear intentions. Florrie relaxed into the gentle movements, letting her head fall against the soft fabric of Diana's gown. She inhaled her scent and warmth, and they moved with more grace than she would have believed. Joining the music, the birds and bees vibrated with the joy of a new day. It seemed fitting for their new beginning. "Thank you, that was wonderful," she said, as the record hissed and clicked around and around at the end of the track. "*This* is wonderful. Thank you for making it special." She raised her head and their lips met. The kiss was slow and unhurried, and Diana licked then tugged at Florrie's bottom lip. She obliged and opened her mouth, letting Diana in. With each second, she was opening to her younger self, to the way she'd been, to the way they'd been: wild and passionate like a stormy sea.

"Mon dieu!"

They sprung apart at Amelie gawping at them, a bag drooping from her hand and her mouth open in shock.

"Ah, Amelie. We didn't hear you come in. Did you knock or just use your key?" There was a slight barb in Diana's tone Amelie couldn't miss.

"I didn't want to wake you. I brought you fresh croissants for your breakfast."

Florrie narrowed her eyes, intrigued Amelie hadn't replied

in French, showing that she did speak good English, as Florrie suspected. Her ears burned, but she was going to make an effort with this woman. "Thank you, how kind."

Amelie's expression remained pinched, betraying her displeasure. "I did not expect this."

"Yet you hoped to catch us out, so you can report back to Edward. He's said the place is mine to use as I like. So I am. How many times did Anthony bring his mistress here? Is this how you reacted?"

Amelie shrugged and mumbled something Florrie didn't catch. She turned around, marched inside with her bag gripped in her hands, and the door clicked shut.

Florrie caught Diana's gaze, and they burst out laughing. "I think we shocked her. I hope she doesn't spit on our croissants."

"Or curdle the coffee." Diana put on another record. "I'll need to tell Edward soon, I suppose, when we return."

Diana's last word weighed heavy in Florrie's heart. This trip was like a fantasy of how she'd always hoped her life would be if Diana had stayed with her all those years ago. Even as the music played on the ancient gramophone and the sunlight streamed onto the stones, casting deep shadows, it didn't feel real. Life at home with Cam and Gloria was real. It was safe, and fun, and fulfilling.

Yet part of her had always ached below the surface. She had yearned for intellectual pursuit, to be loved for who she was, to be special, to be seen and loved fully. Diana was offering her all of that now, and more.

Maybe it was time to stop gripping so tightly to everything she knew. Maybe she didn't have to choose. Perhaps she should simply let go and let the tide carry her.

CHAPTER THIRTEEN

A FEW SHORT WEEKS later, Florrie leaned her head back in the warm water and closed her eyes. Grains of sand gritted between her toes as her feet clung to the bottom. "This is the life. Thank you for bringing me here. I've loved our time together." She opened one eye to check on Diana, who floated completely on her back, spread-eagled, and drifted with the gentle waves. Her large sunglasses covered her eyes, so Florrie couldn't see whether she was looking at her or not.

"You're welcome. Thank you for agreeing to get in the water."

"You're right, it's warm." Florrie swished her arms around, easily and without pain. "I can't believe how well I'm moving here."

"Next time we'll stay longer...if you'd like to come again."

"I'd love to come again, thank you," Florrie said. "I've enjoyed our time reconnecting, finding that we still have the same interests and can still enjoy intellectual discussions, although I don't agree with you about Dinah Shore's 'Buttons and Bows.' I don't like any lyrics that state *where women are women* as a good thing."

Diana laughed and splashed Florrie. She responded by scooping up handfuls of water on Diana's stomach.

"Hey." Diana swam closer to her. "Why aren't you floating on your back?"

"You noticed?" Florrie's cheeks burned. Would she never control her blushing? "I can swim, but I've never learned how to float on my back."

"You must learn. Lie back, and let your feet come off the bottom. That's it."

As Florrie did just that, Diana placed her hands under her back and head, and gently cradled her. "Stretch out your arms and legs like a starfish. Relax."

Florrie stretched her arms then flailed and she splashed, but Diana held her and Florrie eased into her hold, letting her muscles soften.

"I've got you. Sink your head right back so your ears are in the water."

Florrie did so, and water lapped at her cheeks with a soft pressure. Everything was muffled and other worldly. The shriek of seagulls, and children playing, and the thick churning of the gentle sea became muted. It became a different world.

"That's it. Trust me," Diana said, her voice distant.

Something shifted in Florrie, as her feet bobbed at the surface of the water and her limbs became rubbery. Understanding permeated her fear, banishing it to the bottom of the sea. Since they'd been on this holiday, Diana had been nothing but patient and attentive to her needs. Now she was looking at Florrie with such gentle concern, with such obvious love in her eyes, how could Florrie doubt that?

What had really been holding her back? Was it trust or the ache of fear? For too many years, she'd been treading water, enjoying life but not plunging in completely. She'd been keeping her metaphorical foot on the bottom, but in Diana's arms, she was safe. Diana wouldn't let her drown.

Diana raised her sunglasses and met her gaze. Florrie relaxed her muscles, relying on Diana's hand at her back to keep her afloat. "I do trust you, to hold me, to care for my heart. Sorry I've been holding out on you, but I had to be certain before I could release my fear and let go. If this isn't a position of trust and vulnerability, I don't know what is."

"You're talking about more than floating, aren't you?" Diana bit her bottom lip.

"I am. Thank you for waiting for me to be ready. I'm ready to explore more with you, if that's still on the table."

"Truly? I want to kiss you now, here, on this public beach."

How wonderful to be looking up into the eyes of the woman she loved, had loved for years, and had never stopped loving. "I'm not sure the gendarmerie or the Amelies of this world would appreciate that."

"I'd appreciate it," Diana whispered. "And did you notice that I've taken my hands away? You're really floating."

Florrie gasped and floundered, splashing them both. They laughed, and Diana shook her head to dispel the water from her hair. Florrie's feet hit the sand, anchoring her in waist-deep water. Beneath the surface, she reached out instinctively, and Diana's hand met hers. They intertwined their fingers, sure and warm in the pull of the tide. "Thank you," she said. "For waiting, for being patient emotionally and with my physical needs. I love you. I always have, but I was too scared to take my feet off the bottom."

Diana smiled and drew her closer. She smelled of the sea and the faintest tinge of jasmine and ylang ylang. A quiff of hair stood at right angles stiff with salt. Florrie had never seen Diana so unruffled. Though she had many memories of Diana, naked and unkempt, and they flashed into her mind, flooding her body with a rush of arousal. "Let's go home. I think we have something else to attend to."

Diana's eyes widened and darkened as understanding washed over her. "Hurry up then." She tugged at Florrie, almost pulling her over.

They laughed and splashed their way to the water's edge, breaking apart to snatch up their towels and other belongings and hurry back to the car.

Florrie paused with her fingers grasping the handle. "We'd better dry off before we get in."

"Who cares?" She tossed her beach bag in the back. "Put your towel on the seat. I'll get it valeted before we leave for

England. Here let me help you."

Florrie was about to say she could manage, when Diana flicked the towel out so it covered the passenger seat, and then she helped Florrie to settle in.

Diana leaned close, her breath warm against Florrie's cooling skin, and brushed a light kiss by her ear. "I love you too."

Florrie's heart squeezed a little, and blood rushed in her ears in an exhilarating swoosh of joy. "Thank you," she whispered as Diana closed the car door with a soft protective click.

Diana smiled through the window, the first broad, radiant smile Florrie had seen from her since they were younger. Her heart melted. This felt right and certain, and everything fell into place. Diana raced the car back to the villa, but Florrie didn't care. She laughed as Diana swung the car around the hairpin bends until they reached the cliff top. Diana pulled the car into the grounds but didn't park it in its allotted spot by the wall. The engine had hardly turned off before she was out of the car and opening Florrie's door.

Florrie chuckled. "Abandoning the car like this... You must be in a hurry."

"I am."

Still laughing, she tugged Florrie upstairs, urgency and joy hurrying them along to the bedroom. The afternoon sunlight streamed through the slits of the shutters, creating a pattern of bright stripes on the tiled floor and the edge of the bed. The inner curtains flapped in the welcome breeze, stirring the oppressive mugginess.

There was no hesitation and no words in their meeting of minds, of lips, of bodies. The charged silence spilled into the frantic heat and certainty of remembered exploration, the promise of more to come.

Diana pulled out of the kiss and rested her forehead against Florrie's. "You're beautiful." She hummed as she slipped down the straps of Florrie's swimming costume and stroked her nipples over the fabric. "May I take this off?"

"Of course," Florrie said, even though it was too late to pull her tummy in without being too obvious. "I don't want you to be disappointed that my body isn't as you remember it."

Diana reached for Florrie's hand, her thumb brushing softly across the back of it. "Neither of us have the bodies of thirty-somethings anymore, but does that matter? I could focus on how much weight I've lost, the sagginess of my skin and my stretch marks, but I don't. I won't." She brought Florrie's hand to her lips and kissed it chastely, their ardour slowed as they reconnected on a deeper level. "Because I'm here, I'm alive and I'm with you, the woman I love, the woman who inspires me and who I ache to build a life with."

Her eyes searched Florrie's face. "I don't care about a few extra pounds. What matters is that we reconnect and express our love. I do care that you don't feel pressurised and that you're comfortable and feel safe." Diana swallowed hard, her fingers tightening around Florrie's. "If you need more time, I'll wait. God knows I've waited nearly a quarter of a century to be with you, in front of you, like this. On the edge of *certainty*. Because I am certain. I want to be with you for as long as you'll have me " Diana grinned. "Besides, without my glasses I can't see any lines you're so worried about. They're just the signs of a life lived. Now. The shower cubicle is too small for both of us, so I'll let you go first."

Florrie laughed as she removed her swimming costume, ignoring the colour creeping up her neck at being so exposed. She accepted the towel Diana held out to wrap herself in. "Thank you for saying that."

Diana flicked Florrie's behind with her towel. "Hurry up."

"Bossy!" Florrie laughed and entered the cubicle in the en suite bathroom. She quickly showered off, enjoying the warmth of the clean water washing away the salt and sand. When she exited, she snatched up the towel to cover herself. Diana was rinsing and hanging up both of their costumes. She was deliciously naked and totally at ease in her own skin. She was more angular around her shoulders, softer around her hips and belly, equally as alluring, and she moved with the same natural grace. Florrie's skin hummed with anticipation. To see Diana, so exposed and real, caught her breath. "Stunning," she whispered as she was drawn towards her.

Diana cupped Florrie's face in her hand. "Thank you. And so are you. Oh, dearest heart, it's such a joy to be with you again." She leaned forward, her lips brushing against Florrie's neck, stirring the fine hairs on her skin. "I can't wait to feel you under my fingertips, to taste your breath on mine."

Florrie responded in a way she hadn't for years. Warmth uncurled low in her belly. She wanted to reclaim Diana's body, to reacquaint herself, map her skin to rediscover the familiar and the new. "Thank you. Now hurry up before the water and our ardour goes cold."

"It won't, trust me." Diana feathered a kiss near Florrie's ear, a vow of more, before disappearing into the shower cubicle.

Florrie stood in the silence of the room, shivering slightly beneath her towel but not from cold. Anticipation and desire coursed through her, electric and alive, wakening all her senses. She dried off while Diana showered, the water loud and steam filling the cubicle and the bathroom. Diana's frosted form danced in silhouette through the shower screen as she washed her hair, and Florrie watched, completely mesmerised.

Finally, Diana stepped out of the cubicle, her hair wrapped in a towel, and another towel wrapped loosely around her shoulders.

Florrie inhaled deeply. "Would you like me to dry you off?"

"I'll soon dry off, or get wet again." Diana stretched, and the towel slipped from her shoulders, revealing her long, lean body.

She enveloped Florrie in her arms. The faint moisture clinging to her skin made their embrace feel charged and intimate. Florrie smoothed her fingers across Diana's beloved shoulders and down the curve to her small breasts. Tweaking them with her finger and thumb caused Diana to squirm and emit a low moan. Their breathing quickened, falling into a matching rhythm, like they always had.

The absent years melted with the warmth of touch, the scent of arousal, and the desire thrumming in every nerve. Time collapsed into a tendril of connection, strong and pulsing threading through the passage of years. She traced the silver stripes on Diana's stomach, reverently, marvelling at what the human body could endure.

Diana flinched. "I'm also not the same as I was. My scars—"

"Are the signs of a miracle."

Diana chuckled lightly. "It didn't feel like a miracle. It was excruciating and exhausting. They thought one of us might die, and Anthony was clear who he wanted saving."

Florrie took a sharp intake of breath and stilled her fingers. She stepped away, needing to see Diana's face. "Then the miracle was that you both survived."

Diana rubbed her hair with the small towel and shook it out. Damp strands settled loosely around her face. "Physically, yes, but emotionally, I was wrecked. Overwrought."

Florrie touched Diana's skin softly. "I read that happens for quite a few women. They can't cope afterwards."

Diana tossed the towel onto a chair, and it slipped onto the floor with a thud. "I had *always* coped. I'd always been in control—of my life, my business, my writing. Until the damned stock market crash." Her shoulders sagged, her eyes shining with a mix of anger and sorrow. "I lost everything: not only my money, but also my freedom and sense of self." Her gaze locked onto Florrie's, and she reached out. "And you. I look back at those few golden, jubilant years shoe-horned between the bleakness and misery of two wars. We thought they'd never end."

Diana sank onto the bed, pulling Florrie with her. She lay down, and Florrie curled up against her.

Diana pressed Florrie's head close against her chest. "I know you don't approve of my parenting of Edward, and I've failed him. But I'm trying to make amends, even if it's far too late."

Florrie was about to protest, but Diana touched her finger to Florrie's lips.

"When Edward was born, they whisked him away and only brought him to me to feed. But I was too distressed, and exhausted, and overwhelmed, so I couldn't produce the milk. I was a failure there too." Diana's breath hitched. "And Edward cried constantly in my presence. No, that's too benign. He screamed. Every time. It's hard to love someone who screams when they see you...even a baby."

Florrie curled her fingers around Diana's, trying to convey her empathy.

Diana exhaled noisily and cleared her throat. "Anthony arranged for a wet nurse. Edward thrived and put on weight. I told myself that was what mattered, that was for the best."

She spoke so quietly now that Florrie had to strain to catch all her words.

"I bled so much, they advised me not to have another child. And it was tolerable, I suppose, because Anthony didn't want to touch me again."

The unassuaged pain seemed to leach out of Diana, the air becoming thick with regret and sorrow. Florrie squeezed their entwined hands to bring Diana back to now, when she was safe, where time separated her from the trauma. She pulled her head back to study Diana's face. "Who looked after you in all of this?"

Diana raised an eyebrow as if Florrie was being stupid. She swallowed visibly. "No one."

All arousal had fled, replaced by a fog of heaviness settling around them, tinged with guilt and sorrow. "No wonder you struggled with melancholy," Florrie whispered, her fingers tightly laced with Diana's. "I should've been there for you, looked after you."

Diana turned her head, the pillow rustling below her. "Even

after I broke your heart?"

"You did it to save the company and your employees. I should've been able to step over my pain and see yours."

Diana let out a breath seeming to contain the weight of years. "That isn't how pain and grief work. There is no should or what if; that brings madness and despair, as I know. But the real miracle is we found each other now, and we're here with all our scars, the signs of a life lived, decisions made and regretted, and knowing we can make a different choice. I choose you."

Florrie released Diana's hand and snuggled closer, revelling in the warmth of her body against her own. "You always could woo me with your words."

"That's where I've been going wrong. Instead of trying to romance you with luxurious train rides and trips to Paris and Antibes, I should have read my latest manuscript to you. I should've shared the emotions dripping onto the page, all the longing, and the lost time, and regretting how I hurt you."

"And those scars are who we are," Florrie said, "and they're just as beautiful as the silver lines on your stomach." She kissed the scars with reverence and inhaled the heady fragrance of Diana's arousal, the scent so familiar and intoxicating, it overwhelmed her senses. They were here; they were together in raw, open intimacy.

Her desire quickened, and—oh, the surprise and exhilaration— she was wet, where previously she'd been a desert. Their breaths came faster, their hearts pulsing hard in harmony. Her blood rushed in her brain, and she trailed her fingers over Diana's body, familiar but different, down to the thinning curls. Diana's writhing was less frantic now, but the insistent desire urged her on, tracing her tongue down to Diana's core, delving into the intimate folds, she slipped in slick and seductive juices. She paused to look up. "I thought you said you'd need lubrication?"

Diana raised her head and stared at her with unfocused eyes. "I may later but I— Oh, yes...there."

That Florrie could render this intelligent woman so inarticulate swelled her heart. With each touch, and lick, and suck, she shifted back in time to passion, overwhelming desire, and the open vulnerability of trust. All the years slipped away as they merged into a mess of arms, and legs, and all-encompassing sensuality. The world narrowed to this moment, their two bodies and souls entwined in a dance of rediscovery.

Diana's legs clamped around Florrie's head, sweaty and still strong. The taste of her, the firmness of her clitoris as Florrie licked and sucked had her on the edge. *Focus.*

"Inside, please."

Diana's tone, so raw and vulnerable, pulled at Florrie's sensibilities, causing her blood to race, and her heart swooped as her body responded. Almost without thought, she slipped her fingers inside Diana, but she wouldn't be able to sustain the rhythm for long without her fingers seizing up. She glanced at Diana lost in the sensation. Her eyes were closed, almost in prayer, her lips moving, as she matched Florrie's thrusts with her hips, stroke for stroke.

They had always been like this, completely in sync. It all came back so easily, until the dull ache in her hand began to scream, and her back spasmed. "Sweetheart, I'm so sorry I need to stop and regroup. Sorry to leave you dangling." Her cheeks, neck, and chest burned, but she couldn't hide it in her naked state.

Diana's eyes flew open, her pupils still huge, leaving only a ring of brown. It seemed to take a second for her conscious brain to reassert itself, and she smiled. At least she didn't look disappointed.

"Dearest heart, are you uncomfortable?" Diana asked quietly. "Don't worry, we've all had a lost climax. It's precisely to assist us in this that I had Oscar send me the package from Paris." She slipped off the bed and crossed to the dressing table.

The glistening of her arousal in her curls was so evident. Florrie squeezed her own legs together as the warm trickle of desire painted her thighs. She'd forgotten how visceral everything was, but the thick scent of sex was an instant reminder. Diana returned with the parcel, untied string already dangling, and the brown paper torn. She placed the parcel on the bedside table then removed a tissued object and unpeeled the paper, revealing a smooth wooden object about eight inches long, tapered at the top.

"Let me introduce you to Jill Doe the dildo."

Florrie laughed.

Diana swung it like she was a conductor with a baton. "The ancient Egyptians used these, and whaler's wives called them *he's-at-home* for when their husbands were away for months. Even Shakespeare alludes to them using double entendre to describe the rascal Autolycus in *The Winter's Tale* with his delicate burdens of dildos and fadings. I understand now some are made of Bakelite—"

"Only you could sound like you were giving a lecture about the subject." Florrie giggled. "Please tell me you didn't go to a lecture on this."

Diana raised her eyebrow. "In England? They hardly acknowledge women can have sex beyond reproduction, so no. But we did have some interesting discussions at our reading group."

"What sort of reading group did you go to?"

"An enlightened one."

They both laughed, and the tension eased. The mortification coursing through Florrie abated to a prickle of mild embarrassment and disappointment at having to stop. "We don't have that at the WI."

"And yet you sing 'Jerusalem.' You do know the second verse is about sensual love, don't you? Don't look so shocked, dearest heart. It's true. *Bring me my arrows of desire*. How else can that be interpreted?"

Florrie lay back onto the bed and laughed so hard she thought she might wet herself. "All those prudish, self-opinionated, superior women."

Diana brandished the dildo. "Bring me my bow of burning gold."

Florrie laughed again. "God, I hope it doesn't burn. I don't want to hurt you."

Diana stretched back to the parcel and retrieved a humble jar of Vaseline. "Which is why we have this. Of course, the ancient Greeks used olive oil, thinking it might be a contraceptive. It wasn't. But they found it aided pleasure, and, unlike the English, they believed in pleasure."

As she'd talked, Diana had unscrewed the cap off the petroleum jelly and used it to coat the dildo. Florrie smiled. Diana was so astute to distract her with intellectual rambling. It was adorable. *She* was adorable. The rush of warmth seeped over her, engulfing her. "Thank you," she said before she could stop herself. "You've gone to all this trouble to make this easier for me—"

"Trust me, it's entirely selfish. Will you help?"

Diana proffered the jar, and Florrie sat up and scooped up some of the cool, thick gel and slathered it over the dildo.

Diana's hand, now slick with jelly, slipped over Florrie's. "I meant, will you help cover me." She lay down and spread her legs.

"Oh." Florrie's clitoris responded with a hard pulse. She kneeled beside Diana on the bed. The laughter had gone, and Diana's eyes darkened as Florrie placed her fingers on Diana's centre and massaged the Vaseline over her clitoris and lower, slick and seeking. All the time, Florrie held Diana's gaze, checking what she wanted.

Diana groaned and closed her eyes, lifting her hips to meet Florrie's fingers. "Please, use this. Gently, at first."

Florrie grasped the slippery dildo by the hilt and circled the tip at Diana's entrance. Diana placed her hand over Florrie's and guided her in. She took a sharp intake of breath before relaxing and pushing on Florrie's hand, slowly taking in more.

"Oh, yes. Faster."

Florrie obeyed, watching Diana the whole time. She was so open and vulnerable, Florrie's heart expanded with love that she got to witness this, and better yet, be the cause of it.

Diana gasped and bucked. "More," she whispered, pleading and commanding at the same time.

Florrie obliged, then switched hands to ease her ache. Diana hardly seemed to notice and continued to writhe, breathing faster and more shallowly. Just when Florrie thought she would have to change hands again, she brushed her other thumb over Diana's clitoris. A sharp cry escaped Diana; raw, beautiful, and familiar. A shudder rippled through her body, and her eyelids fluttered as her whole body stiffened. Florrie eased her over the peaks of her climax, devoted in offering all the love and care she could give.

Diana took minutes to ride her release before the shuddering stopped. Her eyes opened, and she stared at Florrie. "Dear God, I don't know what to say. That was phenomenal. Thank you."

"I don't think I've ever seen you like this. Not even when we were young."

"No. That was spectacular." She winced. "But I'm going to have to take it out now."

Florrie released her hold, and Diana slipped the dildo from between her legs, still glistening with Vaseline and Diana's arousal.

"Now, would you like me to wash this first, or..."

She waved the wand at Florrie, making contact with her thighs. It was sticky and still warm from being inside Diana. Florrie rolled onto her back, tugging at Diana. "*Or* is good."

Diana laughed and with her spare hand, took some Vaseline from the jar and smeared a little at the top of Florrie's thighs. Florrie rocked her head back and pushed her hips upwards to meet Diana's fingers, so cool against her hot and swollen skin. She hardly noticed as Diana slipped inside, and thrust harder. "Please, I'd like to try with…"

"Are you sure?" Diana quirked her eyebrow. "There's no pressure."

"Yes, I'm certain. I'm so aroused; it's like twenty years of pent-up tension is screaming at me."

"Okay, but if anything is painful or uncomfortable, tell me, and I'll stop."

"Sure." Florrie gasped as the dildo rubbed against her entrance. "Please." But instead of complying with her begging, Diana circled her clitoris with her other thumb. Florrie's nerve ends hummed as Diana seemed to be everywhere at once. "Please, don't tease. It's been too long. Oh…" She widened her eyes as Diana guided the thick object inside, filling her but not uncomfortably so. Her muscles contracted and pulsed. She took a steadying breath. "More. Oh, that's… I…"

"Good?"

"Very. And different." With each thrust, Florrie welcomed it in, welcomed Diana into the core of her being. It wasn't just physical; it was deeper, older, a coming home to her true, whole self. "Yes. Oh, God, yes. That's…" Her voice caught. "I'm coming."

The tension built and broke too quick, too sharp, like a wave cresting before she was ready, engulfing her. A roiling surge of ecstasy bubbled up, pulling her under before cascading her into release. She laughed and laughed as joy broke from somewhere wild and wanton, until unbidden tears streamed down her face, hot and salty.

"Sweetheart, did I hurt you?" Diana asked, her eyes wide.

"No, no. I'm so happy," Florrie said, her voice thick and raspy. She met Diana's gaze, which was full of concern as she searched Florrie's face. "But I'm also sad for all the lost years." She wiped at her cheeks. They were probably blotchy and swollen now, but it was too late to worry about how she looked. "Thank you. I never thought I'd do this again, and certainly not with you."

Diana said nothing as she gently extracted the toy and snuggled closer. The way Diana held Florrie now was tender and protective, as if she didn't want to let Florrie go. And Florrie loved it.

"Rather than regret the unwritten pages, we should celebrate that we get to write our story from here."

Florrie nodded. Diana was correct, of course. As she usually was. "Mm, I could do that again. Somehow I've found an energy I didn't know I had."

Diana kissed her forehead, now hot and damp. "We have all afternoon and evening," she murmured, her lips vibrating warm against Florrie's skin.

Later that evening, they watched the sun go down over the softly lapping sea, and the clouds shifted from orange and pink tinged to indigo, then black. Although it was still mild, Florrie wrapped a cardigan around herself against the breeze and inhaled her surroundings.

With old age came the gift of silence, to have the time to listen to the waves and the cicadas, to not make idle chatter for the sake of stuffing gaps in the conversation. She watched and smiled as Diana traced out words in neat script into a leather notebook. Florrie wanted to tell her how beautiful she looked, but she didn't want to break the spell. Finally, Diana closed the notebook with a snap and looked up.

"It's wonderful to see you writing again," Florrie said, her voice tinged with awe.

Diana reached over and interlaced her fingers with Florrie. "It's wonderful to feel inspired again. It's only an idea now, which I hope to expand and grow into a full novel. I think I'll call it *Starfish on the Shore.*"

She paused and fixed Florrie with her intense gaze. "The trust you placed in me when you floated, when we were intimate... You were so vulnerable, and I feel honoured. Thank you."

Gone was the haughty imperiousness and the intellectual disdain wrapped in generations of superiority. What remained were two late-middle-aged women, weathered by time and sorrow, caught up with each other and completely in love.

Diana shuffled in her seat. "I'd like to share my life with you." She cleared her throat and inhaled sharply. "I've never said it before. Never really meant it." She grasped Florrie's hand and held it like she needed to anchor herself. "I love you. If that means we live in your place in Cambridge, or the cottage in Sussex, or here, it matters not. I don't care where we are as long as we're together. You nurture me like no one else ever has." Diana frowned. "Why aren't you saying anything? Have I misjudged this completely?"

Florrie laughed. "I couldn't get a word in edgeways. I love you too. I always have." She squeezed Diana's hand. "But as you may have gathered, I'm not as flexible as I was before. Are you sure you want to be saddled with me, when I'm so old before my time?"

Diana waved her hand dismissively, a gesture that had once been so familiar. "Maybe if we came here during the winter months, it would be less painful for you than England. Or we could go to southern Spain. I've always fancied going to Granada. Or we could tour Italy by car," she said and grinned. "And I promise I'll drive like a snail, so you don't have hysterics next to me. Please say yes."

Florrie laughed like she was young again, and as gracefully as she could, she leaned towards Diana. "Yes. A thousand times, yes." Then she kissed Diana. She didn't care if Amelie was watching, or if Edward disapproved, or if Cam didn't like the change. She was happy, she was living, and she was in love.

She kissed Diana like it was the first time, with a certainty it wouldn't be the last.

CHAPTER FOURTEEN

Cambridge, 1950

IT SEEMED FITTING THEY'D chosen to meet up in the same Cambridge tearooms where Diana had caused a seismic shift in Florrie's life. Today, they sat inside, while a drizzle formed snail trails of water down the tiny diamond-shaped windowpanes. The interior was gloomy, partially illuminated with dim electric bulbs and half obscured by tasselled cloth lampshades. Florrie hoped the dreariness wasn't a portent.

The bell tinkled as someone entered. She looked up, but it wasn't them. They were late, and Florrie was trying not to make it significant. Her tea was going cold, and doubts heaped up like the leaves at the bottom of her cup. Had Diana changed her mind now they were back home? Or had Edward reacted badly to the news that his mother was with another woman?

Florrie turned her napkin over and over until it was creased beyond recognition. Gloria reached across the table and stilled Florrie's hand.

"Don't worry, Aunty, if Edward's obnoxious, we'll set him right. I don't care what title he has."

Florrie lowered her shoulders a fraction. No matter what happened she had their support. "Thanks, Gloria."

Cam nodded in agreement, but a flicker of doubt crossed her eyes, and her fidgeting leg indicated something was on her mind. Florrie nodded at Cam to speak.

"I only want you to be looked after properly," Cam said. "Are you sure you'll be all right living with Diana? Will she treat you well? Didn't you say she left you a long time ago? What if she does the same again?"

Florrie patted Cam's arm. "You're such a kind soul. I understand your doubt and concern. Initially, I wasn't sure myself, but the years have mellowed her. She's always been kind, in a rather haughty way, but when we were in France, she was gentle and attentive too." She smiled and squeezed Cam's arm. "If we move, I'll miss you and how wonderful you've always been to me. I'll miss my morning cup of tea in bed, but there would be advantages for you too; you won't have to put up with me drinking it out of the saucer."

"I'll miss you, and I don't know if she'll care for you, like we do."

Gloria put her cup down with a flourish. "What we're trying to say is that we want you to be happy, but if it doesn't work out, you'll always have a home with us."

Thank heavens for Gloria. Without her being beside Cam, Florrie would never have contemplated uprooting her life. "Thank you, and for being so supportive. I couldn't do this without you."

Cam frowned. "You've always done everything for me. How could we be anything else?"

Florrie's heart expanded with Cam's simple statement as absolute truth. "Nevertheless, I'm grateful."

"It's grand to see the happiness on your face. Nay, don't deny it, Aunty, you've gone quite pink now."

"Yes, thank you, Gloria, I know." But she couldn't be cross in the face of such genuine warmth and love. She poured another cup of tea to cover her embarrassment and was delighted she didn't spill any.

Gloria's expression became serious. "We don't mind what you decide to do, although obviously we'd prefer to have you in Cambridge."

"Are you sure you want to cause this upheaval in your life?" Cam asked.

Florrie was unsure whether the question was rooted in Cam's

own anxiety about change rather than concern for her aunt.

Gloria squeezed Cam's hand. "Whatever you do, we'll be fine. I promise I'll care for Cam as she cares for us. Now's your time to shine and enjoy life instead of caring for others."

"I'll miss you both if we do move to Sussex or France. I'll miss all your kindness and how you've kept me company all these years."

"We'd prefer you to stay in Cambridge," Cam said.

Gloria interlocked her fingers with Cam's and began stroking her knuckles. Florrie's heart ached. She hated to be the cause of such distress, however well she was trying to hide it. "I understand, but the house is a bit small for Diana, and she'd have nowhere to write." It was difficult to imagine Diana in her little cottage or caring for the chickens; she was always so much larger than life, more exotic than the pall of domesticity, someone more suited to grand French villas than tiny cottages.

And yet the change in Diana *was* undeniable. She'd lost her haunted look, and the tension around her mouth had dissolved. She'd softened with age and settled into her old persona, but the edge of superiority had gone, leaving a woman truly herself: intelligent and curious, present and kind.

Florrie churned the napkin over in her hands again. Diana had said she didn't mind where they lived, but would she grow restless? Would she begrudge the lack of space for walls and walls of books, and no separate room for her to write? Florrie wanted to coax that creativity to spark and for words to settle on the page, especially as Diana was now writing again. She sighed. "I think we'll flit between different houses, but we'll certainly spend time here with you. We'd love it if you came to Sussex or France too." Life was such a tightrope between competing needs. She didn't want to desert Cam, who was doing what she could to remain stoic and supportive, but her disquiet was telegraphed by her knee jiggling and the tapping of her finger and thumb.

The bell dinged again, announcing a new arrival, and Florrie's heart did a little skip as Diana swept in, with a scowling young man in her shadow. Edward was like a younger version of Anthony, all chinless arrogance, but his clothes looked too big for his thin frame. Judging by his expression, Diana's conversation with him had not gone well. Diana flashed Florrie a resigned smile that broke her heart. She'd been praying it would all go smoothly.

Florrie rose, with Cam's assistance, to greet Edward, determined to give him a warm welcome. Diana brushed her hand against Florrie's as she walked past, and Florrie gave it a quick squeeze.

"I'll order another pot of tea," Cam said. "We probably have enough cake for all of us."

She shot off before anyone could contradict her, and Diana made introductions.

Florrie smiled at Edward. "How do you do? So pleased to meet you. I'm sure you've been told you look exactly like your father."

His scowl deepened. *Oh dear.* This must be hard for him. What must he be thinking? Whatever it was, it wasn't bringing him joy. He looked like he needed a big hug, but he'd probably hate that.

On her way back from speaking to the waitress, Cam nabbed a couple of chairs from nearby and placed them around their table. Diana took the seat next to Florrie, and Edward sat between Diana and Gloria. She gave him a broad welcoming smile, and his frown lightened at her attention. He clearly didn't have a clue he was barking up the wrong tree as he ignored everyone else and focused on Gloria. Surely Diana would have told him about Cam and Gloria, but perhaps the opportunity never arose.

He smoothed down his hair. "How do you do? I understand you graduated recently?"

"Aye. I did that, and I've joined the mathematics faculty with Cam."

The look Gloria endowed on Cam was so warm and adoring, their connection was obvious to anyone paying attention. But Edward appeared to only pay attention to the person who interested him.

He flicked a glance in Cam's direction before returning his attention to Gloria. "I like a bright girl but give me a pretty girl anytime."

Cam gripped her menu so tightly that the paper scrunched up.

"Edward, for heaven's sake." Diana's tone was sharp and sliced through the tension. "Open your eyes. I wanted to introduce you to Florence and her family, not for you to make a fool of yourself. I want you to get to know them all if we're all going to be in Cambridge for at least part of the year."

The lightness that had briefly flickered across his face vanished, and the scowl returned like a light bulb had been switched on.

Cam, still and silent, was now the colour of beetroot. Beside her, Gloria gently caressed the back of her hand, seemingly in a gesture of comfort and reassurance.

Diana's mouth tightened into a thin line, and a tense silence hung between them. "I didn't bring you up to be rude and have a closed mind—"

"You didn't bring me up at all," Edward said and scoffed. "You left me in the care of a string of batty nannies before packing me out of sight at boarding school."

Under the table, Florrie gently stroked Diana's hand, offering what comfort and support she could. Diana closed her eyes. Florrie shuddered at the interaction between mother and son. Children always knew how to strike the deepest, and Edward seemed to excel in that skill. Yet the tugging at his collar hinted that the bravado of his response merely hid a great deal of hurt and discomfort.

There was a tremor in Diana's fingers, which revealed her

anguish more than words could. If this strained interaction was them being civil to each other, Florrie hated to think how their relationship must have been beforehand.

Surprisingly, Cam cleared her throat. "My parents wanted to send me to boarding school too, but Aunty Florrie saved me and looked after me. I'm very grateful for everything she's done. Thank you." She turned, meeting Florrie's gaze with a small, sincere smile.

Perhaps Oscar had been right when he said that Cam might be the way to get through to Edward.

Florrie returned her smile. "I wouldn't have had it any other way, Cam."

The waitress laid down the teapot and extra cups on the table with a clatter, then fled. She could probably pick up on the tension, taut like a wire about to snap. Florrie poured out a cup each for Diana and Edward, even though her hand shook a little with the effort. She hoped the familiar ritual might ease the atmosphere. "Milk? Two sugars?" she asked, guessing at Edward's preferences.

He nodded and mirrored his mother's thin-lined lips. Perhaps he was Diana's son after all. He looked so young at nineteen, with clothes that swamped him and an attitude he'd adopted that didn't seem to fit him either. He'd lost his father at an early age, so it was no wonder he was angry and upset, and all of this must've come as a shock to him.

Florrie gave him a small smile and handed over his cup and saucer. "Edward, dear, we live just outside Cambridge, and we'd love you to come over for tea and cake. I'm sure you'd love home-made cake made with real eggs. Do you play chess? Or sing and play a musical instrument?"

For a second, confusion washed over his features, like he was uncertain why he'd been invited to a stranger's house. But at the mention of cake, his eyes had lit up, and there was the faintest twitch of his lips.

"Yes," he said, not specifying which question he was answering.

"Oh, good. Both Cam and Gloria are brilliant at chess. Perhaps you could have a little tournament. And they both sing, and Cam plays the cello and piano. Do you play an instrument?"

He nodded. "The violin."

Florrie clapped her hands together, desperately trying to get him to release his stiff stance. "Perfect. There are a number of pieces you can play with the violin and cello. Maybe you could do a concert like they did in the war. What's your favourite cake?"

"Coffee," he said, still not looking her in the eye.

"I can easily rustle you up a camp coffee cake," Florrie said.

He slammed his hand down on the table, making them all jump and the teacups rattle in the saucers. "Why are you doing this? Is it true about you and my mother?"

He turned bright red, and Florrie hoped she didn't mirror his colouring. She glanced at Diana, who gave the slightest of nods. Her expression was closed off, as though she was struggling with this conversation.

"If you're asking if we're together, then yes, we are. Part of the reason we wanted to get together with you all is that you're the people we love most in the world, and we want you to get along—"

"And what do you think?" Edward turned to Gloria and Cam, his nostrils flaring.

Gloria placed her hand on Cam's arm. "We think it's grand. We want Aunty Florrie and your mother to be very happy together."

"Are you happy with this?" He waved at Florrie and Diana as though they were weeds to be rooted out.

Gloria grinned. "It would be a bit hypocritical if we weren't." She tangled her fingers with Cam's, and they shared a smile.

Edward's eyes widened. "You're... Oh, Jesus!"

Diana snapped her handbag shut. "Edward Packard Smith,

you're no better than some Victorian albatross. Lord knows what poisonous attitudes they fed you in that very expensive school. What would Uncle Oscar say? Cambridge is stuffed with men of a certain persuasion." She glanced around, but her volume was far beyond a discreet whisper.

He sneered and looked down. "Men, yes, but women? You?"

"You have truly absorbed some of your father's worst attitudes. This rudeness stops now."

"Or what? It isn't like you can cut off my allowance."

"And where do you think most of your inheritance came from? From the sales of avant garde books, challenging books, from books written by all sorts of authors including gay men and lesbians." Diana paused as people on the adjoining tables stared at her. She smiled and waved her hand, like the king waving to his subjects.

Gloria giggled, which set off Cam, and Florrie fought to control her snigger while she carefully avoided Gloria's eye.

"Well, that's put the cat among the pigeons." Gloria exhaled through a wheezing laugh and turned to Edward. She exhaled slowly. "It seems to me, Edward, that you have a choice. Either you accept your mother and Aunty Florrie, and you'll be welcomed into our quirky little family, or you'll lose your family entirely. Both Cam and I have been ostracised from our closest family, and trust me, it isn't pleasant. You also have another connection with Cam."

Edward frowned. "What?"

"Your uncle Oscar was Cam's tutor for many years."

He cocked his head on one side, then realisation seemed to dawn as his eyes widened. "You're *that* Cam? His favourite pupil? I always thought it was short for Cameron."

Cam shrugged. "How is he? I haven't heard much from him since Aunty and your mother visited him in Paris."

He glanced down and traced his fingers along the rim of his cup. "I think he's okay."

He looked so unsure of himself, like a boy trying to find his place in the world, heavy with expectations of who he should be and how he should behave. But he needed to know he was safe to explore his identity and role within their little family. Florrie smiled and offered him another slice of cake. He accepted readily and devoured half of it with one large bite.

"We seem to have got off on the wrong foot," Florrie said. "I'm sure it's all a bit of a shock, and maybe we should have arranged to meet at our house rather than in public. But we thought you might find this easier. How about you think about everything and our offer for tea, cake, and chess is always open. We'd love to get to know you better."

He swallowed the remainder of his slice and wiped his mouth with his napkin. "What about the music?"

"That too. Now, we said we'd talk about our living arrangements." Florrie glanced over at Diana. "We plan to split our time between Cambridge and Sussex, giving us all some time together, and apart, and to give Diana space to write when she needs it. Edward, you're very welcome to come over to our home whenever you want and during holidays. All I ask is that you respect everyone who lives there, including our chickens."

He nodded and tugged at his collar. "I'll think about it."

Florrie tried to catch his eye. "Good. You're a very fortunate young man, yet you don't seem to appreciate it." She gestured toward Cam and Gloria. "Here are two wonderful women who've both faced prejudice and been ostracised by their family, yet they've gone on to thrive. You have material wealth and the kind of privilege most would kill for. You have a mother who loves you and an open invitation to be part of a family. I hope you'll do more than consider it. Come for tea and get to know us." She flicked an anxious look at Diana, wondering if she'd gone too far. Diana stared at her son with glassy eyes, the fast blinking indicating how upset she was. Florrie pressed her knee against Diana's, desperately trying to convey her sympathy.

Edward's bravado slipped away, and he looked like a little boy whose boat was facing directly into wind, his uncertainty flapping around him like an untethered sail. "Am I being an ass?" he asked.

"Yes." The chorus was loud and caused other patrons to look over.

"Well," Florrie said, wanting to hug him, "perhaps just misguided. Your mother loves you, and we've become a little family of happy misfits. You're welcome to our home on a visit or to live if you'd prefer. Please don't tell me you bounce around in your Warwickshire Hall on your own in the holidays?"

He straightened as if to demonstrate he was an adult. "No, I take friends there, or I go to theirs when I'm home from Cambridge. Last holidays, I stayed in halls."

Diana stiffened beside Florrie, who found her hand below the table and linked fingers. "You were welcome to come to Mead House."

"Which is boring. All you did was hole yourself up in your Wendy house and pretend you were writing. At least in halls, I saw friends, and there were activities going on." He leaned forward again, the situation on the tip of escalating again.

Florrie cleared her throat. "You could stay at our home—"

"Mother said it was small."

Now it was Diana's turn to colour pink. "I only meant it was more modest than you're used to."

Florrie squeezed her hand to reassure her she wasn't offended. Prickly youngsters didn't faze her, but she hated to see all the other women around the table, her family she loved, upset or withdrawn, so she wouldn't let him get under her skin. "We only have three bedrooms, it's true, and the third bedroom is used as Cam's boxing gym."

His eyes went wide. "You box?"

Cam nodded.

"I've always wanted to learn," he said.

Go on. Say you'll help him. We need to give and take a little in this standoff.

Cam pinched the crease on her trousers then laid her hands flat out beside her plate. "I've been sitting here thinking about how we can rearrange the house to accommodate everyone's needs. If I build another shed in the garden, like our hen house but away from the chucks, I could split it in two. One side could be my gym, as long as I reinforce it for the punch bag, and the other side could be a writing studio for Diana, which would leave the third bedroom for Edward, if he wants it."

"Grand idea, Cam, although I think Diana would struggle to concentrate if you're pounding away on the bag."

Gloria had been surprisingly quiet during the conversation, but perhaps she didn't want to get involved in a family dispute. She'd had enough of her own in the past.

"We can work around each other," Cam said. "I'm happy to work out early in the morning before everyone gets up if that suits Diana best."

Florrie's heart expanded with love and pride that Cam had come up with a solution and embraced the change. She mouthed her thanks, and Cam flashed her a rare, genuine smile.

Diana placed her hand over her heart. "I'm sure we can make something work. Thank you, Cam, for seeing possibilities and being willing to make it happen."

Diana trembled beside Florrie, whether from relief or gratitude or simply coming out of her torpor, Florrie was unsure. Perhaps it was all three. Sensing the moment had shifted, it seemed like time to quit while they'd made some progress, however fragile. Florrie smiled at Edward. "Think about it. Now, do you want them to box up the rest of the cake to take home?"

The gleam in his eye was enough of an answer, so Cam rose to speak to the waitress.

Within minutes, they'd paid the bill, said goodbye to Edward, and set a firm date for Cam to start teaching him how to box.

Diana drove them home, and they settled for a cup of tea rather than another heavy meal, as they were all full from earlier. The evening unfolded with no reference to the confrontation with Edward, and Florrie wondered if Diana was going to gloss over it completely. It was a novelty to have Diana sitting in her home—soon to be their home—because parts of her life had crashed together and hadn't quite melded into place. Cam and Gloria sang and filled the room with their wonderful, blended harmonies, which always made the hairs on the back of Florrie's neck rise.

Diana threaded her fingers through Florrie's, only untangling to clap politely when Gloria and Cam had finished a piece. They'd both been so busy recently that they'd hardly had time to practice, but it wasn't obvious from the way they sang, which had the synchrony of a well-choreographed dance. They even breathed in perfect unison.

It wasn't until they retired to Florrie's room for the night that Diana sagged onto the bed, her head in her hands. "I've never been so ashamed of him. I shouldn't feel that way about my own son, and you were all so welcoming and accommodating. It put me to shame. I was beyond touched at Cam's offer to build a writing room for me."

Florrie sat beside Diana and put her arm around her. "Let's see how it goes. He may well come around for tea, and Cam's promised to teach him how to box. I'm sure Gloria will charm him into submission, and my cakes always seem to go down a treat. Possibly too well." She jiggled a little excess flesh. It normally made Diana smile, but she didn't even raise her head.

"Did I make him like he is?" Diana asked. "Underneath it all, he's a good boy—young man, I should say—but he seemed to be his worst self today. Is that my doing? "

"Give him time. He was upset and shocked by our news. We'll work on him. I do think he'll come around when he realises we don't bite. Well, you do when you're aroused." Florrie grinned to release the tension, and Diana gave her a wan smile.

"You enjoy it."

"I do."

Diana's smile faded. "You've all been so wonderful. I don't deserve this."

"Of course you do."

Diana shook her head. "He basically told me I was a terrible mother, and he's right; I wasn't there for him. I'm not surprised he's like he is. He was rude and arrogant."

Florrie stroked Diana's back. "He's hurt and upset. We can't change the past, but we can forge a new relationship. Learning how to box will probably help him; it certainly helped Cam when she wasn't much younger than he is now. Does he row?"

"I think so."

Florrie didn't show her surprise that Diana didn't seem to know anything about her son's likes or dislikes. Perhaps they could all help to mend their relationship. "That's another thing they have in common then. Cam rowed for her college. They can talk about it, or rather Cam can talk about the techn calities and minutiae. She'd never say, but she was disappointed Gloria never took to rowing. Gloria tried it once and said it was full of stuck-up rich girls who didn't want her there."

Diana turned. "She can't have had it easy. You must tell me her story some time."

"I will, or she will, I'm sure." Florrie chuckled. "She makes no secret of it. What do you need right now?"

Diana visibly softened. "Just hold me."

Florrie leaned back onto the bed and pulled Diana beside her. They kicked off their shoes, and she folded Diana in her arms and rubbed her back. Diana murmured something Florrie didn't catch. "Pardon?"

"Thank you for being you, for opening your arms and your home to me. Do you forgive me for my ungrateful son and for insulting your house?"

"Edward will come around, I'm sure of it. The lure of boxing, music, and cake is too much for any young man to withstand. And I'm not insulted. It's the truth. It's small compared to your houses—"

"I love your home," Diana said. "It's vibrant and has such a warm energy, like it's absorbed your personality. I look forward to spending more time here. Thank you."

Diana kissed Florrie, and what started as chaste became fevered and desperate. Before Florrie realised, she was naked, panting and arching at Diana's touch and tongue, working in tandem to elicit a climax so deep and strong that she shuddered for minutes with glorious aftershocks. Much as she wanted to reciprocate, her eyelids drooped into half-lidded bliss.

"I've got you," Diana whispered. "Go to sleep, dearest heart. Relax and let go. I love you."

"I love you too," Florrie mumbled as she felt herself drifting.

She awoke with a start from pain in her hands and her hip. Damn the arthritis. With a struggle, she twisted to sit up. The bed beside her was empty and cool to the touch, and a soft glow came from a small lamp on the desk under the window. Diana was hunched over, writing on small slips of paper.

Florrie smiled. "My second favourite sight in the world."

Diana turned in her seat and returned the smile, the soft one reserved only for Florrie. She raised her eyebrow. "Second favourite?"

"My favourite is waking up to you beside me in my bed. What are you writing?"

"I was reflecting on the nature of love, our love specifically; love we've rediscovered at this stage of our life, with all the complications that brings. Yet it's so much deeper and well-rounded now. Can I read you something?"

"Always. I love your work, and I love it even more when you read it out in your rich, sexy voice." That earned her an eyeroll, but Florrie didn't care. She'd been intimate with the woman she loved, and upstairs, judging by the squeaking of the bedsprings, Cam and Gloria were doing the same.

"Are you listening?"

"Yes. Sorry. I was thinking how wonderful everything is being here with you—"

A low wail emitted from upstairs, and they both laughed.

"I suppose that's the disadvantage of a small house." Diana pushed her glasses up her nose and glanced at the ceiling. "Assuming there are no more noises, shall I begin?"

"Please. I'm listening. Oh wait, let me just grab another pillow."

Diana tutted good-naturedly and threw a pillow at Florrie.

She caught it and plumped it up before relaxing against it. "I'm all ears."

Diana inhaled, shook her paper out, and peered over her glasses, the tilt of her head exposing her long neck. The soft concentration in her gaze made Florrie's heart flutter. She was still so alluring.

"Sometimes, love hides in the spaces between the lines, in the unspoken words, in the pause at a comma and the inhalation of breath when you read aloud. Every crisp syllable, every falling cadence is a declaration of a love that isn't bold or brash but deep-rooted and can pass unnoticed unless one is really observing. Too often we glance and assume, eager to assess and categorise but not to study and see. But to truly love is to be curious and open to the full orchestra of emotion. It is the detail, the nuance that colours everything we do and who we are. Our love is blended in friendship and companionship, and all the tiny acts of service and support: the cup of tea in the morning, the catch of our loved one's gaze, the stories we share. Only we know, in our hearts, the truth, the certainty of love."

Florrie clutched her chest, as if she could stop her heart stuttering. Diana was certain? That was the first time she'd intimated that, and it warmed Florrie to her soul. "Thank you. That's so beautiful and true for me too. You always had a wonderful genius with words, but that was more than writing. That was seeing me, seeing us." She rose from the bed and went over to Diana, needing to touch her, to connect on the physical as well as the metaphysical plane. "I used to think love was all bold declarations, but it's in the tiny acts you do. You remember how I like my tea, you check I'm comfortable, and you write me a piece like that, which says, I see you, and I love you." She enveloped Diana in her arms. "I have no doubts about us. I'm certain. I'm here for the pauses, for the commas, and every word in between." She nuzzled against Diana's ear and pressed closer, feeling the rise and fall of Diana's chest beneath her, letting the pause stretch and the world outside shrink until there was just them, in this heartbeat. "Read it to me again, please."

Time seemed to bend so they were simultaneously young and middle-aged, curled in the crux of love, and Florrie held her breath, waiting for Diana's voice to fill the space, knowing that in the gentle cadence was the promise of everything still to come.

EPILOGUE

Antibes 1954

From outside on the patio came the low rumble of conversation and clinking glasses. Diana was hiding away in the hardly used internal dining room with Florrie. Everything was upside down today, and the room was stacked with pool furniture and other items they didn't want the public to see—or break.

Oscar and Maurice, who had arrived from Paris less than an hour ago, had brought a very nice champagne, and they were secreted away from all the visitors, sharing the bottle, ostensibly to give Diana extra courage, but Oscar seemed to be drinking most of it.

"Darling, this is going to be a wonderful bash," Oscar said, "and now you've got rid of that dreary woman in black, th s place is a delight to be around. Especially with your new hire, young Jean. I'll have to keep him away from my beau." He slipped his arm around Maurice's waist.

Maurice stepped away and pointed to the door. "Oscar, there are twenty journalists out there who would love to dig up a scandal. Please behave."

Oscar raised his hands. "Sorry, I forgot we weren't alone."

Diana put her half-finished champagne glass to the side and smoothed the non-existent wrinkles on her dress. "Amelie handed in her resignation when I bought the villa from Edward."

Oscar flashed his cheeky boy grin. "My, you must have had a large advance for your new book to afford this place."

She gave him a wry smile. "It was. They're convinced it will do very well, but I'm not so sure."

Florrie rested her hand on Diana's arm, her thumb moving in slow reassuring circles. She leaned in, their heads almost touching. "It's okay to be uncertain. It takes courage to put your heart and soul on the page."

Diana gave a small huff and waved her hand.

Florrie took Diana's hands in her own. "Whatever happens, I'm here, cheering you on and willing it to be a success. And if the world doesn't like it, that's their loss. I love every word of it, just like I love every part of you."

The trembling in Diana's fingers eased, and she gazed at Florrie intensely. "Thank you," she whispered.

Oscar set down his empty glass and strode towards the door. "It will do fabulously, and you'll win over all the journalists. Do us all a favour though and think like a poet rather than the genius novel-writer you are. Keep your speech short, then we can hit the champagne with no beady eyes or ears listening in and have a wonderful evening together on our own. Break a leg, darling."

"I doubt some journalists can be swayed," Diana said. "But thanks for coming down to support me."

He blew her a kiss. "We need to find the coldest champagne, Maurice. That wasn't enough to wet my whistle. We'll see you later."

Oscar exited with a flurry of scarf trailing behind him. Maurice shrugged and followed him out after wishing Diana bonne chance.

"He must be hot in that scarf," Florrie said to direct Diana's attention away from the upcoming event.

"Yes, but it gives him the opportunity to make grand entrances and exits. It's also silk. No doubt, courtesy of Maurice."

Florrie smiled, thinking back to all those years ago when Oscar tutored Cam, and he'd been so broken and lonely. Who knew he would end up a kept man with a suave financier? It gave her hope that even the most unlikely relationships could last if there was love. "It's wonderful to see them so happy together."

"Yes."

Florrie put out her hand to still Diana's rearranging of her costume. "You look perfect."

Diana blew out a breath. "This is so important, dearest heart. I don't think I can bear it if they hate the book. It will feel like they're hating you, hating us." Despite her words, her tone sounded more confident, more herself, with every word.

"I'm sure the people invited here will love it given how much the publishing house is paying for this launch event. I still don't understand why they didn't have it in London—somewhere nice, of course."

Diana gave her an arch look. "Have you lost your romanticism? It's because Antibes is where the novel was conceived."

Florrie squeezed her hand. Tempting though it was to kiss her, journalists were on the other side of the window, laughing and quaffing expensive champagne, so she tried to convey everything by the brief touch. "I know. I remember. It's when I learned how to let go, to fall and be supported." She touched her forehead to Diana's. "When I learned how to love again."

Diana smiled and held eye contact, and their souls connected. The pull to kiss Diana almost overwhelmed Florrie. They both jumped apart as the young assistant publisher, Tamara, bustled into the room brandishing a clipboard. Fortunately, she was staring at that rather than at them.

"Miss Stratford, I need you to have your face touched up before you go on."

"Please call me Diana, and I prefer to have only light make-up, which I've already applied myself. There's no point disguising my age. Most people will know I haven't written anything for nearly thirty years, if they know who I am at all."

Tamara gave a sigh that dripped exasperation. "It's all been arranged, and I have the make-up artist in the next room waiting for you. It's all written down here on your checklist."

"Heaven forbid you should go against the checklist," Florrie muttered under her breath, causing Diana to smile.

Tamara flicked a glance to Florrie then consulted her checklist again. "You may as well sit down now and encourage others to do the same, as Miss Stratford will be busy until the event begins. Come along." Tamara headed towards the inner door.

Florrie knew a dismissal when she saw it. "Break a leg."

"Thank you."

As Diana passed Florrie, she trailed the tips of her fingers across Florrie's back. It was the lightest of touches but signified the deepest of emotions and a shiver rippled through Florrie's body. Diana gave an exaggerated sway of her hips as she left the room, clearly knowing that Florrie would be watching. She chuckled and picked up her cane, which she was using today as there'd be a lot of standing around.

A few people looked towards Florrie as she emerged onto the patio, though they quickly turned, disappointed she wasn't the celebrated author. Jean had done a wonderful job with the garden. It looked glorious in the sun, with geraniums, heather, thyme, and lavender adding to the colour and the sweet aroma. The sound of the sea was obscured by the music, chatting people, and clinking glasses, but she could almost imagine the rumble and hiss of the waves as they hit the rocks.

She drifted amongst the various groups of the literati, talking books and boasting of their knowledge, and it reminded her of the day she'd first met Diana so many years ago. Like then, she wasn't part of any particular group. Edward and his girlfriend, Libby, were around somewhere, and she hadn't seen Cam and Gloria for a while. Cam was probably hiding out to avoid the noise and crush of people. At least they were staying a few days, and they could have a proper catch up.

Their whole life seemed to have revolved around this launch for the last few weeks. The publishers wanted everything to be perfect, although Florrie was getting rather tired of being bossed around by Tamara, who considered herself the mistress of ceremonies.

The day was going to be hot, and Florrie was glad for her floppy sun hat to keep the rays away from her delicate sk n. She made her way over to the refreshment table sagging with punch, champagne, and freshly prepared lemonade. She took a drink, then stood in the shade and sipped her lemonade. She didn't want to get drunk this early as she was likely to be needed to help schmooze later, however much she hated it.

The tart crispness of freshly picked lemons zinged around her mouth, and she smacked her lips quite involuntarily. She surveyed the gaggle of people around their patio and saw Gloria waving to her. Florrie raised her hand, but Gloria waved more frantically and beckoned her over. She and Cam were chatting to the pilots of the private plane that had been hired to bring the guests over from England at some extortionate cost.

As she approached, Gloria reached out to her. "Aunty Florrie, you must meet Beryl and Odette, the pilots who own the air chartering business that flew us all down here. We met them at the end of the war in that club we told you about."

Florrie hadn't got the faintest idea what Gloria was talking about, but she smiled and greeted the pilots, both very smart in their uniforms.

"You know the special club that we're all members of " Gloria inclined her head and raised both eyebrows as Florrie shook the pilots' hands.

Understanding dawned. "How delightful to meet you and your partner," she said to Beryl the taller, broader woman. "I understand you flew in all the VIPs today?"

"We did," Odette said. "It's lovely to meet you too. Do I take it you and Diana could attend the club too?"

Florrie's face burned. If only Gloria wouldn't be so enthusiastic about including everyone. Given her background, it was surprising Gloria was so forthcoming, but Florrie supposed that she must feel safe with these women. Florrie relaxed and gave them both a warm smile. "Perhaps, but we haven't told anyone here."

Beryl tapped her nose and grinned. "Understood. I think you're all being called to take your seats." She pointed to where Tamara was waving frantically.

Florrie sighed. "I've probably upset her timetable. See you afterwards. Welcome." She took Cam's arm and shuffled towards her place on the front row and lowered herself down. Cam and Gloria sat beside her, and they waited.

"So much for needing to sit down immediately," Gloria said and huffed. "Wasn't it grand to meet Beryl and Odette again?"

Cam nodded.

Florrie fidgeted with her watch and glanced across at the door where Diana was to emerge with her publisher. Should she go and check on her again? Tamara probably wouldn't like that one bit. Florrie's heart pounded though, as if she was the one about to take centre stage in front of all these people.

Cam flashed her a quick smile. "She'll be fine."

Oh dear, her worry must be obvious for Cam to notice, but she seemed to be more tuned in to emotions recently. Gloria's influence seemed to spread with every passing day.

Finally, the music stopped, and Tamara pushed open the door. A small, dark-haired man preceded Diana, whose face looked flawless with the heavy make-up. That would be unpleasant in this heat. Florrie caught her eye and gave a thumbs up sign, which Diana acknowledged with the briefest of nods. She pulled at the hem of her jacket sleeves —Diana's tell that she was nervous— and Florrie wished she could sit beside her and hold her hand to reassure her. Diana and the man sat on the comfy chairs on the makeshift stage, and Tamara took a place at the side.

The man waited until everyone settled down. "Good afternoon, ladies and gentlemen, and welcome to Antibes." He spread his hands above his head like he'd scored a winning goal and was personally responsible for the South of France. "My name is Rupert Englebury, and I own Englebury Waters. This is an unusual setting for a book launch but very apt, as it was here where Ms Diana Stratford started writing again. We're thrilled to be publishing this new work. There's been such a huge buzz around it, along with the refreshed versions of all of Ms Stratford's back catalogue, which have graced the *New York Times* bestsellers list, and we think this new book, *Starfish on the Shore*, will top them all."

Interesting to hear how he focused on the business side rather than the literary content. Florrie had a horrible feeling he may be another Anthony in the making, and Diana was putting all her trust in his hands. But if he maximised her royalties, that was a good thing, although good reviews and literary accolades would mean so much more to Diana.

He started with the obligatory life history and summary of Diana's novels. They weren't expecting anything difficult in this part, so Florrie peered around at the attending press. Of the twenty carefully selected reporters, five or six were already drunk. *Good.* As he turned to ask questions about Diana's life and motivations, Diana gripped the chair arms so hard that Florrie could see her fingers go white. She wouldn't catch Florrie's eyes, but Florrie still attempted to slow Diana's shallow breathing by deliberately slowing her own.

"Tell me about the late twenties. It was such a heady time, and that's reflected in your previous work, *On the Edge of Uncertainty*, which many critics say was your best. It was so exuberant, despite the ambiguous ending. What motivated you to write that?"

Diana exhaled visibly. She paused a little too long, and even Tamara raised her head from her clipboard. "Love." She smiled, wide-eyed, as she clearly realised that she had to say more to stave off the supplemental questions. "Love of life, of youth, of what we were doing with Euston Press and the exciting, groundbreaking projects we worked on. It was intoxicating."

Rupert went on to detail some of the exciting projects Diana had referred to. Florrie was tickled that some of those were ones she'd flagged up: the dystopian novel was even lauded as being a classic.

Diana's shoulders lowered an inch.

"So, what happened in the thirties?"

"I married and had a child; what do you think happened?"

Some people tittered, but they could sense her brittle defensiveness and maybe determined there was blood in the water. Diana still didn't look at Florrie.

He laughed. "You didn't write for years."

"No," Diana whispered.

The audience had to lean forward in their seats to hear her above the sounds of the calling birds, the buzzing insects.

"I lost everything in the Great Crash of 1929."

"Everything?"

Diana squinted and held her hand to her eyes to block the afternoon sun. Her make-up must be beginning to melt by now.

"My love," she whispered.

Florrie held her breath. Diana couldn't say that. It was too exposing, and she needed to protect herself. They had to remain hidden. A trickle of sweat broke out on Florrie's forehead, and she brushed it away.

"I thought you married not long afterwards?"

Was he really going there? He was supposed to be protecting her and promoting her, not getting her to unravel before their eyes. They'd been very clear beforehand that Florrie must remain a secret, and that if one of the journalists did go snooping, they were to laugh it off as a fling before she settled down.

"Yes. I meant my publishing house," Diana said and gave a rueful smile. "After the recession, we had to concentrate on the bestsellers, the books that would keep us in business to keep the presses turning. I handed over control to my husband, and as you've pointed out, I focused on being married and raising a child."

"Didn't you have staff?" The *Times* journalist called from the audience.

Diana frowned and peered into the small crowd. "Yes. But it's not a secret that I was visited by the blackness of what Freud called melancholia. I couldn't write."

"What got you writing again now?"

Diana smiled. "I'm a widow, and my son is up in Cambridge, so I don't have those responsibilities anymore. Every woman needs space and time to fulfil her potential."

"Or a good man," one of the drunk reporters shouted.

Florrie wrinkled her nose, thinking that he was probably from the *Express*.

Diana shot him a withering look. "On the contrary, a man is often the cause of a woman subjugating herself and her needs to him. To explore her potential, a woman should be unshackled and free to pursue the purpose for which she has the skill and aptitude."

The man from the *Express* grumbled something about feminist claptrap. Florrie suspected Diana's book wouldn't be getting a great write up in his paper. No loss. Who knew why he'd been invited in the first place, or why he'd accepted? Alcohol and a break in the South of France, probably.

"Tell me what gave you the idea for your new novel, *Starfish on the Shore*?" Rupert asked, desperately trying to redirect the narrative.

All the journalists had received a preview copy of the novel, so in theory, they knew it if they'd bothered to read it. These questions were supposed to be the fillers to provide additional flavour to their articles. They had discussed a press-friendly version of the genesis of the book beforehand. Diana wouldn't reveal the intimacy of it being inspired by Florrie letting go and finally being open to love.

"Starfish cling to the rocks. They can move using suckers under their bodies, but they don't float. Sometimes in a big storm, they are ripped off the rocks and carried by waves onto the shore. Although it's not advisable to touch them, if they're stranded, you can put them back in the water and save them."

Rupert nodded slowly. "So is the book an allegory for being saved?"

"No. It's an allegory for letting go and going with the tide, even if you get stranded. It's about trust."

Diana finally cast a quick glance at Florrie, and her breath stuttered at the yearning contained there. This was all too exposing. Perhaps they should have had the public launch in a bookshop in London, where they could have sold and signed lots of copies, though doubtless, that would come as Tamara had organised a schedule of events over the next few months. But they needed to get through this one and to keep their secret. If Diana kept on looking at Florrie like she was, it would be blown wide open.

"Both this and your previous book seem to be about love and longing. Are they about specific people?"

Diana squinted at the questioner, the man from *The Times* again, and she paused, one breath, two. "Yes. The same person."

Now the journalists sat up, sniffing a story more scandalous than the prosaic cultural piece.

"To make sure I understand this correctly, the two books are about love for the same person?" the *Times* chap asked.

Diana nodded.

"But not your husband?"

Diana quirked her eyebrow, implying he'd asked a stupid question. Florrie held her breath as Diana negotiated the minefield. Was she planning to divulge what they'd agreed to keep secret?

Rupert leaned forward to speak into the microphone. "Thank you for raising that, Jeremy. Yes, the two books are about love.

On the Edge of Uncertainty ends without resolution, whereas *Starfish on the Shore* ends on a note of hope. And we're certain that there will be more books like these in the future."

Diana touched Rupert's forearm. "Not my husband, no. And I'm sure you all want some salacious story you can slap into your papers to maximise your ratings." She rolled her eyes. "I'm sorry to disappoint you. Sometimes, love is not the rage of waves upon the rocks, all turmoil and torrent that overwhelms and then stagnates when the storm of passion is gone. Sometimes, love is the trickle of a mountain stream, clear and silent, purifying and refreshing, constant and ever-present. It is the devotion and constancy over the years, even when all hope seems lost. That is what inspires and intrigues me. How to capture such simple love."

"Who is he?"

That's all they wanted to know, to complete the prurient details, hoping for a juicy scandal to rock the literary world.

"I cannot say and will not say," Diana said simply. "It is not my story to give or yours to divulge. You were invited here as my guests, and I expect you not to break that trust. Thank you. I'm being flagged by Tamara to say it's time to close as your buses have arrived to take you to your hotel. Thank you for your time."

Rupert closed out the meeting and left with the journalists for the next part of their junket, enticing them with the promise of free drinks. Within minutes, the area was being cleared by the catering staff, and tables and chairs were being stacked and loaded into vans.

While Diana saw off the caterers with a smile, her thanks, and a large tip, Florrie rested against the railing and stared down at the constantly moving sea, now lapping gently against the rocks. No doubt the journalists would guess at who Diana had referred to, and it was only a matter of time until the full story came tumbling out, along with the inevitable scrutiny and judgement. She was unsure how she felt about that. Anxious, primarily.

But as she stood there, a wave of certainty washed over her. Everyone who mattered knew already. She didn't care about Nora and Charles. They hadn't been a feature in her life for years, and she wasn't a public person whose approval ratings would fall. If Diana was prepared for it, so was she. She exhaled in relief. They would be all right, whatever happened.

Diana's soft steps echoed on the patio flagstones, and she slid her arms around Florrie from behind. Diana nuzzled her neck, and Florrie stretched to give her access.

"Mm, the taste of salt, and you smell divine. Do you know how beautiful you look, standing here in the glow of the first blush of sunset, with the wind flicking your hair and skirt? It's something I want to remember for the rest of my life."

Florrie placed her hands over Diana's and pulled her closer. She was so content to be enveloped by Diana's scent, and warmth, and love.

"I wanted to say more. I almost did, but I couldn't give you away without your blessing. I don't care if they know and condemn us. I've been a coward too long, and I hurt you so badly. It means everything to me that you're with me now, and I hope you've forgiven me."

Florrie turned in Diana's arms and stretched up to claim her lips in a kiss that deepened into a spark of desire. Now wasn't the time, when they had guests drinking wine around the corner, and they'd need entertaining shortly. She pulled back with a small smile. "I've forgiven you for that, but I'm not sure about our love being a mountain stream. It sounds so mundane and unpassionate. Not romantic at all."

Diana kissed her on her nose. "Have you climbed in the mountains in a storm, or after the snows when the stream becomes a torrent, deep and powerful? That's our love too. But the journos don't need to know that." She grinned. "Nor do they need to know that we shared two orgasms this morning, for all your worrying about being able to cope with the physical. I told you all we needed was a little ingenuity." Her expression sobered. "That's our truth."

The memory flashed in Florrie's brain and warmed her to her soul. She would never take for granted being loved and loving this stunning woman, seeing her unravel in the most glorious way. She stared deep into Diana's eyes. "So, you're not disappointed with what we have now? Don't you wish for the sea rather than the stream?"

"Not at all. I love you, and I want to share my life with you. You give me joy and inspiration."

"Are you certain?"

"I'm certain." Diana rested her forehead against Florrie's. "I just wanted to check you were okay standing here alone."

"I am. I was thinking about us and about getting older. Who cares who knows? The joy of old age is not worrying about expectations and having to fit in. If you want to announce us to the world, you can, although the story may then be more about us than about your book."

Diana kissed Florrie lightly. "Thank you for saying that. Maybe it's something we can consider for later. Now, if we don't want Oscar and Maurice to cause too much mischief, I think we should rejoin the others."

Diana took Florrie's hand, and they slowly returned to the outside dining area at the side of the house. As they approached, they were awarded with a wolf whistle from Oscar and a round of applause. Diana raised their joined hands in acknowledgement, and they took two empty seats.

Florrie smiled, her chest tightening with tender appreciation as she swept her gaze around the small group. Oscar and Maurice were already deep into another bottle of champagne, regaling Cam and Gloria with stories of living in France. Even Jean had accepted an invitation to join them for supper, a cold compilation of ham, cheese, salads, and French bread. And more champagne, of course.

Conversation was easy, and even Edward and Libby gradually relaxed. Edward was still formal around them, but he'd blossomed under Cam's mentorship in boxing, rowing, and maths. He was about to start his career in finance, much to Diana's disappointment, but with a gentle nudge from Florrie, she'd given him genuine congratulations.

Diana squeezed Florrie's hand, then stood, her chair scraping against the flagstones. She caught the eye of everyone at the table. The chatter and clattering of cutlery ceased and was replaced by the steady breath of the waves acting like the heartbeat of the moment.

"Thank you all for coming to support us today. Thank you for standing by us, not only today, but always. Thank you, Cam and Gloria, for welcoming me into your family and for helping to heal my relationship with Edward. And Edward, thank you for forgiving me and being willing to start again. To all of you, this life wouldn't mean half as much without you in it. You'll always have a place here, as this is your home too. You are all family. And to the heart of the family, around whom everything revolves, thank you, Florence, my dearest heart." Diana swallowed hard as if she was trying to push down the emotion in her throat. "To family."

Everyone raised and clinked their glasses and said in unison, "To family."

Diana sat, and Florrie took her hand.

"Is there any pudding?" Cam asked, and they all laughed.

"Hear, hear," Edward said. "Or one of Florrie's cakes?"

Jean rose. "I made some crème brûlée earlier. I'll go make the caramel."

"You're a godsend," Oscar said, peering at an empty bottle. "This calls for more champagne. Can I peep into your cellar, Diana? Family privilege, I would've thought."

Diana shook her head, but she was laughing. "Am I going to have to hide my best wine from now on?"

Oscar's eyes twinkled. "Ooh, a treasure hunt. That could be

fun."

"Help yourself, Oscar, and could you bring out the cognac too?" Diana asked.

Oscar followed Jean to the kitchen. Edward asked Cam about rowing, and Gloria chatted to Maurice and Libby, and the conversation flowed to and fro in the warmth of companionship and the flicker of the citronella candles.

Florrie smiled at Diana, and they leaned towards each other. "I thought life was wonderful until you came hurtling in and upended everything, expanding my world and filling it with colour."

Diana raised an eyebrow. "Is there a but coming?"

"No," Florrie said, her voice thick with emotion. "Without you, I never would've trusted again, never overcome my doubts. I would never have loved again or been truly alive again." She drew in a breath then lifted her eyes to gaze at Diana's "With you, I'm ready for whatever the future holds."

She touched her forehead to Diana's, and everything else faded, leaving only the warmth of Diana's breath on Florrie's lips, the promise in her eyes, and the certainty that they would be together, through every pause, every footnote, and every word still to be written.

~ The End ~

Author's Note

If you would like to find out more about Cam and Gloria, check out *Encrypted Hearts*, and for Beryl and Odette's story download *Virgin Flight*.

I really hope you enjoyed reading *The Edge of Uncertainty*. If you did, I'd be very grateful for an honest review. Reviews and recommendations are crucial for any author, particularly one early in her career. Just a line or two can make a huge difference.

Thank you.

E. V. Bancroft

Other Great Butterworth Books

Encrypted Hearts by E.V. Bancroft
Can they survive the chaos of war, or will secrets tear them apart?
Available from Amazon (ASIN B0DKG7BHMJ)

Love Under Fire by Valden Bush
Two agents. One mission. Zero patience.
Available on Amazon (ASIN B0FGK291DZ)

Here in My Heart by Jo Fletcher
In the golden glow of a South of France autumn, two very different lives collide.
Available on Amazon (ASIN B0FCHNLK9W) B0FGK291DZ

The Heart Remembers by Ally McGuire
One wedding. One ex. And a week that might just lead to forever.
Available on Amazon (ASIN B0F932F8LZ)

The Sister Act by Helena Harte
She's faking it for one sister...but is she falling for the other?
Available from Amazon (ASIN B0F4KSVCZ9)

Sapphic Eclectic Volume One to Six edited by Nyx & Willows
Because everyone deserves love.
Available free from the Butterworth Books website

The Extractor Trilogy by RJ Nyx
Working in the past is hell on your future.
Escape in Time (Book One) ASIN B0DSJFDZ7R
Change in Time (Book Two) ASIN B0DWG24C66
Death in Time (Book Three) ASIN B0DWG24C66

Racing Hearts by Sydney Lear
When love takes the wheel, there's no hitting the brakes.
Available from Amazon (ASIN B0DZP9X3G2)

Driving Me Barking by JP Preston
Sometimes the one who got away never really left.
Available on Amazon (ASIN B0DWG1LLXN)

Breakout for Love by Valden Bush
They're both running from their pasts. Together, they might make a new future.
Available from Amazon (ASIN B0CWHZ4SXL)

The Helion Band by AJ Mason
Rose's only crime was to show kindness to her royal mistress...
Available from Amazon (ASIN B09YM6TYFQ)

That Boy of Yours Wants Looking At by Simon Smalley
A riotously colourful and heart-rending journey of what it takes to live authentically.
Available from Amazon (ASIN B09V3CSQQW)

Of Light and Love by E.V. Bancroft
The deepest shadows paint the brightest love.
Available from Amazon (ASIN B0B64KJ3NP)

An Art to Love by Helena Harte
Second chances are an art form.
Available on Amazon (ASIN B0B1CD8Y42)

Let Love Be Enough by Robyn Nyx
When a killer sets her sights on her target, is there any stopping her?
Available on Amazon (ASIN B09YMMZ8XC)

Dead Pretty by Robyn Nyx
An FBI agent, a TV star, and a serial killer. Love hurts.
Available on Amazon (ASIN B09QRSKBVP)

Nero by Valden Bush
Banished and abandoned. Will destiny reunite her with the love of her life?
Available from Amazon (ASIN B0BHJKHK6S)

Warm Pearls and Paper Cranes by E.V. Bancroft
A family torn apart by secrets. The only way forward is love.
Available from Amazon (ASIN B09DTBCQ92)

Judge Me, Judge Me Not by James Merrick
One man's battle against the world and himself to find it's never too late to find, and use, your voice.
Available from Amazon (ASIN B09CLK91N5)

Music City Dreamers by Robyn Nyx
Music brings lovers together. In Music City, it can tear them apart.
Available on Amazon (ASIN B0994XVDGR)

Scripted Love by Helena Harte
What good is a romance writer who doesn't believe in happy ever after?
Available on Amazon (ASIN B0993QFLNN)

Call to Me by Helena Harte
Sometimes the call you 'east expect is the one you need the most.
Available on Amazon (ASIN B08D9SR15H)

What's Your Story?

Global Wordsmiths, CIC, provides an all-encompassing service for all writers, ranging from basic proofreading and cover design to development editing, typesetting, and eBook services. We specialise in helping self-published authors get their books into the world but also help authors find a traditional publisher or agent.
Another part of our work is charity and community focused, delivering writing projects to under-served and under-represented groups across Nottinghamshire, giving voice to the voiceless and visibility to the unseen.

To learn more about what we offer, visit: www.globalwords.co.uk

A selection of books by Global Words Press:
Desire, Love, Identity: with the National Justice Museum
Aventuras en México: Farmilo Primary School
Times Past: with The Workhouse, National Trust
Young at Heart with AGE UK
In Different Shoes: Stories of Trans Lives
Our Pride: with Nottinghamshire Healthcare Trust